Praise for the work of Jaci Burton

"Realistic dialogue, spicy bedroom scenes, and a spitfire heroine make this one to pick up and savor." —*Publishers Weekly*

"Sexy and fast paced. Jaci Burton delivers." —Cherry Adair, *USA Today* bestselling author

"Exciting, intense. A ride you don't want to miss. Burton has written a reality blast that will leave you breathless." —Lora Leigh, *New York Times* bestselling author

"One hot novel that I could not put down until the last word. This story has it all: mind-boggling sex, unique and unforgettable characters, and a wonderful plot that will grip your heart . . . raw, dynamic, explosive. Wow!" —*Just Erotic Romance Reviews*

"Lively and funny . . . The sex is both intense and loving; you can feel the connection that both the hero and heroine want to deny in every word and touch between them. I cannot say enough good things about this book." —*The Road to Romance*

"Burton's book packs an amazing wallop! It's rich with passion, excitement, intense emotion, and a sense of love that's utterly palpable." —*Romantic Times*

"[An] exhilarating novel . . . flaming hot . . . This is one sweet and spicy romance." —*Romance Junkies*

"A fabulous read. [Burton] delivers, in every possible way." —*A Romance Review*

"Sizzling hot sex that will have you panting. I highly recommend this story to anyone looking for a hot read." —*The Romance Studio*

RIDING WILD

Jaci Burton

Heat | New York

THE BERKLEY PUBLISHING GROUP
Published by the Penguin Group
Penguin Group (USA) Inc.
375 Hudson Street, New York, New York 10014, USA
Penguin Group (Canada), 90 Eglinton Avenue East, Suite 700, Toronto, Ontario M4P 2Y3, Canada
(a division of Pearson Penguin Canada Inc.)
Penguin Books Ltd., 80 Strand, London WC2R 0RL, England
Penguin Group Ireland, 25 St. Stephen's Green, Dublin 2, Ireland (a division of Penguin Books Ltd.)
Penguin Group (Australia), 250 Camberwell Road, Camberwell, Victoria 3124, Australia
(a division of Pearson Australia Group Pty. Ltd.)
Penguin Books India Pvt. Ltd., 11 Community Centre, Panchsheel Park, New Delhi—110 017, India
Penguin Group (NZ), 67 Apollo Drive, Rosedale, North Shore 0632, New Zealand
(a division of Pearson New Zealand Ltd.)
Penguin Books (South Africa) (Pty.) Ltd., 24 Sturdee Avenue, Rosebank, Johannesburg 2196, South Africa

Penguin Books Ltd., Registered Offices: 80 Strand, London WC2R 0RL, England

This is an original publication of The Berkley Publishing Group.

ISBN: 978-0-7394-9281-9

PRINTED IN THE UNITED STATES OF AMERICA

To Charlie,
for teaching me the joy of the wind in my face
and the road on two wheels.
Thank you for your patience,
your love,
and for all the wild rides on our Harley.

one

AS ASSIGNMENTS WENT, THIS ONE WAS ODD. BUT AS A PRIVATE investigator, Lily West did what she was hired to do. Her latest mission was to attempt to break into the museum, test the night security team, and see if they were doing their job.

Easy enough. She'd been casing the museum for the past week. The day shift was tight and doing a fine job handling the large crowds coming in to see the traveling Star of Egypt exhibit of artifacts. The day crew was also busy enough to allow her to wander around and study everything, map it all out, so she'd know what to look for at night.

She'd gotten her answers. The night crew was severely lax, and the museum's overall security system sucked. No one patrolled outside, and the guys mostly sat on their asses in the front lobby and talked to each other instead of making rounds. Lucky for them, not a damn thing had been going on.

These guys should be fired, which is probably what her client already suspected. She intended to hang out awhile longer and keep watch on the off chance the donut-eating morons inside might get up off their asses and decide to do their jobs for a change, though it was probably a waste of her time. She could do cartwheels naked across the front lawn and those guys wouldn't notice her.

A motorcycle roared by, its loud pipes obliterating the quiet. That low-throated rumble never failed to get her attention. Or remind her of Mac. Not that he was ever far from her thoughts.

Bored and restless, she leaned against a tree and watched the front entrance. It didn't take long for thoughts of Mac to enter her mind.

She'd always fantasized about riding him on his Harley. She stayed hidden within the darkness, remembering how many times that particular fantasy had brought her to a blistering orgasm.

She'd hear him first—the roar of his bike rumbling in the distance. Her body would come alive. Like the vibrations of the machine, she'd tremble and hum. Her clit would purr, her nipples quiver, her pussy quake with the force of a rocketing engine. He'd pull up in front of her house and shut the engine off, but the steady beat of its power would still growl within her. He wouldn't bother to knock, because he knew she'd be waiting for him.

She was lost in the fantasy now. The wind from the open living room window blew over her naked pussy, heightening her arousal. She'd worn her sundress and nothing else, wanting to give him easy access to her body. She clenched her hands, awaiting the moment he would touch her aching heat, relieve the burning need flaming inside her.

The front door opened, the light from the table lamp backlit his tall frame. Worn jeans lovingly framed his muscled thighs. Too hot for his leather jacket. Just a T-shirt stretched tight over his broad shoulders and wide chest. The harsh planes of his face drew her eye. He had that bad boy look. Always had. That had been the first thing to attract her to him. Sexy. Forbidden. Oh, she'd wanted him.

As soon as he reached the sofa he dropped to his knees, placed his hands on her thighs just under the hem of her dress.

"You smell like spring, baby," he whispered.

She gazed at him, drinking him in like cool water on a hot summer afternoon. He quenched her thirst like no man ever could.

"Hurry," she said.

"You need it."

"Yes."

He raised her dress over her hips, baring her pussy to his gaze. God, he turned her on when he looked at her like that—hungry, his whiskey brown eyes going dark. He licked his lips, bent over her, and kissed below her belly button. Her abdomen quivered and she let out a whimper.

"Shh," he breathed against her skin, then reached for the strap of her dress, drawing it down and freeing her breasts. Her nipples peaked and hardened as he covered one of the mounds with his palm, gently rubbing back and forth. She arched into his hand.

Hot, flaming her desire to an inferno.

He swept his mouth lower, kissing her mound before delving into her cleft with his tongue, finding the hood of her clit and circling it.

Maddening. She tangled her fingers into his hair, trying to direct him. He said something, his voice muffled against her skin. The words were unintelligible, almost like a chuckle.

He was teasing her. She loved it. She hated it. She wanted to climax, to come in his mouth, to pour her cream over his tongue. She'd denied herself too long.

"Mac, please."

"Tell me what you want," he murmured against her thigh.

No man ever challenged her like this, brought out the wildness within her. But Mac did. He made her crazy, made her want to tell him exactly what she needed.

"Lick me. Make me come." She squeezed her buttocks and lifted her hips, offering herself to him.

He dragged his body over hers and parted her legs, then covered her sex with his mouth. She moaned when he slid two fingers inside her pussy, then sucked on her clit while he finger fucked her.

Yes! This is what she needed. The pulses began to sharpen, heat building and melting inside her. She thrashed around on the couch, unable to hold still as she built to a crescendo with every hot lick of his velvety tongue against her throbbing flesh.

He knew just where her pleasure points were. *Yes, right there.* She was going to fly. She didn't want it to end, yet she needed it.

"I'm coming, Mac! I'm going to come in your mouth."

She heard his groan, felt it vibrate against her bare skin, and then she couldn't hold back, crashing against him as the waves of orgasm coursed through her. She held his head against her pussy, rocking up and down as she splintered into a million pieces, shuddering and shaking.

No man could make her come like Mac could. She sighed in utter satisfaction.

The sound of the motorcycle returning shook her out of her fantasy. She blinked, fanning away the self-induced heat that spiraled up inside her.

It had been ten years since she'd last seen him, but just thinking about him could still make her hot, could take her out of herself and turn her into some wild, hungry creature so unlike her real self. She wished . . .

Ah, whatever. She could wish all she wanted, but she needed to focus on reality.

She saw the bike flying fast and furious down the busy main street, its silver chrome a flash of lightning under the streetlights.

Shit. Here she was, dreaming about Mac and she was supposed to be working. The moronic, so-called crack security team was still hanging around the lobby. Eating snacks, no less.

Getting in was going to be easy.

She skirted through the trees, though stealth wasn't really required since no one was on the lookout. Then she heard the motorcycle again, closer this time. She darted behind a tree and watched as the rider cut his engine and pulled into a dark alley about a half block away. She waited to see if he'd appear out of the alley, but he didn't. Still, instinct told her there was something not quite right about this, so she stayed hidden among the trees.

Five minutes later, he walked his bike to the museum's delivery entrance.

Her heart skipped a beat. There was something hauntingly familiar about this man—the cocky way he tilted his head, the way he leaned to one side and hooked his thumb in his belt loop as he studied the door. The way he brushed his hair off his face—a weird case of déjà vu. She studied him, trying to make a connection. Did she know him?

Then it hit her. He looked so much like Mac Canfield it was uncanny. Was it because she'd just been thinking about Mac? Memories of all those years ago washed over her in an instant. Lily placed her hand over her heart to stop the thudding beat she was sure he could hear.

Oh, shit. And then her fast-beating heart skidded to a halt as she watched him expertly jimmy the lock and slip into the building. She waited for the alarm to sound, ticking down the thirty seconds before it would go off. Nothing. He'd obviously deactivated it.

Well son of a bitch. He'd just broken in. In less than a minute and a half he had circumvented what was supposed to be an expert security system.

Now what? She had to check this out. She had to call the police.

She headed in the direction of the door, reaching into her purse to grab her cell phone, but something made her pause.

Of course it wasn't Mac, even though she could clearly picture him riding a mean-looking Harley like the one this guy had pulled up on.

Don't be stupid, Lily. Make the call. Mac was in Texas, where she'd left all the pieces of her past. Plus it had been ten years. The man she was looking at now was taller, broader, and he had a mighty fine ass.

Then again, so did Mac.

Three minutes. He'd been in there three damn minutes and was out again. No security team running like hell after him, either. He'd managed to slip in and steal something without the night watch even knowing he'd been there.

Those guys really sucked.

He had something under his arm. The telltale white sheen and its unusual shape meant it was one of the artifacts! Why the hell hadn't she called the cops? Because this guy reminded her of Mac?

Idiot, idiot, idiot! She was so fired. Of course, even the cops couldn't have gotten here in time, and calling for the dipshit security guards would be useless. She'd have to stop him first, then call the police.

She hurried the remaining distance across the well-manicured lawn, pulling her gun. As he turned toward the bike, she pointed it at his back.

"Freeze. I've got a gun pointed on you."

"Fuck," he whispered. He raised his hands above his head, the artifact held tight in his left hand.

She exhaled in relief, then smiled. This had been way too easy. "Put the item down and turn around slowly." She'd put him face-down on the ground, then call the cops.

He pivoted.

The past mingled with the present, and Lily felt dizzy. She almost dropped the gun, her worst nightmare come to life. *This* was why she hadn't called the cops. Something inside her had sent off warning bells and she hadn't wanted him to get caught.

"Mac."

Ten years had changed him, but not enough. Six feet of prime male flesh was instantly recognizable. Wicked sexy and hot enough to steal a woman's panties, and her heart, right out from under her.

"Lily?"

She was relieved to see his eyes widen with shock. The rush of pleasure from her fantasy of a few moments ago was doused by the cold reality of facing the man who stood in front of her right now. He was still the bad boy of her dreams, still a thief, who'd stolen something vital from her ten years ago that she could never get back. A very special gift. Okay, maybe stolen was too harsh a word, since she'd practically begged him to take it. But that was just semantics. He'd known what he was doing, and she'd been naïve and stupid and too damn much in love with him to know better. He'd gladly taken what she'd offered, then run like a thief in the night.

Just like he was doing now. Only it wasn't her virginity in his hands—it was a damned valuable piece of property.

"You've just stolen a priceless artifact."

His look of shock faded to a sharp frown. "What the hell are you doing here in Chicago? What are you doing at this museum?"

"I'm the one holding the gun so I'll ask the questions." She held out one hand, keeping the gun steady and trained on the center of his chest. "Hand over the artifact."

His gaze darted around, then back at her. "I don't think so. Lily, you have no idea what you're doing. Get out of here before you get yourself in trouble."

She stuck her hand out farther. "Give it to me, goddamit."

Now his posture relaxed, and danger signals boinged all over her body.

"I remember you saying something similar about ten years ago, but back then you were demanding my dick."

Asshole. Did he think she was going to go running into his arms as soon as she recognized him? Then again, that could actually work. Time for a little payback. She lowered the gun. "You're right. What am I doing?" She stepped closer. "It's really you."

As soon as she got within breathing distance of him, his scent registered and memories assailed her. He still smelled like Mac—a combination of earthy male and soap, a lethal blow to her olfactory senses. How could something so simple fire her up so quickly? And his body heat—she could feel it even though he stood inches away.

Get a grip, Lily!

Mac dropped his hands at her approach, and when he did, she grabbed the artifact and jumped away from his grasp, lifting the gun and pointing it at him once again.

"I can't believe you did that."

She shrugged. "I can't believe you fell for it. Turn around and face your bike. Keep your hands where I can see them."

"You won't shoot me."

She cast him a venomous glare and raised the barrel of the gun a little higher. "You in the mood to try me?" She thought about saying "make my day" but figured that'd be just a bit too corny.

Besides, while she might want him to suffer for screwing then dumping her ten years ago, she didn't want to kill him.

OF ALL PEOPLE TO RUN INTO AND OF ALL PLACES. MAC KNEW everything there was to know about this museum, about the traveling exhibit—how long it would be here, where it was located— night security and what to expect.

Yeah, he had every expectation covered. Everything except finding Lily here. *Goddamn.*

Mac stared down the barrel of the gun in Lily's hands, not at all afraid for his life. It might have been ten years since he'd seen her, and he might have done the cruelest thing a guy could do to a woman the last time they were together, but he knew without a doubt she'd never pull that trigger.

Lily wasn't a cold-blooded killer.

He'd broken her heart. He knew it and she knew it. But she wasn't about to fill his chest with lead as payback. If she'd wanted to make him suffer for what he'd done to her, her rich daddy could have taken care of that years ago. Mac could be rotting in jail right now on any number of trumped-up charges. Or for that matter, real charges. He had been a thief. John West had considerable influence in Dallas and could have pulled plenty of strings to see to it that Mac paid for what he'd done to his daughter.

But the night Mac had tossed Lily out of his apartment had been the last he'd seen of her until right now. He'd dumped her so she'd go to the Ivy League college she'd been accepted to and fulfill her destiny. He thought she'd become a lawyer or the head of her father's business.

He never thought he'd run into her again in an alley in Chicago. Or that she'd pull a gun on him. Just looking at her now made his jeans tighten in ways they shouldn't, broke his concentration in dangerous ways. She'd been bad news ten years ago and still was. Her eyes were still the brightest blue, and her hair, though shorter than it had been years ago, still shined like sable silk.

"Mac, turn around and put your hands on the seat of the bike," she said again.

"And if I don't?"

She paused for a second. "I'll shoot you."

His lips curled. "No you won't."

Apparently she realized he'd called her bluff. He took a step forward. Her eyes widened and she turned tail and ran, but Mac was on her before she was halfway across the lawn. He grabbed her and rolled onto his back, taking the impact onto himself and making sure Lily landed on top of him.

The artifact went flying over her head, landing with a crash and disintegrating into several tiny pieces.

From her position on top of him, Lily's head shot up and she gasped.

"Look what you did!" She pushed off his chest and scrambled on her hands and knees toward the broken object. Mac rose and calmly walked over to the container she hadn't noticed had rolled out from the center of the object.

"The artifact is a fake," he said. "This is what's valuable."

He held up the vial of green liquid contained within a thick Plexiglas container. The contents were well protected, just like he knew they'd be.

Lily sat back and stared at it. "What's that?"

"It's a virus."

She frowned. "A virus?"

"Yeah. Deadly virus. Like an open-it-breathe-it-and-everyone-dies kind of virus."

She cocked a brow. "Right. Does it come with little green aliens, too?"

"I'm dead serious here, Lily. No bullshit."

She stared wide-eyed at the vial for a few seconds, then back at him.

"It's fluorescent green."

He nodded. "Yeah."

"Why?"

He shrugged. "Hell if I know. I guess because it's toxic."

She visibly shuddered. "Jesus, Mac, what are you into?"

"I'm not into anything. It's not mine."

"Whatever it is, it belongs to the museum. Give it to me."

"You're not listening. It doesn't belong to the museum. You've been had. I don't know who hired you or what you're doing here, but the last thing you want is this vial."

"Still thinking you know what's best for me, I see."

He was about to answer, but she leaped forward, launching at his legs. Off balance, he went down like a falling tree. His back hit the ground, knocking the wind out of him.

Well, damn. He hadn't expected that. Where did she learn those moves?

Lily climbed up his body and grabbed for the serum.

Goddamn, she was a wildcat. While still struggling for breath, Mac rolled her over and pinned her to the ground.

Now this was a familiar position. His cock remembered it well, too. His mind screamed *danger* and *get the hell out of there*, but he wanted answers first.

OLD FEELINGS RUSHED TO THE SURFACE AS LILY FELT MAC'S body against hers. *Dammit.* She might hate what he'd done to her ten years ago, but her body clearly remembered all the good things about being with him, especially how he made her feel. Restless, hot, wet, and needy. And she felt it all right now, as well as really irritated that he'd just gotten the best of her.

"Get. Off. Me."

"You sure are a lot tougher than you used to be," he said, his breath warm against her cheek.

She inhaled deeply, but all that did was press her breasts against the hard wall of his chest. *So not helping.*

"Please let me up, Mac. I can't breathe."

He stared at her for a few seconds, and she was lost in the depth of his eyes. So easy for her to tumble back in time, remember the last moment they had been this close and he had been on top of

her. Only they'd been naked. And he'd been inside her. The flood
of moisture between her legs annoyed her.

They were history, no matter what her body thought.

"Tell me what you're doing here," he said.

"Get off me first."

With a sigh, he rose and held his hand out to her. She grasped
it and started to pull up, but at the same moment a shot rang out,
spraying up grass and dirt inches from where they lay. Not a loud
shot, either, but someone using a silencer. Mac fell on top of her
again with a hard thud, pulled a gun, and fired back in the vicinity
of the assailant.

"Stay down!" he ordered her, covering her body.

Lily held her breath. Who was shooting at them? More importantly, where was her gun?

"Let me up, Mac!" *Dammit!* She'd been a cop. She knew how
to fire a weapon. If he'd just move his big body off her, she could
use it. She did a quick scan of the area, spotting her gun on the
lawn just a foot or so out of her reach. But Mac was too heavy and
she couldn't throw him off. Now was not the time for chivalry.
She could help.

Instead, he tucked his arm around her back and rolled with her
behind a thick tree, then slammed her up against it, keeping her
covered as another spray of bullets sent bark flying a few inches
from her head.

Okay, someone was pissing her off. She wanted her gun and
now.

"Let me go!" she hollered.

"Stay still before you get hurt."

She pushed at him, but he had better leverage and it was like
trying to move the tree. He wouldn't budge.

"Is it museum security?" she asked.

"No. No one in uniform. Someone dressed in black."

Oh, hell. This wasn't good. Who was shooting at them? And

where was security? Goddamn useless, donut-eating morons! They were probably cowering under the lobby desk after they heard gunshots.

Mac shot off another round. "Do you see anyone else?"

She craned her head around him, searching both sides. "No. Just the single shooter."

Mac aimed, fired, then said, "I think I might have hit him. Let's move!"

Before she could object, he grabbed her hand and hauled her to her feet, dragging her along behind him. Bullets sprayed the dirt near their feet. No time to argue or grab for her gun along the way.

They tore down the alley toward his bike. "Get on!"

She didn't even think this time, letting common sense prevail. She hopped on the back of his bike, wrapped her arms around him, and held tight while he revved the engine and tore off down the alley, escaping the barrage of bullets as if the hounds of hell were chasing them.

Lily was afraid maybe they were. She didn't exhale the entire time Mac wound them around side streets and clear out of the city limits. They rode for hours, Lily's mind whirling the entire time. She didn't speak, and neither did Mac. Her body was too frozen with shock to move or talk or notice where they were headed. Not until they were well out of town and she realized they were in some remote location. Since no bullets had whizzed by her ears, she assumed they weren't being followed, but she wasn't about to unbalance the bike by shifting around to look.

There were no streetlights and the road had changed to two lanes. The trees were taller and more dense and the temperature had dropped, making her shiver from the chill. They'd moved from city to country, the smell of pine and clean air much more evident than in a smog-choked city.

After what seemed like hours of riding, evidenced by her rather numb tender parts, Mac finally turned onto a dirt road and into what appeared to be a deserted campsite. She hoped he knew where he was going, because she was hopelessly lost. When he pulled over, Lily resisted the urge to whoop for joy. He turned off the engine and waited for her to slip off the bike. He followed after her while she bent over to stretch her tight muscles. He pulled a bottle of water out of a saddlebag and took a long swallow, then tossed it her way.

She drank greedily, soothing her parched throat. And she finally exhaled.

"You okay?" he asked.

"Yes. Who was shooting at us back at the museum?" she asked.

"I have no idea. I thought maybe you would."

She shrugged. "No clue." But now that she had her wits about her again, she gave him a scathing look. "Are you out of your mind? Did you feel it necessary to play hero back there? We could have both been killed."

He stared at her, not even moving while she advanced on him. And he didn't say a word. Fine then, she had plenty to say. "For your information, I spent three years on the police force before leaving to become a private investigator. I know how to handle a gun. The one you knocked out of my reach. I could have helped. But, oh no. You had to throw yourself on top of me like some freakin' superhero and prevent me from grabbing my gun."

"You were a cop?" His eyes widened.

"That's not what we're talking about. We're discussing your macho show of overprotectiveness back there."

"I was trying to prevent you from being shot."

"I didn't need your help."

Ignoring her outburst, he unzipped his jacket and slowly started peeling it off his shoulders, as if he wasn't paying the slightest bit of attention to her.

"Are you listening to me at all, Mac? Are you hearing what I'm saying? I am competent, goddamit. I am not some airheaded idiot who needs protecting. And where's the vial?"

Once he had the jacket off, she zeroed in on the dark stain on his arm and a river of blood pouring off the ends of his fingers. Any anger she felt dissipated in a rush of panic and concern.

"Oh. shit. You were shot?" She rushed over and began to pull up his shirt.

"I'm fine," he said, but he didn't try to stop her.

"You're bleeding."

"Bullet just grazed me."

Her gaze rocketed to his. "Oh, and you're some kind of psychic doctor, I suppose. How do you know?"

He shrugged. "I've been shot a few times. I know."

She shuddered at the thought. "Spare me the details. Let's get this shirt off." She drew the shirt over his head, then peeled it gently away from his shoulder, taking special care when she pulled the fabric down his injured arm.

"We need more light." She looked around the campground, spotting a gray brick building with a single overhead light a short distance away. *Bathroom.* "Have you got a first aid kit in the bike?"

"Yeah. Left saddlebag."

She hurried over and fumbled through the bag, found the first aid kit and a flashlight, then pushed him toward the bathroom. The light switch revealed a dim bulb hanging from the ceiling. Thankfully there was a sink and paper towels in there.

"Sit," she ordered, pointing him toward the wooden bench next to the shower.

"Bossy," he teased, grinning up at her.

Ignoring him, she wet some paper towels, turned on the flashlight, and placed it on the edge of the sink so it was pointing toward his arm. She cleaned the wound, wiping away the blood so she could get a look at the injury.

Like he said, it was a graze. Mean looking and about three inches long, but not deep enough to need stitches. He was lucky the bullet had barely scraped the flesh of his arm. She cleaned it, applied pressure until the bleeding stopped, and after spreading some antibacterial ointment on it, placed a bandage over the wound.

The hot rush of adrenaline she'd felt after she'd seen the blood dripping down his arm calmed somewhat. She was surprised at the fear she'd felt seeing him bleeding like that, having long ago convinced herself she was immune to ever having feelings for Mac Canfield again. She should have known better than to think he would ever mean less to her. She sighed.

"You're going to be fine," she said, pushing her emotions deep as she cleaned everything up and turned to him.

"I could have told you that." He stood. "But thank you anyway."

"You're welcome."

MAC COULDN'T BELIEVE THE WOMAN STANDING IN FRONT OF HIM. The one who'd faced down a barrage of bullets, hopped on the back of his bike for a quick escape, then yelled at him because he'd prevented her from diving for her own gun.

She sure as hell wasn't the same Lily West he'd known so many years ago. That girl had been sweet and gentle and fragile. The woman who stood in front of him now looked similar, though obviously more grown-up—and a hell of a lot tougher. Curvier, too, with low-slung jeans hugging her hips, a snug-fitting polo shirt that accentuated fuller breasts and a slender waist. But what was completely unrecognizable was her attitude.

She stared at him, not speaking. Hell, he didn't know what to say. She licked her lips and he followed the track of her little pink tongue swiping across her full bottom lip.

His gaze went from her mouth to her eyes, and the past mingled with the present.

God, she really was here. He moved toward her and she took a step back, stopping when she hit the wall. But her gaze never left his. Even in the darkened bathroom the look she gave him was unmistakable. She was thinking the same thing he was.

Ten years ago. The heat between them. The fact they'd just been shot at a little while ago.

Aw, fuck it. He never was much good at thinking things through. He braced his hands on either side of her head and moved in closer, crowding her.

"Your arm," she said, looking at the bandage, then back at him.

"Is fine."

Her lips were still parted and he heard her breathing. Rapid little pants in and out, like she was having trouble catching her breath. But this time she wasn't pushing at him to let her go.

"Mac," she whispered, whether in warning or invitation he didn't know.

Before it became a denial spilling from her lips, he slanted his mouth over hers and took possession.

TWO

MAC DRANK IN THE SOUND OF LILY'S WHIMPER, ADDING A GROAN of his own.

A thousand reasons why he shouldn't be doing this fired through his brain. He shut them out. Fuck them all. He *was* doing this. She wasn't a young girl anymore. She was an adult. And until and unless she said no, he was barreling full steam ahead.

Christ, she tasted good. Hot and sweet and wet. He shifted, wrapping his uninjured arm around her back to pull her against his body. He rimmed her lips with his tongue, then slid it between her teeth to find hers, lapping against the velvet softness. She wasn't saying no. Not with the way her body sank into his.

Lily palmed his chest, smoothing her warm hands over his skin. He couldn't think rationally, just wanted her naked against him. He skimmed her belly, feeling the muscles there quiver while he lifted her shirt and jerked it over her head. A sexy little black bra barely contained her breasts. He traced the swells where they dipped into the satin enclosure. She shuddered.

Her eyes—soft, wide pools of dark blue—registered surprise.

He'd always loved her eyes. They told him so much about what she was thinking.

Don't say a word, he pleaded mentally. He didn't want anything to stop this.

She didn't speak, instead grabbed his belt buckle and unhooked it, then released the snap from his jeans. His breath came out in short rasps as she drew the zipper down and slid her hand inside, wrapping her cool fingers around his heated cock.

He pulsed against her hand, surging forward, loving the feel of her skin against his. But he wanted more. So much more. He buried his face in her neck, inhaling the scent of her, drawing his tongue along the column of her throat.

He remembered the taste of her, like an intoxicant entering his bloodstream, drugging him into a wild frenzy of untapped lust. He skimmed her flesh, sliding his fingers into her jeans.

The scent of her filled the air around them, a heady, potent aphrodisiac. He already knew how she'd taste and he wanted that sweet honey on his tongue.

Christ, he wanted it all and right now. It had been too damn long.

"Wait. Stop. Mac, stop."

His motor was running, his engine revving in high gear, and she wanted to slam on the brakes?

Shit. He slowed down, withdrew his hand from her pants, and pulled back, studying her eyes. Eyes that spoke volumes—that read *no. No, no, and no.*

"What's wrong?"

"We can't do this. I can't do this." She released her sweet, tight grip on his cock and started fixing her disheveled clothes.

Ah, hell. She was probably right, though his throbbing dick wanted to argue the point in a big way. He shoved it in his jeans and zipped up, staying silent while he gathered his composure, trying to figure out why the wildcat in his arms had suddenly tucked its tail and run.

Where had his common sense gone? One look, one whiff of her scent and he was off and running at high speed. He was on a case, not on vacation. This wasn't the time to pursue Lily, to take up where they'd left off ten years ago. He had a ton of questions. Like who she was now and why she'd been at the museum.

"Okay, we won't do this. If you'd rather talk than fuck, I have questions," he said. "Why were you at the museum tonight?"

She whirled on him, the heat, the passion of a few moments ago gone from her eyes, replaced by a cold hardness. "No. I have questions for *you*. And I'm not saying a damn thing until I get answers to *my* questions first."

So much for warmth and sex. He felt every bit of the chill in the night air. Or maybe that was coming from Lily, who'd definitely turned on the cold, hard freeze. "Then I guess we're not going to have much to say to each other, because I can't tell you anything."

She crossed her arms. "Ditto."

Shit. He couldn't exactly hold Lily captive without explaining why, but he sure as hell couldn't reveal who he worked for and why he'd stolen the vial. Which meant she was going to believe he was still a thief. He hated that, but it was how it had to be.

Wild Riders was a secret. No one outside their organization knew they even existed. Hell, their own government didn't even know. And it had to stay that way, which meant he'd have to lie to Lily.

Again. Just like ten years ago, when he told her didn't care about her, didn't love her, didn't want her in his life.

And just like ten years ago, she was going to hate him.

LILY WAITED FOR MAC TO SAY SOMETHING, ANYTHING. TELL HER he had a reasonable, logical explanation for breaking into the museum and stealing the artifact. Or, rather, the virus. This was so confusing.

"Well?"

He stared at her for a few seconds, then shook his head and left her standing in the bathroom.

Oh no. He was not going to get away with blowing her off again. She stalked out after him.

"You know, stealing someone's wallet or a few bucks here and there was bad enough when you were younger," she said, stepping around to the other side of the bike. He grabbed a clean shirt out of the saddlebag and put his jacket back on, then started lifting other things out. "I had hoped you had grown out of that petty thievery. What are you into now, Mac? Luxury cars? Fine art? Knocking off a bank here and there?"

He didn't answer. Instead, he tossed a lump of something on the ground, then gathered pieces of wood and started a fire in the campsite's pit. After that, he grabbed a roll and unraveled it.

"What are you doing?"

He looked up at her from his position on the ground. "You were always a smart girl, Lily. What does it look like I'm doing?"

She scanned the area, finally making the connection. Campsite. Tent. Oh hell no. "I am *not* staying here with you tonight."

"Yeah, you are, since I'm not taking you anywhere else. You didn't give me much choice after showing up . . ."

She waited for him to finish the sentence. Of course, he didn't. "And screwing up your theft of the artifact? Or the virus? Tell me about the vial. How did you know it was inside the artifact? What do you plan to do with it? How much are you making on this deal? Do you have any idea what terrorist organizations will do with something like that?"

He left the tent pieces and stood, approaching her. Just having him stand near her was unnerving. A few minutes ago she'd held his cock in her hand—hot and hard, his mouth and hands on her, reminding her of the all the reasons she'd fallen in love with him before. Sexy, uninhibited, and thrilling, he'd promised adventure and a trip to the dark side, a place she'd never been. But this wasn't ten years ago. Now was reality, not a teenager's fantasy.

If she hadn't gathered her wits about her and stopped him, she could have easily fallen into the same trap again and had sex with him. Maybe she hadn't learned a thing in ten years.

His eyes were warm, but his voice was cold. "I did steal the virus. But I can't tell you why or what I'm going to do with it, other than I'm not selling it and it's not going to fall into the hands of terrorists."

She was so confused. What she really needed was to talk to her boss and her client. Did the museum even know what was inside that artifact? Oh, why didn't she just call the police when she saw Mac pull up at the museum? She was in deep shit now.

She knew Mac's history, and if she had a choice, she'd choose her agency to turn the vial over to, not Mac. Not a once petty, now probably professional thief.

"A virus like that could be worth a fortune." She shuddered to think what someone could do with it. Countries looking to create chemical warfare. Terrorist organizations. The possibilities were endless.

"I can't tell you what I'm going to do with the virus. But trust me, it's nothing bad," he said.

"And I'm supposed to believe you."

He shrugged. "You have no reason to, but yeah, I'd like you to."

The look hadn't changed at all—street toughness mixed with charm. God, it was so sexy, had always served to dissolve her hesitations. It had worked so well back then. It didn't now, and that actually hurt. He had stolen something dangerous and destructive. Despite their connections to each other and to the past, she couldn't allow it. She grabbed her bag from the ground and pulled out her cell phone. Thank God she'd looped the long strap of her purse around her neck and shoulder or she'd have lost her purse in the scuffle in addition to her gun.

"I'm sorry, Mac, but I have to call this in. There's no way I can allow this virus to get out, no matter what you'd like me to believe."

She started punching numbers to call the agency, but Mac moved like a stroke of lightning. He was on her in seconds, jerked the phone out of her hand, threw it on the ground, and stomped it to pieces. She stared dumbstruck at the crumbled remains of her phone, not sure if she wanted to cry or kill him. Judging by the trembling anger bubbling up inside her, probably both. She forced a calm she didn't feel, refusing to break down in front of him.

"I'm sorry, too, babe, but I can't let you make that call. If you were calling your boss or the cops, that would spell bad news for me."

Gathering her wits about her, she said, "You should have thought about that before you broke into the museum."

"Tell me who your client is."

"I was hired by the museum to check night security. Which obviously sucked since you managed to get in."

Unbelievably, he grinned. She shook her head. He was proud of his prowess as a thief. Frustration ate at her, making her pace back and forth in hopes of releasing some of the furious tension boiling inside. Long-term passion and feelings for Mac or not, she was a law-abiding citizen, a former cop. She followed the rules. Mac had never followed them. She'd found that exciting about him once, to her detriment. She wasn't about to make the same mistake again.

"I'm not doing anything wrong, Lily."

"Give me a reason to believe you." This was why she had paused when she saw him at the museum, why she had delayed making that call. Instinct, maybe, but she'd somehow known it was him, couldn't bear turning him over to the police. Now she was kicking herself and needed some kind of proof, needed him to tell her anything at all that would make her believe in him.

"I don't have one. But you know me."

She laughed. "Yeah, I do. I know you're a thief."

"Okay, you're right. But do you really think I'm the kind of person who'd sell a killer virus to terrorists?"

She didn't think so, but ten years could change a person. Had Mac changed that much? "I don't know."

He reached out and skimmed his knuckles across her cheek. So gentle, the action so incongruent with his bad boy image. That's what always made her insane about him. He was unpredictable, never fit into any kind of a mold—part of what was attractive about him. And she'd always been able to see beyond the surface, past what everyone else had seen of Mac Canfield. She'd seen the goodness in him. Was that part of him still there?

He hadn't hurt her, and he could have. If he'd changed enough, become bad enough, he could have shot her, or left her behind to fend off the shooter. Instead, he'd grabbed her and taken her with him. He'd thrown his body over hers, making himself vulnerable to protect her.

"Don't believe everything you see, Lily. Things aren't always as they seem on the surface."

She sighed. "Then if there's a reasonable explanation for what you're doing, tell me." She wanted to believe him, wanted to accept that he'd changed, that what he was doing was some kind of superhero act, that he was working for the good guys.

"Sometimes you have to rely on faith and your instincts. What do your instincts tell you?"

"They didn't serve me so well ten years ago," she muttered, more to herself than to him.

"I'm sorry," he said. "For a lot of things. For ten years ago, for this. I can't change the past, and I can't change you being in the wrong place at the wrong time tonight. What happened tonight was a fuckup and you got caught in the middle. Now you're going to have to come with me. I know you don't like it—I don't like it. But I don't have any other choice."

She paused, her mind replaying what he'd just said. "You can't mean to kidnap me."

He moved back to the tent and resumed erecting it. "I'm not sure what I'm going to do with you. I hadn't expected to run into anyone—especially not you—but I sure as hell can't let you go."

Her frustration returned. She couldn't believe she'd almost had sex with him. What the hell had she been thinking? Oh, right. She hadn't been. Just like when she'd offered her body like a sacrificial lamb, as if giving up her virginity to Mac would somehow open his eyes and make him realize she could be the greatest thing in his life.

It hadn't made a damn difference to him. He'd taken what she offered and still dumped her. She'd been stupid then, just like she'd been stupid a few minutes ago in the bathroom. What was it about him that made her IQ drop a hundred points and turned her into a quivering mass of bimbo?

"I'm not going anywhere with you voluntarily, and I can't believe you'd stoop to kidnapping."

He tightened the tent ropes and stood, wiping his hands on his jeans before he approached. "Look, Lily. I wish I could give you answers. I'm not into anything illegal, but I can't tell you what I'm going to do with the virus and I can't let you go, so you're just going to have to ride along."

She was about to start another argument with him, but that was pointless. He was obviously lying and probably into "illegal" up to his neck. But it occurred to her if she went with him it would be a perfect opportunity to bide her time and recover the virus. If she didn't go with him, the virus was gone. And no way could she let that deadly virus get out there in the world. While she was at it, maybe she'd figure out what Mac was really up to. If she was clever enough, she could wait until just the right moment, uncover his secrets, and steal the virus before he made delivery to . . . whom- ever. Hell, she could bust this case wide open.

Then again, she'd be bringing Mac down while doing it, and that wasn't something she wanted to be responsible for. She'd fig- ure that out later. First thing she had to do was cooperate, gain his trust. Maybe even ply him with a little seduction.

After all, men thought with their cocks most times, anyway. She wasn't above using her feminine wiles to get Mac to give her what she wanted. And what she wanted right now was informa- tion, the virus, and her freedom. And it would make her agency happy. Good PR, right?

Okay, so maybe she still carried a big, bright burning torch for Mac. That much was obvious after the episode in the bathroom. Her pussy quivered at the way he'd backed her up against the wall, the promise in his touch and in his kiss. She wanted more.

But he'd used her ten years ago. Payback time.

As soon as he trusted her and let his guard down, she'd be history—along with the virus.

"Lily," he said, breaking her thoughts. "I'm sorry this hap- pened . . ."

She shrugged and sat in front of the fire, not saying anything. She didn't want to give in too easily. He sat next to her and added another log, the additional flame calming the chills shivering through her body. The night had grown cooler, the wind picking up around them adding a bite. It wasn't quite summer yet and late spring nights up in the hills could still be cold.

"I remember when you took me up to the point to see the stars," she said, glancing at the sky.

He smiled. "You said you'd never been out in the country be- fore. I was surprised."

"Hey, I was a city girl. It wasn't like my dad ever took camping trips or treks into the hills."

"You had your head tilted back for so long you ended up with a crick in your neck. You must have gaped at those stars for hours."

"They were so beautiful. Like tonight." The bittersweet memories washed over her. Sitting in Mac's convertible, the sky clear black and the stars so close she felt like she could reach up and touch them. She'd never seen anything like it. They were like that tonight, too. And the same man was next to her again. He'd been the only one to give her adventures. She'd had to create her own excitement after Mac, and even then it hadn't been the same, because he hadn't been with her.

"So you were a cop?" he asked.

She nodded.

"How did that happen?"

She lifted her lips at the incredulity in his voice. "I majored in police science in college, then went to the academy after graduation."

"What about law school?"

"That was my father's dream, not mine."

Mac shook his head. "Bet your dad was pissed about that."

"Oh, he was so angry." She grinned at the memory. "Threatened to cut off my funding, refused to pay for college. His way of getting me to toe the line. It backfired on him. I got loans instead, determined to do what *I* wanted to do. When he realized I wasn't going to back down and return to the fold with my tail tucked between my legs, he relented and paid for my education." She looked at her hands. "Not that it did me much good."

"Why not?"

"Three years on the force, and he used his influence to keep me off the streets. I got tired of his interference, tired of being assigned desk jobs and fighting him. I quit."

"And now you're a PI?"

"Yeah."

"How did you end up in Chicago?"

"I couldn't get hired anywhere in Dallas. Dad's power was too great there. I moved to Chicago to get away from him, so I could actually do my job without him sticking his fingers in everything I did."

"You own the agency?"

"Not yet. I figured Dad would hinder me less if I just worked for an agency right now, so I found someone who I thought couldn't be bought or manipulated. Maybe someday I'll start my own. We'll see how this goes."

"You like it?"

She shot him a sideways glance. "Actually, I do. A lot."

"And here I thought you'd end up a lawyer in your father's company."

"That's what he wanted. Hence the 'pissed' part."

"You always enjoyed digging at him."

She lifted her chin, thoughts of her father inflaming her nerve endings. "He deserves it."

"Yeah, he does." He shifted on the log. "You turned out so damn different than what I thought."

She wanted to say "and you dumping me did no good, did it?" Insead she kept silent, knowing it would come across shrewish and petty, but she couldn't help wondering how different things would have been if they'd stayed together, if he'd given them a chance.

"I turned out exactly the way I wanted to." *Sort of.* "I did what I wanted to do. Nothing you did ten years ago stopped that." *There.* She'd said it.

"I guess not. All those years ago you talked about taking a walk on the wild side. Did you ever do that?"

Had she? She'd changed direction in her life and career, taken risks, but done anything wild and crazy? "Not really."

"So how about doing it now?"

She studied him, trying to decipher his meaning. Did he mean the trip to deliver the virus, or something else entirely? Was this about sex, about picking up where they'd left off . . . where they'd never really had the chance to go all those years ago? They'd barely started before he walked out of her life.

This was her chance to experience bad boy Mac Canfield. In the flesh. At least for a while . . . as she furthered her career.

He might be a thief and he might be going to jail when this was all over with, yet she couldn't help but want what she hadn't had ten years ago.

The experience, the lifestyle. She admitted it—she craved it, wanted to know what it was like to ride on the back of Mac's Harley and just live the wild life with him.

And she'd get answers at the same time. It wasn't like she was going to allow him to get away with anything illegal, so why the hell not? As long as she considered it part of her job and didn't let her foolish heart get involved, then she could handle it, right?

Heat seared her as she met the promise in his dark gaze.

"What about it, Lily? You game?"

"It's insane." She shook her head.

"You used to be all-in for adventure."

He was baiting her. "I used to be a lot of things I'm not anymore."

"Don't hesitate. Don't think about it. Just do it."

He had no idea what he was asking. Then again, he had no clue about a lot of things. She looked up at him, unable to believe how much her body still swelled with heat just looking at him.

She nodded. "Okay, Mac. You're on. I'll take that walk on the wild side with you."

THREE

MAC DIDN'T BELIEVE FOR ONE SECOND THAT LILY HAD JUST HAD an about-face and agreed to go with him. She had a plan in mind, no doubt to lull him into some false sense of security, steal the virus from him, and return it to her client. Which, of course, was in direct opposition to his assignment.

Not only did she think he was a thief, she also thought he was stupid. Whatever idea she had in her gorgeous head didn't matter. As long as she came with him without argument, he could deal with anything she tried to pull.

He moved through the thick woods, having used the excuse of hunting for more firewood to put some distance between himself and Lily. He needed to make a call—one she couldn't listen in on. He had to call General Lee.

As the head of Wild Riders, General Grange Lee was not a patient man, and Mac was already late phoning in his report. His cell had been buzzing incessantly for several hours, but no way could he take a call with Lily lurking nearby.

Grange answered on the first ring.

"What the hell took you so long?"

"I ran into a little trouble." Understatement, since it was a dump-truck-of-shit kind of trouble. He filled Grange in on what happened at the museum, including being shot at and running into Lily and the fact she was a blast from his past. He also told Grange about Lily's former occupation as a cop and current job as a PI.

"Christ, Mac. This was supposed to be an easy lift."

"So you said."

"Any clue who was shooting at you?"

"None. My guess is someone else who wanted the virus. But who?"

"That's the billion dollar question, isn't it? What about your friend Lily? Could she be involved in this virus thing somehow? Do you think she's dirty?"

Mac laughed. "Lily? Not a chance." It might have been a decade since he'd last seen her, but no way had she changed that much.

"You did the right thing under the circumstances. I don't like that she knows as much as she does, little that it is. You sure as hell can't let her go now. Not until you make the delivery. If she's involved in this somehow, then she jeopardizes your mission. And even if she's not, she'll go running to the cops or back to her agency and client with information we don't want them to have. She'll have to stay with you."

"That's what I'm thinking." Though it would make his job a lot harder trying to hold onto her while traversing the countryside. Not impossible, just difficult.

"Keep her with you, travel around a day or two longer. Make a few stops here and there so she doesn't know exactly where or when you're making the delivery, then dump her. I don't want her getting anywhere near her client or her agency until after the delivery is made. And it would be nice if we could somehow fig-

ure out who was shooting at you. I'd like to know who wanted
that virus. We'll do what we can from this end to figure that out,
too."

"Got it."

"And stay in touch. Holler if you need backup."

"Will do." He hung up, scrounged for some firewood, and
made his way back to the campsite.

He hated keeping secrets from Lily, especially this one. He'd
like to show her just how much he had turned his life around in
the last ten years, but he owed his allegiance to Grange and the
Riders. He had to do whatever was necessary to maintain the integrity of the program, and that meant not telling Lily anything.
With a resigned sigh, he broke through the brush and into the
campsite. She was sitting on a log near the fire, shivering.

Cold night. He made a mental note to stop tomorrow for
clothes and supplies. And if they were going to be riding he'd need
to reconfigure the bike so she'd be more comfortable.

She turned her head as he walked up to the fire. "Took you
long enough. What? You didn't shoot a deer for me?"

He grinned. "Forgot my rifle. Sorry. I have some cheese and
crackers in my jacket, though. That'll have to do for tonight."

"Yummy."

They sat and ate while the fire kicked up. Unfortunately, so did
the wind, and the light clothes Lily wore were no protection. "We
need to get into the tent. It's getting colder out here."

Lily nodded, wrapping her arms around herself. "Good idea.
I'm freezing."

They crawled inside the tiny tent that really was only designed
for one person, which meant a very tight squeeze. One blanket,
too. Mac traveled light. He hadn't expected to be housing a guest
in his tent. Then again, Lily wasn't very big. They'd make do. It'd
be cramped as hell in there, but they'd manage.

He slipped off his leather jacket, making sure to hide the vial and his cell phone out of Lily's reach. "Put this on," he said, wrapping the jacket around her.

"Then you'll be cold," she said.

He couldn't see her face in the darkness. He really liked looking at her, because her eyes told him so much. "I'll be fine. You're freezing. I can feel you shivering."

She shrugged into his jacket and he pulled the blanket around her legs. He settled himself onto the icy canvas floor of the tent, resigned to a cold night. He'd suffered worse than this before.

Once they were situated, everything went quiet, the night sounds outside and the crackling fire the only noises. Mac listened to Lily's breathing, wondering if she'd fall asleep fast or if she was uncomfortable. She lay still for the longest time and he thought she was asleep, but then she let out a deep sigh. He waited for her to say something, but she didn't.

Yeah, it was cold, and the ground was damned uncomfortable. This wasn't exactly a cozy setup for sleeping, but under the circumstances it was the best he could do. Tomorrow they'd stay someplace warmer but tonight was about getting someplace remote and fast, and making sure no one was following them. He preferred the outdoors anyway, where he could keep his ears open, hear cars or footsteps, listen to the sounds, and pick up anyone who might be sneaking up on them.

Finally, she seemed to settle down. Mac closed his eyes and mentally planned the route he'd take. Off the beaten path, no main roads, except tomorrow when they'd stop at a bike store to swap seats and then another place to get Lily some clothes. He'd stay on the back roads, mainly because he liked to wind around and enjoy the ride. Plus he didn't like traveling the highways, and since they'd gotten away with the virus, he could almost bet whoever had shot at them would be on the lookout for them. Which meant the less traveled roads were safer.

He startled when Lily moved, shuffling around next to him.

"What are you doing?" he asked.

"Hang on."

She shifted, surprisingly, on top of him, laying her body over his and pulling the blanket over them both. Instant heat enveloped him.

"What are you doing, Lily?" he asked again.

"There's no sense in both of us freezing," she said, her voice low as she faced him. "You were shot tonight and need to stay warm."

"My shoulder doesn't even hurt."

"So? I won't be able to sleep knowing you're cold and I'm wrapped up in your jacket and the only blanket."

"I think you're trying to find the vial. Or my phone." Or his gun.

"You don't trust me." There was a tinge of shock in her voice.

"Duh."

"I'm not after either. I'm trying to keep you from freezing."

He didn't believe her. And he wasn't cold now—not with her breasts pressed against his chest and her pelvis rubbing against his crotch. In fact, his cock was warming pretty damn fast. "This isn't a good idea."

"Am I hurting your shoulder?"

"No. I told you it doesn't hurt at all. And I'm plenty warm."

"And now so am I. This feels good, and I'm even warmer now."

If she kept wiggling around on top of him things were going to get even more heated. Was she deliberately trying to torment him? If so, it was working. He still thought she was trying to maneuver her way toward the vial and his cell phone. Not that it would do her any good. He had tucked them safely out of her reach, so even in her current position she wasn't going to find them. But damn, who could think straight when her warm, lush body was sliding over his? She was going for distraction—and it was working. Damn, was it ever working.

"Lily, you're playing a very dangerous game."

His vision had adjusted to the darkness now and enough moonlight filtered through the tent that he could see her cocked brow. "Who's playing? It's cold outside. This is basic survival."

He lifted his lips. "We're hardly in the Arctic."

She shrugged against him, splaying her hands out. She was searching the tent for the vial and he damn well knew it. "I'm cold natured. I need the extra warmth. This is purely self-preservation. You wouldn't deny me that, would you?"

Right now he'd deny her nothing. She wasn't going to get what she was looking for, but she was going to get something entirely different if she kept playing this game. He was at her mercy as she surged against him. Her soft hair brushed his face, her breath wafting against his neck. He slid his arms around her, pressing down on her lower back to feel more of the contact of her body along his.

He decided to test her by letting his hands wander lower, cupping the globes of her ass and gently kneading them. She gasped and stilled.

He waited for her to roll off now that she knew she wasn't going to find the vial or his phone, but he didn't remove his hands from her ass. Instead, he kneaded her butt cheeks, pulling her against his erection, letting her feel what she was doing to him.

He was damn shocked when Lily laid her head on his shoulder and moaned, rocking against his now fully erect cock.

"Mac," she sighed.

He'd expected retreat, not a full-on attack. So now what? Undressing in this tiny tent was out of the question. And fucking her? So not a good idea for way too many reasons. But he owed her. He owed her big-time. And he could help her sleep. She was tensed up from everything that had gone down tonight—he could feel it in every muscle of her body. So was he, but at the moment he wasn't thinking about himself—he was thinking only about Lily, and the way she felt on top of him, sliding her jean-clad pussy against his cock, wanting what he desperately wanted to give her.

But not this way, and not tonight.

"That's it, baby," he whispered against her ear. "Ride my cock. Does it feel good on your clit?"

"Mmm-hmmm," she mumbled, her face buried in his neck. She had a death grip on his shirt as she pitched forward.

She needed better contact. He reached between them, finding the button of her jeans. With a quick flip of his fingers the button was undone and he drew the zipper down. Hey, he was a thief. He was good at getting into things. And getting someone out of things. With a hard tug, he jerked Lily's jeans down her hips, maneuvering underneath her to drag them down her thighs.

Damn, he wished he was naked so he could feel the silky smoothness of her skin against his. This would have to do.

"Now rub against my dick. Make yourself come."

She lifted, her gaze searching, curious. "Don't you want to . . ."

He grinned, swept her hair behind her ears. "More than life itself, baby. But this isn't the time or place, and there's no room in this tiny tent for a rollicking fuck session. Besides, I want to enjoy you. I just want to hear you, feel you get off. Now do it."

Those eyes of hers . . . so vivid. She might want, but she was unsure whether to trust him. He asked a lot of her, exposing her like this, and he knew it. Once again, she was the one taking all the risks. But she was also the one who'd reap all the rewards. She needed this. Her muscles were taut with tension and she needed to unwind.

"Come for me, Lily," he whispered. "Let me do this for you."

She stayed like she was, braced up with her hands on either side of him, then moved forward, her pussy brushing against the rough denim of his jeans. Against the hard rock of his dick, which throbbed in response, pulsing in protest.

Yeah, yeah, it could complain as much as it wanted, but no way was he going to roll her under him and fuck her. Not tonight and not like this. Too much history, too much mental wrangling he wasn't prepared to deal with. Besides, it was pure heaven soaking in the response in her eyes, the way her lips parted and she gasped as her clit found what it needed, dragging against his shaft.

"That feel good?" he asked.

"Oh. Oh, yes," she whispered, her voice all gravelly soft and doing terrible things to his balls.

At least he didn't have to worry about being cold anymore. Heat swelled his cock to painful proportions; the sweet burn of her body undulating against him was roasting him. Yeah, he was more than hot now. Lily was fire and he was engulfed.

He lifted his hips to give her better access, and she responded by groaning.

"Mac."

His name spilling from her lips made him shudder. He gripped her hips, helping her slide along his cock. Her panties were wet, the moisture from her pussy soaking through his jeans. The urge to slip his fingers inside her, to feel her tight muscles surround his finger, was prominent in his mind. He wanted to pump her pussy and bring her to orgasm, to feel her clench and writhe around him and scream in his ear while her hot cream poured over his dick.

And why, exactly, wasn't he doing that? Because of some misguided sense of chivalry? When had he developed *that* particular affliction? Hell of a time for him to become honorable.

Especially when her breathing grew sharper, her movements faster as she slid with relentless determination against his swollen cock.

"Mac, I need to come."

"I know." He dug his fingers into her hips and drew her down hard. His gaze was riveted on the concentration on her face, on how her teeth nibbled her bottom lip. The sounds of her ragged breaths intermixed with the tiny moans that escaped as she neared climax.

"Yes, so close."

She was panting now, and he gritted his teeth. Fuck, she was making him crazy rocking against his dick like that. His balls squeezed tight against his body, damn near bursting with the sweet pleasure of her hot pussy all over him. Control was almost nonexistent but he held on, concentrating on her face as she tilted her head back, cried out, and released, shuddering against him.

He could only imagine the sweet relief she felt as her orgasm crashed through her, leaving her trembling in its wake, panting as she fell on top of him, her head on his shoulder.

Mac wrapped his arms around her and let her recover. He kept his eyes closed, the memory of Lily coming apart on top of him so damn sweet.

And not at all comforting to his throbbing cock.

She wiggled around and adjusted her clothes, then looked at him. God, she was incredibly beautiful with her hair disheveled and her lips parted. A ray of moonlight shined down on her, making her look like a wild angel come to visit him.

More like a she-devil temptress out to steal his soul.

She reached for the buckle of his belt, but he laid his hand over hers.

"No."

She frowned. "Let me do this for you." She glanced at his erection.

"Trying to distract me again so you can go on the hunt for the vial?"

With a wry grin, she shook her head. "No, I'm trying to make you come."

He shuddered at the thought. Tempting, but not a good idea. He needed his wits about him and he'd already lost them once.

"I'm fine, babe. But thanks. Just lie here with me and let's get some rest."

"You don't look fine. You look hard."

She really was tempting him. How easy it would be to let go. "Lily, you can see how goddamn much I want you. But this tent is small, and all I wanted tonight was to get you off. Now relax. We'll have time for more later. Get some sleep."

She frowned, but didn't say anymore, just rolled to his side and pulled the jacket and blanket over them both before snuggling against him with a deep sigh.

Good. At least she'd gotten a little relief. Frankly, he was surprised she'd gone for his suggestion. Hell, he was surprised about a lot of things. Whoever Lily West used to be wasn't the woman he'd met again tonight. The Lily of ten years ago would never have rubbed her pussy against his cock and gotten herself off. She'd staggered him with her bold moves just now.

Then again, he didn't know a damn thing about the Lily of now, did he? He had to stop thinking of her as the shy, virginal girl she'd been. That girl was gone. In her place was a competent, ball-busting ex-cop turned private investigator. One who wanted to turn him in as a thief. One who wanted to steal the virus from him.

He looked at her, wishing he could delve into her mind, really talk to her. But that would mean telling her things he couldn't. Not right now, anyway. Maybe not ever.

Her breathing was deep and even, signaling she'd fallen asleep. The orgasm had worked. She'd needed the release. So did he. But Mac hadn't often gotten what he wanted, and what he'd really wanted tonight was Lily. What he'd always wanted was Lily.

Denial built character, right?

Or at least a long sleepless night.

*   *   *

LILY WOKE EARLY, HER BODY SPRAWLED HALF OVER MAC'S. SHE was cold, stiff, and utterly pissed about her behavior the night before.

She'd been after the virus and his cell phone—or even his gun. Instead, she'd gotten an orgasm. No vial, no cell phone, no gun. No freedom.

But yeah, she'd gotten one hell of a climax. Then she'd passed out in his arms, and this morning she was still Mac's prisoner.

Ugh. Some tough PI she was. *Hell of a way to do your job, Lily.*

The odd thing was she felt no embarrassment. He'd offered, she'd needed it, and why the hell shouldn't she have taken it? Anxiety had ratcheted up to screaming level, and she'd really craved a shriek-inducing orgasm. She might not have screamed, but she sure cried out with the release.

Granted, it hadn't been the same as having Mac's thick cock buried deep inside her, but what her body wanted and what it was going to get were two different things.

Besides, she had no business dredging up the past with Mac, at least not emotionally. Physically, well, why not? They were two consenting adults—she was no longer a wide-eyed teenager. She was more mature than the last time they'd played this game. She could handle it now. The logical part of her knew that she and Mac had no future beyond this time they would spend together. Why not use him the same way he'd used her ten years ago? He was great in bed, knew how to use his mouth and hands. She'd never had better orgasms than the ones she'd had with him. Even the one last night had been pretty damned spectacular, and he'd done nothing more than lie there while she rolled around on top of him and rubbed her clit against his cock.

Her body heated at the memory, wanted much more than that.

Tough. Now was not the time. Finesse was required, and a little more teasing. That meant that Mac would have to wait. And so would she.

"You're deep in thought this morning."

She lifted her head and looked into his dark, mesmerizing eyes. "I'm always deep in thought."

"Sleep well?"

"Like the dead. Thanks for the orgasm."

"My pleasure."

She cracked a smile. "No, I believe it was mine alone. Sorry about that."

He grinned back and they crawled out of the tent, Lily heading straight for the bathroom. She realized after she'd used the facilities that she only had the clothes on her back. Not even a toothbrush or a comb to drag through her hair. She rinsed her mouth with water, then looked up and glanced into the dirty mirror, grimacing at the remnants of yesterday's makeup spread across her eyes. They'd definitely have to stop for a few necessities today. She hoped Mac was amenable to that. And where the hell was he hiding the vial and phone? She had to find them.

He was already taking down the tent when she returned.

"Mac, I'm going to need a few things."

"Already got that covered," he said without turning around. "I figured you're going to need some girlie supplies, and I need to get a new seat for the bike. You can't continue to ride on that tiny backseat. Not with the mileage we have to put on the next few days."

Girlie supplies? She smiled at that. *A new seat? Mileage?* "Just how far are we going?"

"Can't tell you." He shoved the folded tent into the bag and stood, facing her. "The ride's scenic though. You'll enjoy it."

She rolled her eyes as she followed him to the bike. *Scenic.* Great. That revealed a lot.

After packing up, he tossed her his jacket and made her put it on.

"Shouldn't you wear it? You're in front."

"I'll be fine until we get you a jacket." He straddled the bike and looked at her. "Get on. We have a lot to do today."

With a resigned sigh, she climbed on the back of his Harley and wrapped her arms around him, holding tight while he sped out of the campground. The first stop was at a little mom-and-pop store where they had a quick cup of coffee—which was thick and strong and tasted wonderful. The breakfast roll was a little dry, but after no dinner last night it was heaven on earth. Then it was right back on the bike again.

It occurred to her as they whipped through the chilly morning breeze that, other than riding a block here and there, she'd never really been on a motorcycle before the adrenaline-pumped journey with Mac last night. Instinct had roared to life and caused her to jump on the back of the Harley as if she'd known what she was doing.

In the bright light of day, she realized as Mac flew around sharp curves, this was a rather terrifying experience. The passenger seat, such as it was, was minimal at best, barely affording a spot for both her butt cheeks. There was no backrest in case she slid backward, forcing her to lean forward and hold onto Mac for dear life.

Funny how she hadn't noticed any of these things last night. The thoughts had never crossed her mind, since bullets had been zinging at the time. Now that she was safe and actually paying attention, the whole bike-riding ordeal was a little hair-raising and not at all like her fantasies of hopping onto the back of a bad boy's bike, the wind whipping through her hair as the engine roared and they zipped down the road.

Well, she was definitely on the back of a bad boy's bike right now. Her fantasies had always centered around Mac and his Harley. And now she was riding with him, living out her dream.

Okay, so maybe it wasn't so bad. The wind was definitely whipping, and she sure as hell felt like she was flying. If she focused on the positives rather than the negatives, she could see that this was a rather liberating experience, actually. The roar and vibration of the bike between her legs was a giant moving turn-on. Her breasts pressed against Mac's back, her thighs aligned with his—oh yeah, this was pretty cool.

After about an hour or so the thrill wore off and she wondered if they'd be stopping anytime soon. Her butt was getting sore. He mentioned getting a new seat—she hoped it had lots of padding.

After two hours nonstop on the bike, Lily was more than ready to get off. In fact, her body was screaming for it. Her back was tight, her butt was numb, and the tender spots between her legs . . . she just wasn't going to go there.

Thankfully, not too long after that, Mac pulled into a bike shop. Lily stretched her tight muscles, resisted the urge to massage between her legs where she was really sore, and followed him inside.

She waited at the counter while he purchased a new seat for the bike, then he pulled her over to the clothing section and made her try on some jackets.

"These are heavy."

"The elbows and shoulders have built-in Kevlar to protect you in case we wipe out."

She arched a brow. "But we won't do that, will we?"

He grinned. "Hell no. But I like the thought of you being protected when we ride. Plus, the jacket will keep you warm. Even though it's nearly summer, riding a bike is chillier than being in a car. And the nights can still be cold."

So she'd noticed.

"You need chaps, too. And boots."

She looked down at her feet. "I have shoes."

"Yeah, and the heat of the pipes is melting the soles. You need boots."

She rolled her eyes and followed him around the store while

he chose gear for her to wear. After he'd picked out chaps, boots, a helmet, gloves, and goggles, he added them to the well-padded leather jacket. She had to admit, he chose a pair of kick-ass boots for her, too. Finally, he called it good and they checked out, new seat in hand.

"What are you going to do with your current seat?" she asked as he switched out bike seats there in the parking lot.

"Leave it here. Nothing else I can do about it. I'll get a replacement for it after . . . later."

After what? After he dropped her somewhere? She almost felt guilty about him losing the original seat to his bike, but immediately shoved that thought aside. It hadn't been her idea to come along on this expedition, so she had no business feeling sorry for him and his lost bike seat.

The new seat looked thick and cushiony, and he'd also purchased a padded backrest that he called a sissy bar. *Hallelujah!*

"Good bitch seat. You should be comfortable now."

"Bitch seat and sissy bar, huh?"

He grinned. "That's what I call them. If you're going to be a biker babe, you need to learn the lingo."

Biker babe. Cute. That was some terminology. She'd known Mac for years and he'd always had a bike, but he'd never let her ride with him. In fact, he'd always tried to push her away, get her to go home, even though she'd insisted on hanging around him.

Like a disgusting, lovesick puppy.

Live and learn. She should have listened when he told her to get lost. How different her life might have turned out.

Yeah, right. If not for Mac, she'd have dutifully followed her father's dictates and gone to college, then law school, never once thinking about what *she* wanted to do with her life.

Despite her broken heart, Mac had taught her a lot about thinking for herself, about demanding the freedom to live her own life, not one that had been decided for her. She'd done that and more, thanks to him. If she'd only learned to guard her heart around him, their relationship could have ended on a good note.

But no. She had to go and fall in love with the bad boy. The one she had no business going crazy over. The one who'd tried his best to push her away.

Lily had refused to take no for an answer. She was her father's daughter, after all. A lot of John West's DNA was deeply embedded within her. Like stubbornness and refusing to yield. Yeah, she definitely had an armload of that. So every time Mac had tried to get rid of her, she'd come back, determined to win him over.

He'd been so wrong for her. Everything he represented was what her father hated. Mac had been poor, in trouble, going nowhere in life. His parents had been warring alcoholics, his dad in and out of prison. Mac had most definitely not been college bound, had no career or educational goals in mind. All he'd wanted to do was hang out, ride his bike, and work on cars. And petty thievery—oh yeah, that was one of his specialties. That's why he was so good working with his hands.

Work with his hands. Lily had been mesmerized by his hands. Watching him every day after school, leaning over the hood of a souped-up muscle car in the garage had made her nerve endings tingle.

All Mac ever said was that she'd get dirty.

She'd wanted to get dirty. She'd craved Mac's grease-stained hands all over her pristine clothes, wanted his work-roughened fingers on her bare skin, his stubbly beard brushing against her cheek, his mouth on hers . . .

The memories alone were like a forest fire on a snow-covered mountain. Despite the morning chill, the memories of Mac thoroughly heated her to the core.

Memories that were best tucked into the far recesses of her

mind and not dredged up. She'd jump his bones later in the physical sense only, because there was no room in her life for an emotional entanglement with Mac. Right now she had to strategize getting that vial away from him.

Then again, since he seemed to have it well hidden and obviously wasn't keen on her ransacking his saddlebags or body at the moment, she'd have to study all the places he might have it tucked away, so that when the opportunity arose for her to do a little digging, she'd know where to start.

"That should do it," he said, tossing his tools back into the saddlebag and straightening. "New seat's in place. Let's see about getting you some of those woman supplies you need as well as a couple changes of clothes."

After the bricklike original seat, the new one was a slice of heaven to her abused butt. Mac drove them a short distance to a nearby store, where she bought another pair of jeans, a couple of shirts, and some underthings, then to a drugstore for some sundry items like toothbrush, hairbrush, and a little makeup. Okay, so she was just vain enough to want to touch up a bit.

She felt better now, having clothes and essentials. She just wished she had her cell phone so she could report in to her client and to her boss, but that would just have to wait. Mac watched her like a hawk wherever they went, so she wasn't able to sneak off to a pay phone. She hoped her client didn't think she was the one who'd stolen the artifact. Hell, for all she knew there could be an APB out on her for art theft.

Her stomach clenched at the thought. She really needed to get to a phone. She had to get the vial and get away from Mac and back to Chicago.

She didn't want to think of Mac on the bad side of the law, but it wouldn't be the first time it had happened. She had hoped by now he would have turned his life around.

Guess not.

Which she had to remind herself wasn't her problem, since she was no longer emotionally attached to him.

Her clothes and toiletries were packed into the saddlebags. Mac helped her into her chaps, then drew out a pair for himself and zipped and snapped them on.

Holy crap. A rush of heat enveloped her as she looked at him standing next to his Harley. Biker dude in leather chaps and jacket, dark shades, and gloves. Now if that wasn't the sexiest thing she'd ever seen, she didn't know what was. Her mouth watered at the look, feel, and smell of the leather on him. She wanted to stand closer, to run her hands over his body—hell, she wanted to strip down on the spot and rub her entire naked body over his.

Damn. Focus, Lily. Pure physical response, right?

Right.

She slipped on her leather jacket, gloves, and goggles, then they hopped on the bike again and took off down the main road.

Lily expected Mac to jump on the highway. He didn't. Instead, he turned off the main road and started down one of the side streets, then hit a two-lane road and stayed on it, bypassing every single main highway entrance.

She leaned forward when he stopped at a light, pressing against him so she could talk against his ear. "Where are we headed?"

"South."

She rolled her eyes. That much she realized. "South where?"

"Can't tell you."

Okay, so she already knew that was going to be his answer, but she had to try. She leaned back, rested her hands on his hips, and decided to just enjoy the ride. Once the sun was fully up, it warmed considerably. She was comfortable in the jacket, gloves, and chaps, which kept the cool wind from cutting into her, and the warm sun on her face lulled her into relaxation. She found herself enjoying the scenery, her body adapting to the turns in the roads and the thrum of the bike between her thighs.

She figured they must be somewhere near the state line, but wasn't exactly sure how far they had ridden, and she wasn't familiar with the road around here.

Where was he taking her?

And where the hell was the virus?

FOUR

BY NIGHTFALL, THEY'D RIDDEN OVER EIGHT HOURS. LILY'S BUTT WAS sore and her thighs were cramping. She'd had enough and prayed at every town they passed that this would be the one Mac would choose to stop at. The only stops they'd made all day were for gas and to grab a quick bite to eat. Convenience store food sucked.

They made a quick detour at a Chinese restaurant and grabbed something to go. Then, saints be praised, Mac pulled into a motel. Not a Hyatt or Marriott, but it wasn't a campsite, either, and for that she was eternally grateful. After riding all day, she was hungry and tired and more than ready for a shower and change of clothes. They checked in, and just the sight of a bed in the room was enough to make Lily want to cry.

"Tired?" he asked as he tossed their bags onto the dresser.

"A little."

"Hungry? I am."

"Starving."

"I hope choosing the Chinese food was okay."

Right now, she liked anything. Her stomach was growling. "Sounds fabulous."

They sat at the tiny round table near the window and inhaled the food. Lily tried to remember her upbringing and manners as she ate, but frankly she was too damn hungry. She dug into one of the little cardboard cartons with chopsticks as if she hadn't eaten in a week.

"You were hungry," Mac said, cocking a brow.

"Clearly." She grabbed a napkin and wiped sauce from her chin, then took a long swallow of bottled water. Okay, she felt partially human again. As soon as she digested a little, the next order of business would be a shower. She felt icky wearing yesterday's clothes, her hair was windblown and stringy, and she shuddered at how she must look.

"Quit doing that. You look gorgeous."

She looked at Mac. "Quit doing what?"

"Fiddling with your hair. It's sexy like that."

She hadn't even realized she was combing it with her fingers. "It's a mess. It's not sexy."

"I disagree. It's wild looking. Like you just got out of bed after spending several hours there with your lover. It's a very hot look."

She knew better. It was a tangled bird's nest. "You're blind."

Mac shook his head. "No, I'm not. I know exactly what I'm looking at."

He'd always been able to do that to her. When his voice dropped low, his meaning all too obvious, the vibration settled right between her legs, making her clit quiver. Just like now, when he looked at her with his half-lidded gaze and spoke to her in that deep voice, the implications of both incredibly dangerous to her libido as well as her emotions.

The libido she could handle. Her emotions she'd have to constantly wrestle with. The sooner she ended the journey, the better.

She took a quick glance at the telephone on the bedside table, wondering how she could manage to call her boss without Mac stopping her.

"I'll wait if you want to take a shower first," she suggested, trying to appear nonchalant about it. She stared into the carton of food, refusing to look him in the eye.

"Nah, you go ahead."

Okay, either way that could work to her advantage. When he was in the shower, she could at least notify her boss what was going on, even filling him in about the virus. And more importantly, that she wasn't the one who had taken it. She could tell him she'd lost her cell phone, and that she'd report in when she could. Then he'd at least have something to tell their client. The thought of showing up on the FBIs Ten Most Wanted list because of the stolen artifact wasn't at all appealing to her.

And then . . . well, Mac couldn't very well take the vial into the shower with him, could he? So if she could find the vial, she could hightail it out of here in a hurry, grab a taxi, and be on her way.

Lots of options.

She grabbed a change of clothes on the off chance she could make the call, find the vial, and get out of there while Mac was in the shower. It was either that or parade around naked, and that she wasn't prepared to do. Though that might distract Mac enough, wouldn't it? She smiled at that thought as she entered the bathroom and turned on the shower, nearly salivating as the steam filled the tiny room. She stripped off her dirty clothes and stepped in, letting the warm water stream over her body.

It felt so good she let out a moan of pure joy. She could stay there for hours, but she had work to do. She grabbed the shampoo and washed her hair, then conditioned it, truly appreciating the feel of cleanliness. She closed her eyes and let the conditioner sit there for a minute or so, leaving her eyes closed as the water ran down her back.

She shrieked in surprise at the rush of cold air when the shower door opened. Her jaw dropped when a naked Mac stepped in.

"What are you doing?" she asked.

"Showering."

She arched a brow, refusing to appear shocked. "Couldn't wait until I was finished?"

He grinned. "I could have. Didn't want to."

Her body flushed with heat. This was the reason she'd thrown herself at Mac ten years ago, why she hadn't been able to stay away from him. The lure. The temptation. The bad boy who took what he wanted, damn rules and propriety. His eyes went dark as he scanned her body, the message in them clear. He'd come in here for her—for sex. He wanted her.

She'd bet he'd come in here to distract her, too. To keep her off balance, or lull her into some false sense of security or feeling of closeness with him. He wanted to bind her to him, to assure her loyalty.

Well as far as wanting, as far as sex, the feeling was mutual. She wanted him. She could do this and keep her heart intact. She was a big girl now and knew how to guard her emotions. This was a means to an end—gaining Mac's trust so she could get closer to the vial. Nothing more. She was offering her body to do her job, using whatever means necessary to keep him from making a colossal mistake that might land him in jail for a very long time.

She had a plan, and her plan included this dance with Mac. If she derived pleasure from it—bonus. But she was only going to go so far—she had limits.

"Don't let me interrupt. Keep doing what you're doing," he said, his voice tight with strain.

His cock was hardening. She wanted her hands, her mouth on him. Last night she'd been denied. Tonight, she wouldn't be. Instead, it was her turn to distract and overwhelm him. And this time she'd get the satisfaction of knowing she'd given him pleasure. She reached for the soap and held it under the streaming water, rubbing her hands together to work up a thick lather, then spread the soap over her breasts, letting the bubbles drift over her nipples. They rolled over her breasts and down her belly. Mac watched the trail with riveted interest.

His gaze on her was like a heated caress, urging her on. She'd never put on a show of touching herself before, but this feeling of boldness shouldn't surprise her. She'd always been braver with Mac than with anyone else. She cupped her breasts, using her thumbs to roll over her nipples. They were so sensitive she couldn't hold in the whimper of delight when she touched her own flesh.

"You need to be fucked," he whispered.

"Yes." She wanted his cock inside her desperately, but the strain of hesitation pulled at her. Dammit, why couldn't she just go for it like she wanted to? Why did the past always interfere?

Take it slow, Lily, see where it goes. Play a little to start. She definitely wanted to play with him.

He reached for her, but she backed away. *Not yet.* She had more to show him, delights to promise that were just within his reach. And now that she'd started this tease, she couldn't seem to stop. Her hands became his as she showed him what she wanted, moving from her breasts to her rib cage, then lower, skirting her abdomen and slipping between her legs. His eyes widened when she found her clit and began to rub in slow, wide circles.

The sparks of arousal blew into an inferno of incredible sensation as she massaged her sex, dipping her fingers between the soft folds and sliding inside her pussy.

Mac's jaw tightened as he clamped his lips shut, his nostrils flaring as he breathed in and out. She felt the tension and it ratcheted hers up another level.

"Oh, God, Mac. I need you."

He took a step forward but she raised her hand to stop him.

Now who was being tortured? Lily wasn't sure anymore. She wanted to come, was so close the contractions gripped her fingers in a tight vise, yet she wouldn't let him do it for her. Not this time. She wanted the control, wanted to show him she wasn't the same girl she'd been ten years ago. She wasn't so easily manipulated.

A tiny spark of fear still lingered at the thought of giving him everything. The last time she'd given him all she had, he'd left her. She couldn't risk the heartbreak again. This time, she'd walk out on him.

God, how could she be so cold and calculating and at the same time feel her body burst into flames, her pussy trembling and so near orgasm? How could she wish he was inside her and know that she was leaving him shortly?

She pushed away the confusion and concentrated only on sensation, on the way he watched her, encouraging her with the heat in his gaze.

With the heel of her palm firmly pressed against her clit, she rubbed and exploded, letting the orgasm inflame her, spreading her legs so Mac could see her finger fucking herself while she rode a wild climax.

Shuddering through the aftereffects, she released her fingers, then brought them to her mouth and licked them clean.

"Christ, Lily."

She stepped forward and dropped to her knees, looking up at Mac as she reached for his cock.

STILL STUNNED AT THE SHOW SHE'D PUT ON FOR HIM, MAC JERKED in response to the first touch of Lily's soft palm around his shaft. He braced his hands against the shower wall and thrust his cock through her hand, pumping slow and easy. She smiled, looking away only to stare at his dick. She stroked it, base to tip, swirling her thumb around the wide crest. Pearly liquid escaped the head and she swiped it with her thumb, all the while watching him, compelling him to focus on her.

As if he wanted to look anywhere else. She was sex incarnate, and he'd rather die than turn his gaze away from her hot mouth. When she brought her thumb to her lips and sucked, he swore, wondering again who the hell this sexy woman was. She'd been so shy about sex before. Willing and eager, definitely, but not bold and confident like the woman before him now.

"Salty," she whispered, then grasped the base of his cock and led it to her lips, flicking her tongue out to roll along the head.

His knees buckled and he pushed harder against the wall for support. She took his cock head between her lips and sucked, and if he didn't have his man reputation to worry about, he might have passed out. Christ, that mouth of hers . . .

Ten years ago Lily hadn't known anything about sex. Shards of jealousy ate away at him at the realization she knew exactly what she was doing now. Then again, what had he expected when he'd dumped her? For her to remain practically untouched on the off chance he might see her again?

She wasn't a virgin anymore. He'd taken care of that, at her request. But she'd sure as hell mastered a few things in the past ten years without him.

Like how to suck a cock—covering his shaft with her lips, swirling her tongue underneath as she drew him into the dark, hot, wet recess of her mouth. All the way to the back of her throat until she couldn't take anymore.

Then she swallowed, the action squeezing his cock head until he felt like he was going to burst down her throat.

"Lily." He couldn't take this for much longer without shooting a hot stream of come into her sweet mouth. And he didn't want to keep thinking about how, where, and with whom she'd gotten her practice, because she was a goddamn expert at cock sucking.

She was gifted, that was it. When they were together before

she'd never sucked him. Maybe she had a natural ability all along, but they'd never taken the time to explore it.

Yeah, right. And he'd been a Boy Scout the past ten years, too.

Her mouth was a volcano, sucking him into a vortex of heat. She rolled her tongue along the seam, backed off to examine it, then rotated her hands around his tortured flesh. He wasn't going to be able to take much more of this—he wanted to fuck her now. But when he tried to lift her, she resisted.

"No," she said, tilting her head to look at him. "Let me do this."

The water raining down over her, steam rising from the floor of the shower, made her look like she was coming up from hell itself, a tantalizing succubus there to steal his soul.

He smiled at the visual that conjured. His very own devilish seductress, tempting him, teasing him with her lush mouth and hot, wet tongue. She licked the throbbing crest, lapping at the slit and capturing the cream that spilled from him. He jerked and pushed into her mouth, grasping her head between his hands.

If she wanted to do this, he'd let her. He pumped between her lips, driving his cock deep. She took it without complaint, devouring him with hungry abandon. When she reached for his balls and began to lightly massage them, he knew he was going to lose it and soon.

"Baby, if you want to stop this you'd better move away, because I'm about to come in your mouth."

He waited, his balls pulsing, his cock jerking with the need to erupt. She leaned back, smiled, then took him all the way in, sucking him hard as she grasped his shaft and squeezed.

The orgasm ripped through him like a barreling freight train at high speed. He jerked against her lips, driving his cock in deep as his come jettisoned into her warm mouth. She tightened her lips around him, her gaze meeting his. The look on her face was pure heat. Mac could barely breathe. Intense spasms rocketed his body as Lily swallowed, keeping up with the relentless pulsing of his cock.

It would be damned unmanly of him to faint, but his legs were shaking. He sucked huge breaths through his mouth, then dragged Lily to her feet and pulled her in his arms. He planted his mouth over hers and kissed her long and hard. She moaned against him, sliding her fingers into his wet hair.

Goddamn. He was still hard, and nowhere near ready for this to end. He reached for her leg, intending on fucking her right there.

But Lily backed away from his embrace, shaking her head. "Oh, no," she said, a teasing glint in her eye. "Some things you'll have to wait for."

Mac frowned, not understanding what she was saying. "Lily," he warned, moving toward her again.

She pressed a palm to his chest and grinned. "Come on, Mac. Anticipation is half the fun."

He didn't want to anticipate. He wanted to have her. All of her. Right here, and right now. But he read the "no" signal loud and clear. Lily was done playing.

"Your call, babe," he said with a shrug, then grabbed the soap, handing it to her to finish washing herself. She did and scurried out. He watched her through the clouded glass door. She dried off in record time and hightailed it out of the bathroom, shutting the door securely behind her.

Had he just been used? Maybe he should be pissed, but hell, how could he be after what she'd just done? His cock still hadn't calmed down after her sexy performance. Maybe she had done it to distract him.

Then again, maybe not.

But she sure put a halt to the fun in a hurry. Like she had something else more important to do. He smiled, knowing exactly what she was after. He took his time, enjoying the remnants of the hot water. No reason to rush. Whatever Lily thought she was going to do, she was wrong.

He wasn't that stupid. And he knew exactly how smart Lily was. By the time he'd finished washing and the water had turned cold, he stepped out of the shower and was greeted by a naked, very perturbed-looking woman leaning against the bathroom door.

She tossed him a towel.

"Dammit, Mac. What did you do with the motel room's telephone?"

He took the towel from her hands and feigned an innocent look. "Phone? What phone?"

"You know damn well what phone I'm talking about. The one that used to be on the nightstand. Where did it go?"

"Maybe it made an escape while we were otherwise occupied in the shower. We should report that."

She rolled her eyes and stalked out of the bathroom, snatching his clean T-shirt on the way out. He followed, watching her pull it over her head and place the clothes she had laid out on top of the dresser. She jerked the comforter to the end of the bed, flounced onto the mattress, and grabbed the remote, glaring at him. He grabbed his boxers, slipped them on, and sat beside her.

"You hid the vial and your cell phone, too," she said, her voice low and laced with irritation.

"Well, yeah."

She busied herself with flipping channels, refusing to look at him.

So much for cuddling after sex. She sure blew hot and cold. Not that he could blame her. He knew damn well she'd be after the phone and the vial, so while she was in the shower he took care of getting rid of the motel room telephone and made certain the virus and his cell phone were well hidden. Like locked outside on the bike where she couldn't get to them. Then he stuffed the bike keys somewhere she couldn't find them. Not that she could ride it, but hell, he wouldn't put anything past her. She might just try to get away.

"Lily, what did you expect?" He slid closer. Lily scooted farther away. And she didn't answer.

Unless "hmph" was an answer.

"I can't turn over the virus or let you contact your people. Right now I don't know who to trust. We don't even know who was shooting at us. It could have been someone from the museum. It could have been your client. I just don't know."

"Uh-huh," she mumbled, flipping channels and staring at the television.

If it was possible, a layer of frost would have coated the sheets. Man, was she ever pissed. "I know who I work for, and it's one of the good guys."

"I work for the good guys," she said.

"So you say. But do you know that for a fact?"

"Yes." She didn't even hesitate. "I don't work for people I don't trust. And I'd never take a case I thought was shady."

Lily had always been honorable. Her biggest downfall. "Maybe you were misled."

She shot him a glare. "I'm not an idiot, Mac. I know what side of the law I work on. And what side *you* work on."

"I am on the right side of the law, Lily."

"Uh-huh."

"It's the truth. But I understand your lack of trust."

"Really? That's so magnanimous of you."

Her sarcasm wasn't lost on him. She had absolutely zero reason to trust him.

And when he was finished riding her around several states,

when he had to drop her off without the virus—when he had to dump her yet again—she'd have even less reason to trust him.

Most days he loved his work, the freedom it gave him, the excitement and pure adrenaline rush of living the life of a thief, but doing it legitimately.

Sometimes, like now, he really hated his job.

FIVE

BY MORNING, LILY DIDN'T EVEN WANT TO SPEAK TO MAC. THE HOTEL only had one bed, so they'd shared it. Lily had thought about grabbing the blanket and pillow and curling up on the chair, but it looked hideous and uncomfortable. And why should she suffer just because she was angry at Mac? She didn't care where he slept. So she took her side, and he took his. Despite the bed's warmth and comfort, she tossed and turned the entire night.

Besides being utterly pissed at him for hiding the motel's telephone, his cell, and the vial, she'd slept next to Mac all night and hadn't done what she really wanted to do with him—make love.

Not that it was his fault. Oh no, the blame lay entirely at her feet. Or more appropriately, in her head. Because her stupid mind was stuck in the stupid past where it stupidly shouldn't be. For the love of God, she was an adult woman, no longer a teenager in the blushing throes of her first love. She was levelheaded and understood the dynamics of a physical-only relationship. Last night she could have fucked him, could have felt the utter bliss of his cock inside her. She could have spent the night wrapped up in his arms, having the best sex of her life.

But oh no. She was afraid. What a moron. It was time for her to grow up and get over it, because Mac sure as hell *was* going to dump her again. Big deal. She'd survive. They had nothing together, just like they'd had nothing together ten years ago. The least she could get out of this was some decent sex. And the vial containing the virus, because she was most definitely going to come out of this the winner. And maybe, just maybe, she would leave Mac with some lingering memories of what *he* was losing and leaving behind this time. It was time to stop acting like the victim and start taking control of this situation. He might be hiding the vial and his cell phone from her, but there were other ways to play this game.

She had learned quite a bit in the past ten years. After Mac had fucked and dumped her, she'd made it her quest not to spend her life wallowing over a guy she couldn't have. Oh sure, she allowed herself time to mourn, had even thought that maybe there was a way for her and Mac to work things out.

But when the months passed and he hadn't once tried to find her or contact her, she knew she was living a child's dream, that it was time to grow up and become a woman. It was then that she put Mac in the past. Determined to move on, she'd tackled men with gusto, figuratively anyway. In college, she'd had a few lovers, though they were mostly inept, drunken frat boys sorely lacking in the finesse department. None of them had resulted in a relationship because frankly, she hadn't been interested and neither had the guys. After college, she'd dated here and there, mostly cops, but none of them had generated enough of a spark to carry on a lasting relationship.

She had learned about sex, though. What she liked, what she didn't like, and how to please a man. She wasn't an unpracticed virgin any longer, and she intended to use everything she knew on Mac.

When he left her this time, he'd leave still wanting her. This time she'd be the one to walk away without looking back.

Okay, maybe it was petty. So what? She deserved at least a little payback, didn't she? And anger seemed a lot more productive than angst.

They ate breakfast, then packed up the bike and checked out of the motel. She climbed onto the bike behind Mac, feeling a little hum of excitement when he cranked up the engine, the pipes emitting one incredibly loud roar that made every nerve ending in her body tingle. When he took off, she rested her hands on his hips, enjoying the cool morning air whipping through her hair. Riding a motorcycle was damn thrilling.

Once again, Mac headed south.

"Are you going to tell me where we're headed today?" she asked, already knowing his answer.

"We'll stop in a little while," he said, completely avoiding her question. "I think you'll enjoy this."

Oh sure. Flying blind while semikidnapped was her favorite pastime. She'd probably end up fired, too. Why was she doing this again? Oh yeah, for her job. The one she'd thought would be adventurous and exciting.

Then again, it couldn't get much more adventurous and exciting than this, could it?

THE DAY WARMED UP IN A HURRY, BUT LILY WASN'T UNCOMFORTable. The scenery was gorgeous. She was used to traveling by highway, the typical views those of concrete, billboards, hotels, and fast-food joints. Traveling the back roads was entirely different. No boring highway signs. Only scattered signs, houses, and the occasional town, though she kept track of the road marker in case she did manage to make an escape or find a phone. At least she'd have a faint clue where she was.

Tall trees, houses nestled deep into the dense woods, with the nearest neighbor sometimes a mile away. Kids played in expansive yards, with endless freedom to run and hide and live out their childlike fantasies of Robin Hood or whatever games kids played these days. No city limits restricted them. It was remote, peaceful, and she even saw deer leaping across the road a couple of times. Lily sat back and breathed in the clean, smog-free air, feeling every muscle in her body relax.

They passed the state line into Missouri, crossing the interstate and staying on the two-lane road. They rode for several hours, stopping for a drink and break every now and then. The road seemed deserted, though she was certain a few cars must have passed them. She was probably just oblivious.

Some private investigator she was. Give her some fresh air and country road and she lost all sense of reality. For all she knew, they could have been followed the last hundred miles and she wouldn't have had a clue.

If she didn't start paying attention, she really *was* going to get fired. Though she probably already had been.

No, not true. She wasn't going to be fired. She was going to be a hero when she returned with the virus. But she had to be alive to do that, so she'd better make sure no one was on their tail. She did a quick half turn and noticed no cars behind them. Okay, that part was good.

It was early afternoon when Lily started seeing more motorcycles. Then more. And even more, all heading in the same direction they were. Puzzled, she started counting them. Guys by themselves on their bikes, some with women, and even women riding their own bikes. When Mac paused at a four-way stop sign she leaned forward and tapped him on the shoulder.

"What's going on?"

He tilted his head back. "You'll see. We're making a stop."

She hated mystery, yet she couldn't help but feel a thrum of excitement as they ended up joining a group of bikers. The roar of the engines was deafening. Lily felt like she was part of a pack as they sped up and passed other bikers, then others passed them. So many she stopped counting. And everyone seemed so friendly, smiling and waving as they passed by.

Did Mac know these people? Was he going to be off-loading the virus here, or was this really just for fun? She was definitely paying attention now.

Following the rest of the bikes, he turned off the two-lane onto a smaller country road. Lily could already see more bikes parked in what looked like nothing more than a cow pasture.

Lots of bikes, too. Hundreds, maybe even a thousand or so. He parked, they got off, and Mac packed up their helmets. Lily shook out her hair while she looked around. More bikes were coming in, the sound of their pipes so loud she had to sidle up close to Mac so he could hear her.

"What is this?"

"Bike rally," he said as he started down a path toward a bunch of tents. "They hold it here annually."

Lily gaped at what she saw. Lots of leather, definitely. Men, women, loud music, vendors everywhere selling food and drink, artists doing tattoos and body piercings, some people selling T-shirts and bike accessories. Basically, anything and everything.

And the people . . . oh my the people, especially the women. Some so scantily clad they might as well have been naked. Leather chaps with nothing underneath but a G-string, tiny little bikini tops, or see-through shirts that left nothing to the imagination. Lily wanted to cover Mac's eyes so he couldn't ogle the smorgasbord of feminine delights on display.

But that would be ridiculous. Mac didn't belong to her—she wasn't his woman and he could ogle . . . or even touch, if he could get away with it. He could mingle with any woman he wanted to, and there was nothing she could say about it.

Didn't that just irritate the hell out of her.

Get over it, Lily. He's not yours. And you're not his. She smiled at the latter, because it meant she could look at the guys in tight jeans or equally snug leather pants, T-shirts stretched taut over well-muscled chests, men who looked like they worked on their bodies with the same care they worked on their bikes.

There were some gorgeous guys here. The problem was, the only man Lily was interested in looking at, being with, or touching was Mac. And just like ten years ago, she knew better, knew how futile that was, yet she could do nothing about how she felt.

Much better idea to focus on what they were really doing here. She had to figure out if Mac was going to deliver the virus to someone here. And hopefully, she could get hold of a phone or slip away in this crowd. She'd have to keep a really close eye on him.

The music grew louder as they approached the grandstand area. The people were thicker here, bodies crowded together, talking, laughing, drinking, and dancing. The sun was high and much warmer now. It was a gorgeous day with enough of a breeze flitting through the crowds to keep it from feeling too hot. Good thing the temp was higher today, too, considering how some of the women were dressed. Or not dressed. She still couldn't get over the rampant exhibitionism on display. Some women had a lot of guts. They were braver than her, that's for sure.

But what a fun event. There were signs posted on a huge bulletin board announcing various bike events, from a bike competition by class to various fun excursions throughout the day and into the evening. There was even a wet T-shirt contest for the women scheduled for later this afternoon. Lily snorted.

"You going to enter?" Mac asked, reading over her shoulder.

"Not on your life," she said with a shake of her head, turning to face him.

"You should. You'd be a sure winner." He took a quick glance at her breasts, winked, and slung an arm over her shoulder. "Let's go get a beer."

They grabbed some food and a beer, then found a spot to sit and listen to the band play. Though she didn't know any of the people sitting around her, Lily felt comfortable, enjoying the company of this fun group. Mac didn't seem to have any trouble talking to the people, since they had bikes in common. And that's all he seemed to be doing, chatting about bikes. No nefarious activity as far as she could tell.

She listened to all of them, Mac included, tell stories of rides they had taken, rallys and events they'd attended. There was an entire biker community Lily knew nothing about, a sense of family she had never felt before. Though this was her first time, she already felt accepted. It didn't matter what you wore, how you looked, clean-cut or scraggly, you were one of the "gang" as soon as you showed up on your bike. There was no social class distinction amongst bikers. You rode a bike, you were part of the family.

She felt guilty for judging people on the way they were dressed. No one was judged here, and no one was what or who they seemed to be. Everyone was simply here to have a good time, no matter who they were or what their background was. Lots of people stopped and talked to them. Some were construction workers; others were lawyers, waitresses, or schoolteachers. Lily was amazed. All walks of life, and all of them were bikers. They were all equals at this rally.

A lot different than the way she grew up, and the polar opposite of the way her father thought. With her dad it was all about your background, what your connections were, your family, your money. Who you were inside didn't matter. Who you associated with was always important—one of the things she'd disagreed often with her father about.

She felt more connected to this group of strangers than she ever had to people at any function she'd attended with her father.

And she wasn't attired in a designer dress, dripping in diamonds, and attending the opera or a thousand-dollar-a-plate charity function. She was sitting in the grass drinking beer out of a plastic cup listening to a rock band bellow out a song.

"You're quiet," Mac said, leaning into her.

She turned to him and smiled. "I'm having a great time." Such fun, in fact, that she'd forgotten about her job. For the past couple of hours she hadn't tried to find the vial containing the virus, or Mac's cell phone. In fact, she probably could borrow a cell phone from any one of a hundred people around her if she could slip away from Mac for a few minutes. She'd been so relaxed, so lost in her own thoughts that the one thing she should be doing was the one thing that hadn't occurred to her.

Mac was a really bad influence on her.

Again.

Oh, screw it. She got up and brushed grass off her jeans.

"Where are you going?" Mac asked, looking up at her.

"To the bathroom. And I'm getting another beer. You want one?"

"Sure. I'll go with you."

So much for sneaking off to borrow a cell phone. But maybe in the ladies room? Mac led the way, and Lily's hopes fell in an instant when he showed her to the Porta-Johns. No chance of wrangling a cell phone in one of those. After that they went to the beer tent and bought a couple more cups.

"Mac?"

A decidedly feminine voice stopped them. Lily turned, as did Mac, who lifted his brows.

"Hey, Jessie."

Lily arched a brow and tried to appear nonchalant as the woman threw her arms around Mac and planted one firm kiss on his lips. Could this be his contact for dropping the virus?

Built like a centerfold, she wore low-slung jeans, a midriff-baring, breast-hugging top—and oh my God did she have breasts. Her platinum blond hair was cut very short and spiked out everywhere. It looked gorgeous framing her heart-shaped face, accentuating the most beautiful green eyes Lily had ever seen.

Lily wasn't the jealous type, but even she was salivating over the woman. She could only imagine how Mac was reacting.

"I thought that was you," Jessie said, hooking a thumb in a loop of her jeans. "What are you doing here?"

Mac shrugged and grinned. "Happened to be in the area, so thought we'd stop by." He turned to Lily. "This is my friend, Lily."

Lily offered a wary smile and held out her hand. "Nice to meet you, Jessie."

Jessie grinned and shook Lily's hand with great enthusiasm and a very firm grip. "Great to meet you, too, Lily. I'm so happy to see Mac with someone, finally. He spends entirely too much time alone."

"You talk too much, Jessie," Mac said, frowning.

"Yeah, yeah." Jessie turned and hooked her arm with Lily's. "Mac says I'm like the little sister he never had and never wanted. Always in his business like a buzzing fly."

Now Lily was really curious. How did Mac know Jessie? Did they . . . do business together? They couldn't have met at school, because Mac and Lily had known all the same people, so they had to have met after Lily graduated and went off to college.

"How do you and Mac know each other?" Lily asked as she and Jessie walked back toward the band area.

"Oh, we've known each other . . . forever, it seems," Jessie said, flopping down on the ground and crossing her legs over each other. "Eight years or so. I was fifteen and in serious trouble when I met Mac. He was my savior. But don't tell him I said that. He's already got one hell of an ego as it is," she finished with a whisper as Mac settled in behind them.

"What are you talking about?" Mac asked.

"Girl stuff," Jessie tossed over her shoulder. "Go find some guys to bullshit with."

Lily laughed. She knew Mac was going to listen to every word on the off chance Lily asked for a cell phone.

Okay, so maybe Jessie wasn't Mac's contact for the virus. And she should be profoundly jealous of Jessie, but frankly she couldn't be. She really liked this girl, who couldn't be more than twenty-three at most. Yet there was a hard edge about her that belied her young age. She'd really like to know more about her.

"So do you and Mac work together?"

"Us? Oh hell no. I would drive Mac crazy. But we ride together sometimes."

"You have your own bike?"

Jessie beamed. "You bet I do. I drove this old piece of shit hand-me-down for the longest time, but I've saved for the past few years and just bought a brand-new Harley 883. It's small and fits me perfectly."

Okay, so she was gorgeous, built like sin, *and* rode her own motorcycle? Jessie was every man's dream. The problem was, she was also funny, friendly, and outgoing and didn't seem at all the type of woman other women didn't like. *Dammit.* Surely Jessie had some faults.

"Do you live in Texas?"

Jessie nodded. "I'm on the road a lot, but Dallas is the place I call home."

"I could tell you were a Southern girl by your accent."

Jessie laughed. "You have the same one. You live there, too?"

"Not anymore. I live in Chicago now."

"Ah, but you're still a Texas girl."

Talking to Jessie made her miss home. Not her actual home, per se, because she absolutely did not miss living with her father, but she missed Texas. Maybe because Mac lived there.

Ugh. She had it so bad for Mac. She really had to mentally slap herself more often.

"So how did you and Mac get together if you live in Chicago?" Jessie asked.

"We went to school together. We're old friends."

Jessie's gaze flitted over to Mac's, then back on Lily. "Ah. Old flames, are you?"

Lily felt Mac's beard brush against her cheek as he leaned forward.

"You, Miss Jessie, are entirely too damn nosy."

Jessie stuck her tongue out at Mac. "So you always tell me. Never stops me from asking a million questions though, does it?"

"No it doesn't," Mac said. "Including personal, intimate questions that are none of your business."

Jessie sniffed, but didn't look at all insulted. "Fine. I get the hint. No personal questions about the hot, steamy love affair you two once shared—or maybe still do."

"Goddamit, Jess."

Lily couldn't help it. She burst out laughing. Who wouldn't like Jessie? Even when she was prying she was adorably innocent about it. Lily had always wanted a little sister. Instead, she'd ended up an only child, and lonely. Even her playmates had been scrutinized by her father. Only the "best" for his only child.

She drained her beer, then stood.

"Another?" Mac asked.

Lily nodded. She felt a little buzz from the toasty weather and two beers, but she didn't care. She'd been high-strung and working hard for so long, the stress had finally taken its toll. Yes, she had no business letting her guard down, but she was having a wonderful time and she'd just decided to take the damn day off. Tomorrow she'd go back to stressing and worrying again. As long as she kept an eye on Mac, she figured that was good enough, right?

"I'll get it," he said. "Jessie, keep an eye on her. Don't let her use a phone."

Jessie arched a brow. "Whatever, Mac."

Lily sat and waved him off, keeping her gaze glued to him. When he got in line at the beer tent, she was satisfied. "Like I could think of anything coherent to say at the moment anyway."

"You buzzin' a little, honey?" Jessie asked.

"A little. I never drink."

Jessie snorted. "Yeah, I'm a cheap drunk, too. I'm such a light-weight in the alcohol department." She held up her plastic cup. "It's soda. Two beers and I'll never find my tent tonight. And since I'm traveling alone on this trip I don't like to lose my facul-ties. You know, in case I have to kick some guy's ass who tries to take advantage of me."

Laughing, Lily said, "And I believe you could."

"Hell yeah, I could. You don't grow up on the streets like I did without learning to take care of yourself. And that means learning how to punch, kick, and wield a knife like you mean it."

Lily couldn't imagine a childhood like that. She had lived a life of obscene privilege, so much it was almost embarrassing. And she was sitting next to someone who'd had to defend her honor by learning street fighting.

"It must have been really rough for you, growing up like that."

Jessie shrugged, then smiled. "I'm doing just fine now, honey. I have a great life. Thanks to Mac."

"What did he do? You don't have to tell me if it makes you uncomfortable."

"Oh, I don't mind at all. He grabbed me one night while I was trying to steal a car. Scared the shit out of me, too. I thought he was a cop."

Lily couldn't fathom a fifteen-year-old Jessie trying to steal a car, but kids did get into trouble. "What happened after he caught you?"

"He brought me to a friend of his, who gave me a job, made me go back to school while I was working, gave me a place to stay since I had nowhere to go."

"Didn't you have a home? Parents?"

She frowned. "Yeah, I had a home and parents, if that's what you want to call them."

Okay, so Jessie didn't want to talk about her family. Obviously an unpleasant situation. "Then you graduated?"

Her face just lit up when she smiled. "I did. Got my diploma, even went to college. So I worked and saved money, paid back all that I borrowed, and finally bought my own bike."

"You've done well for yourself. You should be proud."

"I am. I worked my tail off. But I'd have never made it without Mac. He pulled me off the streets, kicked my butt when I wanted to quit, which at the beginning was often. He forced me to look a few years down the road, to what I could be instead of what I thought I was. He's an amazing man—more of a father to me than my own old man ever was."

Tears glistened in Jessie's eyes. Lily felt a tug in her chest, trying to reconcile the Mac she knew with the one from the story Jessie told.

He'd literally saved Jessie's life.

Who was Mac Canfield? Was he really one of the good guys, like he said? Had he changed in the last ten years?

Was Lily wrong about him?

Mac brought a beer for Lily and another soda for Jessie.

"Thank you," Lily said, her gaze fixed on him as he sat.

"What?" Mac asked.

Lily shook her head. "Nothing."

Mac glared at Jessie. "What did you tell her?"

Jessie batted her lashes at Mac. "Why, nothing, Mac. Would I reveal your deep, dark, perverted secrets to just anyone?"

Mac lifted a lock of Lily's hair, rubbing it between his fingers. "Oh, I think she already knows those."

Warmth coiled low in Lily's belly. Mac's gaze never left her face when he said that, and she couldn't tear her eyes away from him.

"Oh, this is *so* my cue to go find my other friends. Before you two get down and dirty right here on the grass and completely gross me out. I could get nightmares from the visual of that one."

Mac's lips curled upward. Lily tore her gaze from his and turned to Jessie. "I'm sorry. Please, stay with us."

"Are you kidding? You two are putting off 'hot sex imminent' signals and it's icking me out. It would be like watching my parents screw. I'm leaving."

Lily giggled.

"I'll catch y'all later. Be good and for God's sake, get a room," Jessie said, waving as she walked away.

"She's adorable," Lily said.

"She's a pain in the ass," Mac replied. "But yeah, she's a good kid."

"She told me what you did for her."

Mac frowned. "She shouldn't have done that. She's got the biggest mouth."

"You saved her life, Mac."

He shrugged, stared ahead at the band. "She was just a confused kid with lousy parents. I knew where she was coming from. All she needed was a little guidance."

Lily laid her palm against his cheek, forcing him to look at her. "You saved her life," she said again.

This time, he didn't look away. He pulled her onto his lap, wrapped his arms around her. "I don't want to talk about Jessie anymore."

His eyes were the finest brandy, molten and intoxicating, and she was utterly lost in him. In this crowd of thousands, there was just the two of them.

He was going to kiss her. She should be thinking about where he'd just been. He might have delivered the virus to someone—but instinct told her he hadn't.

Besides, he was going to kiss her. Some PI she was, huh?

She waited with agonizing impatience for that moment when his lips touched hers, when lightning would strike, when her world would spin out of control as it did every time Mac kissed her.

When his mouth descended on hers, when the tip of his tongue slid between her parted lips to touch hers, she clutched his shirt, her toes curled, and she was lost.

SIX

THE CROWDS, THE NOISE, EVERYTHING AROUND HIM DISAPPEARED
as Mac held Lily in his arms and kissed her.

Wrong place, wrong time, as usual, but he didn't give a shit.
She was soft and warm, her lips giving under his, her tongue lapping against his in a lazy, oh-so-sexy way.

She tasted of beer and of Lily. A little spicy and sugary and a lot
like the woman he could never get out of his head, no matter how
much time had passed.

He shouldn't do this to her, not again. Not use and discard her.
But goddamn, he couldn't help himself. She was the most potent
drug he'd ever come up against and, God help him, he couldn't
resist the temptation. Her scent was the sunshine of a warm day,
leather, and the musky perfume of woman.

His woman. She'd always been his woman, no matter what had
happened when they were apart. Her lips were meant to touch his,
her tongue a perfect match for his, her body fit against him like a
matching puzzle piece. He'd never connected to another woman

like this before. Even when they fought, they still meshed. He knew it—and he knew she did, too.

But just holding and kissing her in the midst of this crazy crowd wasn't enough. He wanted to touch her more intimately, delve inside her, have what he hadn't had in too damn long.

Reluctantly, he broke the kiss, slid her off his lap, and hauled her to her feet.

"What's wrong?" she asked.

"Nothing"—he held onto her hand and leaned in, his lips touching her earlobe—"but I'm going to fuck you and unless you want me to do it right here in front of everyone, we need to find another place."

Her breath expelled in a sigh, her warmth drifting across his neck. He leaned back to look at her. Her lips quirked. Her eyes glittered with passion. She nodded and didn't say a word, just followed him.

Those were definite "oh hell yes" signals.

His cock strained against his jeans, clearly outlined for anyone to see. Let them look. He could care less. Right now finding a spot to be alone with Lily was all he cared about.

Fortunately, he spotted a friend and hoped he had a solution. "Jim."

One of his old biker buddies turned around. In his late fifties, Jim and his girlfriend came to every one of these events.

"Mac!" Jim shook his hand. "Glad to see you here. And I see you brought a pretty lady with you, too."

Mac nodded. "Where's Sheila?"

Jim rolled his eyes. "Wandering around the shopping tents. God only knows what she'll come back with this time."

"You bring your RV?"

"Don't we always?"

"Can we borrow it for about an hour?"

Jim took one look at Lily, then back at him, and grinned. "You sure can."

"I haven't pitched our tent yet and Lily needs to . . . uhh . . . lie down for a bit."

"I'll bet she does. A little hot out here today. Go ahead." He dug his keys out of his pocket and handed them to Mac. "It's parked over by the trees there," he said, pointing. "Door dead bolts from the inside. Sheila and I will make sure no one bothers you. We'll be near the food tent when you're done."

"Thanks, man. I owe you one." He clapped Jim on the back as he walked by.

"He knows exactly what we're going to do, doesn't he?" Lily asked in a low voice as they headed toward the RV.

"Of course he does. But he's also stopped by my place to crash a time or two. Jim and I go way back. Don't worry about it."

Lily leaned into him. "Did I say I was worried?"

Her face was flushed, her lips parted. Maybe it was the beer, but she hadn't had all that much to drink, so maybe it was something else.

Like need. Desire. Desperation. Yeah, he liked to think that's what created the pink across her cheeks.

Jim had found a great parking spot for his RV, set way back from the mass of crowds and secluded behind a thick grouping of tall trees. Privacy. That's what Mac craved right now. He unlocked the door and let Lily climb inside, then he threw the dead bolt after he closed it.

Lily stood in the tiny living room waiting for him.

They didn't need small talk or any words between them. He walked over to her and dragged her into his arms, covering her mouth with his. A rush of expelled breaths, tangling tongues, and they started peeling off their leathers. Mac squatted and undid the snaps on Lily's chaps, then slowly drew up the zipper on each side. She didn't speak, just tilted her head down and watched as he undid the buckle on the belt holding her chaps up.

Damn, he really liked undressing her. It was like opening a Christmas present. Next he removed her boots and socks, then started on her jeans, undoing the button and reaching for her zipper. His knuckles brushed her bare skin and he heard the rush of breath as she inhaled.

Good. He liked that he affected her with just a hint of contact. If he got that reaction from just his knuckles across her stomach, what would he get when they were full-on naked, when he was inside her?

His cock lurched at the thought and a renewed sense of urgency spurred him on. He tugged the jeans over her hips and down her legs, holding her hand while she stepped out of them. Then he leaned forward and reached for her ass cheeks, drawing her toward his mouth so he could bury his face in the vee between her legs. Even her panties smelled sweet, just like the woman inside. Hot, wet, musky—he couldn't resist taking a swipe of her with his tongue. He could taste her through the fabric.

She shuddered and pushed against his face. "Mac," she whispered.

He moved the panties to the side and slid his tongue along her pussy lips, delving between the swollen cleft to dip inside. Her sweet cream poured onto his tongue and she trembled against him, her hand coming down on top of his head to grasp his hair.

Needing more than this, he pulled her panties down, unveiling her sex. Ripe, swollen, wet, she had the prettiest pussy he'd ever seen. Bare at the lips and above with just a small patch of silken hair at her mound, giving him free access to roam. He licked around her clit, then closed his lips around the bud and sucked gently, listening to the sounds she made, eager to give her pleasure.

She leaned back against the couch and spread her legs wider. *Oh, yeah.* He loved a woman who enjoyed sex, who craved that orgasm as much as he did. And Lily wanted it. He could tell with every intake of breath, every lift of her hips, the way she looked on him with such intent—God, it was so sexy the way she watched, encouraging him with her eyes. He kept his focus on her face as he slid two fingers into her pussy. They went in easy, her walls gripping him, the muscles there already pulsing as he latched onto her clit and sucked again.

"Mac, I'm going to come if you keep doing that."

That was the objective. To feel her squeeze his fingers, pour come all over his hand, and let go. He really liked watching her in the midst of an orgasm, to know he was the one in charge of giving her pleasure. He rolled his tongue over the hard knot, moved his fingers in a steady rhythm in and out of her cunt. Her lips parted, her breathing quickened, and her eyes widened.

"Yes, oh yes, I'm coming," she whispered, lifting her hips even higher, grinding her sweet, wet pussy against his face as she climaxed. The muscles tightened around his fingers and he held onto her clit with his mouth, lapping it gently through her orgasm until he felt her relax. Only then did he stand, pull her shirt over her head, and reach around to undo the clasp on her bra, freeing her breasts. He couldn't resist taking a taste of her nipples. The pink buds stood at attention, teasing him. He licked one, sucked it, flattening it between his lips and the roof of his mouth. Even her skin tasted sweet, the low moan she uttered adding to his pleasure. He released one, then sucked on the other, rolling it around on his tongue until it stood hard and wet. He stepped back to admire her.

Now she was completely naked, her body flush with desire.

And he was still fully clothed, with one very angry, very hard cock clamoring to get out. Rectifying that was the next step.

Lily stayed right where she was, leaning against the back of the couch, even teasing him by keeping her legs spread. Her pussy, swollen with the aftereffects of her orgasm, glistened with moisture. She watched him as he toed off his boots, then removed his chaps.

"Those are so sexy on you," she said, expertly arching a brow as she inspected him.

He smiled, unzipped his jeans and pulled them down, making sure he didn't appear in too much of a hurry. They weren't teens anymore, but damn he wanted inside her.

Then the realization struck that he'd only been inside her once. One time in ten years.

The last time she'd been a virgin, and it hadn't exactly been his best moment. He'd been awkward about it then. Oh, he'd tried to make it easy for her. He'd kissed her, taken his time, licked her to orgasm first, and made sure she was relaxed and primed so that penetration was minimally painful, but there had been more to it than that, because he'd known going into it that he was going to ruin her, that he was going to leave her that night.

He hadn't wanted to do it, but she had insisted. Lily had wanted that night to happen, so he had taken her virginity, broken her heart, and hadn't known what to say to ease her emotional pain.

This time, he was going to make it better. This time, though barriers still stood between them, it wasn't the same thing.

But dammit, he didn't want to hurt her again. And he was going to.

He pulled the shirt over his head and cast it to the floor. Naked, he advanced on her.

TEN YEARS. LILY REALIZED IT HAD BEEN TEN YEARS SINCE SHE and Mac had last had sex.

Oh, they'd played the past couple of days—but now they were going to fuck. He walked toward her, all bad boy predator, intent written clearly on his face. No smile, no fooling around. Light banter, teasing, and play were over. This was serious business.

She gripped the top of the sofa behind her and waited for him, a trickle of fear entering her mind.

Don't hurt me again. Her mind said it, and she cast the thought aside as foolish and juvenile. She could handle this, she could keep her emotions separate from the act. It was physical. It didn't have to be earth-shattering.

Just great sex.

"Oh, hell yeah."

Mac threaded his arms around her and jerked her to him. She yelped in surprise as their eyes met. "What?"

"Great sex."

Oh, God. She'd said it out loud. "Oh. Yes. Definitely." Before she said anything else moronic, she kissed him.

And he kissed her back. God, his lips were full, soft, masterful as he moved them over hers. Her world spun, literally, when he tilted her sideways. He invaded her mouth, swiped at her tongue, and took possession of her.

Not earth-shattering? Who was she kidding? She clutched at his arms, feeling the muscles bunch and strain as he held her. She felt like a pirate's war prize being plundered after capture. He was marauding and she was the booty. She might actually be swooning. Not in the past ten years, with any man she'd been with since Mac, had she ever swooned.

Nor had a guy made her light-headed, but she was now, and that had nothing to do with the couple of beers she'd had. No, it was the fullness and heat of Mac's mouth, the expert way his tongue danced with hers, the way he held her in his arms as if he wanted to make her a part of him.

So many men were removed from lovemaking, as if only they were the ones taking part. Mac threw himself into it completely, taking her pleasure as part of his own. She was an extension of him, her pleasure part of his pleasure.

Which is exactly what she wanted to be. A part of him.

He picked her up and held her as if she weighed nothing—and she definitely weighed way more than nothing—and carried her into the small bedroom. He laid her on the bed, left for a second to retrieve the foil packet containing a condom. She watched him slide it over his cock—damn, even that was sexy—then he crawled onto the bed.

Pinning her arms to her sides, he clamped her in place with his hands over her wrists. She thrilled to his possession. Something about his dominance was so incredibly erotic.

He lay on top of her, his cock nestled between her legs, his thighs brushing hers, and she could have cried at the severe need it evoked in her. She bit her lip to keep from begging him to fuck her, to scream that she needed it right now.

But all he did was rub against her. The hairs of his thighs tickled her skin, the head of his cock slid between her pussy lips, then he withdrew, only to rub his cock head against her clit.

She gritted her teeth and glared at him, lifting her hips, demanding he give it to her. Was he really going to make her say it?

He reared back, then slid forward, seating himself fully inside her.

She whimpered, then moaned in utter ecstasy as her body swelled around his cock. It had been so long. So damn long. And before it had been awkward and kind of painful and she'd wanted so much to please him, but it had hurt. And she'd been shy and hadn't known what she was doing. She'd had so many things rolling around in her head that night ten years ago.

Now she was focused only on Mac, only on the sensations driving her. Now it didn't hurt. It was utter pleasure. His cock was thick and hot, pulsing inside her, stretching her. Her pussy gripped him, tightening in protest as he partially withdrew, then thrust. She wrapped her legs around him and lifted her hips, drawing him even deeper.

"You're so beautiful, Lily," he said as he looked down on her.

But she was the one in awe of him. Braced on his hands above her, he was all muscle, all working man. Not an ounce of softness on him, a man who used his hands and his body, whose muscles were forged doing a hard day's labor, not in a gym. He used every one of those muscles to surge against her.

The room was hot, perspiration coating their skin. Mac bent down and gathered Lily close. He lifted her leg and gripped one of her ass cheeks, drawing her tighter against him. Their bodies slid together as he powered against her, kissing her with a ravaging passion that she met with eager abandon.

Release hovered. She forced it back, not wanting this moment to end. She wanted to be held, suspended, just like this, for as long as she could. With Mac's mouth on hers, his hands on her body, his cock tucked inside her, and all the things that kept them apart obliterated from her consciousness.

But, dammit, he ground against her, rubbing against her clit. She tore her mouth from his.

"Mac, stop."

He stilled. "What's wrong?"

"You're going to make me come."

His half smile was devastating. "And that's bad?"

"I don't want to. Not yet." She reached up and threaded her fingers through his hair. So soft, so thick, and damp with his sweat.

"Oh, but I need you to come for me, baby. I want to feel your pussy squeeze my cock so hard that I can't hold back and go off inside you."

Her pussy quivered in reaction to the dark promise in his words. He rolled against her, each point where their bodies made contact a sizzle of sensation, a heated reminder of their connection.

Slick, wet, they slid against each other, undulating like ocean waves crashing against the shore. Mac moved up and Lily met each thrust, no longer able to hold back the tidal wave of her rushing orgasm. She held onto his arms and rode it out. He kissed her as she came, taking in her screams, groaning against her as he pinned his pelvis tight against hers, his orgasm making him grit his teeth. His shudders against her, knowing that he was coming that hard inside her, ratcheted up her own climax to a frenzied level, until she was shaking and spent.

Panting, she held onto him, not wanting to break the contact. They were slick with sweat and she thought about being on someone else's bed, but at the moment she didn't care. She was in heaven and this was perfect, regardless of location.

Mac pressed soft, lingering kisses across her lips, licking her bottom lip.

"You taste good."

She smiled. "Like beer?"

"No. Like Lily. A little hot, a little spicy mixed with sweet."

She sighed.

"And I want to make love to you about a hundred times right now, but we need to give Jim and Sheila their RV back."

This time, her sigh was one of resignation. "I know. Should we wash their sheets?"

Mac laughed and rolled off her. "No. They'll do it. They used my bed a few times when they were first getting together and I did the honors. They know the score."

He held out his hand and helped her up, showed her where the bathroom was so they could clean up.

Now that she sort of had her wits about her again, Lily watched Mac dress, keeping a close eye on him as he slid his jacket on. She moved toward him and slid her arms underneath his jacket, wrapping them around his waist. Mac pulled the gun out of the back of his jeans and tucked it into the inner pocket of his jacket.

Lily frowned. "I was going for a hug, not to disarm you."

"Not true. I find you incredibly disarming, Miss West."

She snorted. "Smart-ass."

He wound his arms around her. "You were trying to get my gun. Or find my cell phone. Or the virus."

"Does that mean you still have the vial? That you didn't deliver it to anyone here at the rally?"

The casual smile he'd been sporting left his face, replaced by the hard-ass look she knew all too well. The impenetrable wall had returned. "The less you know the better."

"Mac, please." She didn't want to push, didn't want to break the idyllic spell of their lovemaking, but knowledge of the vial's contents continued to pound at her. She couldn't let it go. She was a woman and had enjoyed a woman's pleasure, but she was still an investigator, had been a cop. She wasn't going to let this go.

He pulled away from her embrace. "You have to trust me on this, Lily."

She hooked her thumbs in the belt loops of her jeans and blew out a breath of utter frustration. She'd held enough inside. "I want to trust you. God, you have no idea how much I want to. After what Jessie told me about you, I know you care about people. I know you wouldn't deliberately do anything to harm millions of people."

"You're right."

"Then why can't you have enough faith in me to talk to me? Why is that so hard to do? Why has it always been so hard for you to be straight with me?"

He brushed his fingers through his hair. "It's too dangerous for you to know."

"Bullshit. It's too dangerous for me to be with you. You didn't have any trouble dragging me along, though."

He didn't answer her. Of course he didn't, because there was no answer. "This is just like ten years ago." The reality of it slapped her across the face like an ice-cold hand.

He frowned. "What?"

"Ten years ago, you pushed me away. You didn't trust me."

He shook his head. "No, you're the one who thinks I'm going to sell the virus to some terrorist organization. The issue of trust is with you, Lily."

"Is it? Ten years ago you didn't believe in my feelings for you, or my faith in you. You didn't trust that I knew what I was doing when I said I loved you and wanted to be with you. You always thought you knew what was best for me. You thought you knew better than I did. Just like now."

"That's not true."

His voice went low and he looked away, no longer meeting her eyes. She knew Mac. That meant he was lying.

Why did this have to happen? Every time they got close something happened to pull them apart. Maybe they weren't meant to be together. Her head knew that. Logic told her that. She was on the good side of law enforcement. Mac was . . . God only knew what he was, but he wasn't eager to share it with her, and that meant trouble.

Maybe it was time her heart caught up to cold reality. They had great chemistry together, but beyond that, they couldn't sustain more than a couple of hours' worth of happiness without it dissolving into an argument. They were polar opposites in thinking and values.

Maybe her father had been right all those years ago. She and Mac didn't belong together. They had nothing in common, no shared belief systems.

He didn't believe in her.

And right now, she didn't believe in him.

She went to the door and threw open the dead bolt. Mac's hand covered hers.

"Where are you going?"

"Out. The air in here is stifling."

"Then we go together. I don't want you to go out there alone."

She half turned, making sure he could read the expression on her face.

"You don't trust me. You're not being solicitous or looking out for my welfare. You just think I'm going to find the nearest phone and turn you in." She pivoted all the way around. "I could have done that the night at the museum, you know."

At his wide-eyed look, she nodded. "Oh yeah. I saw you break in. My hand was on my cell phone. I could have had the cops there waiting the moment you stepped out of the museum with the artifact in your hand."

He stared at her, a dumbfounded expression on his face.

"Why didn't you?"

She blinked back the welling tears, refusing to let him see her cry. "Because instinctively I knew it was you. The sounds of the motorcycle, something about the way you stood. My heart told me it was you. I compromised my job, probably my career, for you. Because I couldn't bear to see you fail. How stupid was that?"

She turned and walked out the door.

This time, Mac didn't follow.

seven

Mac watched Lily walk out, then dragged his fingers through his hair.

Ah, hell. He knew this wasn't going to be easy with Lily, but he thought they'd reached an understanding, or at least some warmth. To hell with warmth. Things had reached inferno level.

But every time they got hot, each time they seemed to grow closer, something happened to put a wedge between them.

He put it there. And maybe it should just stay there. Keeping distance between them would probably be easier on Lily when the time came that he had to let her go.

Maybe it would be easier on him. Because short of telling her who he was now and who he worked for—which was impossible—there was no choice but to keep her in the dark. Which meant she was going to maintain that level of mistrust, and there wasn't a damn thing he could do about it other than continue to ask her to believe in him, when she had absolutely no reason to.

He'd let her leave the RV, because she needed to cool off. After what she'd said about the museum, he didn't think she'd run and find the nearest phone and give him up.

Because he did trust Lily. If he told her everything, she'd be fully on his side.

But he'd taken an oath, and that meant something to him. No matter how he felt, no matter what his personal needs and wants were, he couldn't betray the Wild Riders. Because it wasn't just his ass on the line. Other people counted on his discretion. He had no choice.

So . . . same frustrating as hell status quo. He returned Jim's RV keys and searched for Lily. It didn't take long to find her, since she wasn't far from Jim. She was hanging out with Jessie near the front of the bandstand, virtually guaranteeing they wouldn't be able to talk. Jessie tilted her head in his direction as he approached. Lily had her arms crossed over her chest and didn't bother to make eye contact with him. She didn't turn around or acknowledge his presence, just kept her focus on the band. Her posture was tight and strained. She wasn't enjoying the music at all, wasn't relaxed.

He knew she was mad and would probably stay that way for a while. Nothing he could do about that and he refused to apologize for doing his job. So he let her listen to the music, let Jessie lean in and talk to her. He stayed behind them, keeping an eye on her and the crowd.

Not that it was unusual for him to keep watch. He'd been doing that from the moment they'd hightailed it out of the museum alley. Since then he'd been keeping one eye behind him the entire time, wondering if whoever had shot at them had been following. He doubted it, because if they had he'd have spotted them by now.

Maybe. He didn't believe in sure things or getting off easily, so he just assumed the bad guys might follow them. He'd continue to keep looking, because he had two things to protect—the virus and Lily. Like it or not, Lily was stuck with him, and she'd just have to remain uninformed until he let her go.

The warmth of the day had long ago been sucked away with the setting sun. Lily pulled on the jacket she'd been carrying, huddling inside it as a stiff breeze picked up. It might be almost summer, but it still got cold at night. And with the cold shoulder she was giving him, Mac figured there'd be no cuddling for warmth in their tent tonight.

He tapped Jessie on the shoulder and leaned over so he could talk in her ear over the band. "I'm going to grab the tent and set it up. Watch Lily."

Jessie nodded and resumed jamming to the music. Mac tracked toward where the bikes were parked, using the opportunity away from Lily and the noise of the music to call Grange and give him a report.

"We've been doing a little recon of our own here at headquarters," Grange said. "We have video surveillance tapes of the cities the artifact had been to before it hit Chicago."

"And?"

"Someone's been in every city since the artifact was first put into play in New York."

That was interesting. "Who?"

"No clue, but we figure it's the same guy based on height, build, and type of walk. All we've picked up is a dark image stalking the grounds outside, and we've confirmed it's not security in any of the locations. Wears a long coat, a hat, and dark pants, stays in the shadows. Smokes."

"How Humphrey Bogart of him."

Grange snorted. "We're studying video of everyone who's passed by the exhibit in each location, trying to see if anyone similar pops up from city to city, but that'll take some time."

"Any thoughts?"

"Someone who knew the virus was in the artifact."

"Do you think he was casing each location, looking for an opening to do a heist?"

"Maybe. Maybe not. I'm not really sure yet, but we're looking at all the angles."

Why else would someone be monitoring each museum? Mac shook his head, deciding to leave the big picture stuff to Grange. "What's the word on Chicago? Anything on Lily?"

"Big news on the theft of the artifact, of course. The heat went down on the night security team. Media's focused more on that than anything and the museum is taking shit in a big way. Nothing about Lily West or her involvement."

"Good." Mac didn't want any press on Lily or her absence, and he was glad her agency hadn't implicated her. Her boss was probably covering his own ass, but Mac would bet the agency Lily worked for wanted her back and probably suspected Lily in the theft. Maybe they were even working with the local police to finger Lily for it.

"Grange, we need to make sure Lily isn't targeted for the theft at the museum."

"It's already taken care of. According to what we've found out from intelligence we've gathered at her agency, they're concerned since her gun was found at the scene that she was kidnapped by whoever did the job. She's not a suspect."

Mac smiled. Grange had contacts everywhere. "Great news. Thanks."

"She still in the dark?"

"Pitch-black." And hating every minute of it. In her shoes, he'd feel the same way.

"Keep it that way. And watch your back. Since they know you have the virus, they're hunting you."

"I'm on alert." Mac pocketed his phone and grabbed the tent from his bike, then circumvented the crowd to find a spot to erect it. He set it up in the middle of a grouping of trees, still within the area of the other tents, but a bit separate from every-one else. He moved his bike, just like everyone else did, making sure to park his alongside Jessie's and all the others he knew, so they'd all be parked near the tents. After he had the tent in place, he went back to find Lily and Jessie. They weren't in the band area any longer, so he hunted them down and found them in the food tent.

Jessie passed him a burger, fries, and a drink. "I figured you hadn't eaten either, and Lily looked like she was about to drop."

"Thanks." He realized after he downed the burger in three bites that he was hungry. Eating made him feel better. He looked at Lily. Her skin was pale and she had dark smudges under her eyes.

"Tired?"

She shrugged and took a sip of her soda.

"Are you tented here somewhere?" he asked Jessie.

"Yeah. A group of my riding buddies and I are over by the river. You?"

"Near the RVs."

"You can tent up with us if you'd like."

"Thanks, but we're fine."

Jessie glanced at Lily, then back at him. Her lips quirked. "Yeah, I'll bet you are. Your girl is about to fall asleep in her pop, so why don't you take her to bed?" She threw an arm around Lily for a quick hug. "Night honey."

Lily hugged her back, managing a faint smile. "Good night, Jess. Thank you."

Mac stood and pulled some money out of his pocket, holding it out to Jessie. She looked at it, then back at him, and shook her head. "You're such a dick sometimes. I've got it covered."

He laughed and leaned across the table to kiss her cheek. She winked and strolled away.

The table went silent. Mac blew out a breath, wondering if he should ask her if she wanted to talk, then changed his mind, figuring Lily was exhausted. And he didn't want to fight with her. She really did look wiped. "You ready to get some sleep?"

She shrugged. "I guess so."

He led her to the tent. She climbed in without a word and lay on her side. Turned away from him, of course. He pulled the blanket over her, then lay on his back, staring up at the dark canvas of the tent ceiling.

The noise of the band played on, the sounds of the crowd still going strong. They'd go all night, some of them anyway.

"You can go out there with them, you know."

Mac turned his head toward Lily. "Huh?"

"You can go out there and party with your friends. I'm fine here."

He shifted to his side. "I don't want to be out there."

"Trust me. You don't want to be in here, either."

"Lily, you've known me a long time. You know I do exactly what I want, when I want." He touched a curling end of hair from her ponytail. Like silk. "If I wanted to be out there, I would be."

She went quiet then, but he knew she wasn't sleeping.

"Just let me go, Mac. I can't stay here with you. I won't give you up to the police. You have to know that."

He did know it. "I can't."

She turned around to face him. "Why?"

He started to reply, but hell, what could he say that hadn't already been said? Or not said. It was the same conversation over and over again. The conversation they couldn't have. He really hated this, but no one could know about the Wild Riders.

"There are things I can't tell you."

"Will you ever be able to talk to me?"

He hoped she could read his face in the semidarkness. "Honestly? I really hope I can. Someday."

But even as he said the words, he knew he was lying to her. And it actually hurt him, like a physical pain, to know he couldn't. This was bullshit. Something was going to have to change.

LILY SAT UP, DRAWING HER KNEES TO HER CHEST AND WRAPPING her arms around them. Moonlight lit up the tent enough that she could see what she didn't want to see. Frustration ate at her, the sensation of feeling closed in and unable to breathe.

She knew Mac so well she could read the lie on his lips. He'd never tell her the truth. How could she care about him, make love to him, when she had no idea what he was going to do with a deadly virus?

How could she reconcile her feelings, this draw she felt toward him, with the possibility that he could be unleashing a disaster of epic proportions on the world?

She tossed him a glance over her shoulder. "That virus could potentially kill millions of people."

"I know."

"Children, too."

"Yes."

She blinked back tears again and looked away from him. How had she gotten involved in this? Wrong place, wrong time.

Wrong man. But what if she had called the police and they had recovered the artifact? What then? Whose hands would it have fallen into? There was no doubt a plot was in place to move the artifact from city to city. It didn't take a rocket scientist to figure that part out. But who was moving it and why? For what purpose?

And why couldn't Mac see they could do so much better working on this together than apart?

Men were so stupid sometimes. Fine. If he wouldn't let her in, if he wouldn't divulge information, she'd just figure it out on her own.

"Lily."

He had moved behind her, drawing her hair to the side so his breath washed across her neck. She shivered, tried to brush him off, but he held firm to her shoulders. She hated that she could be so pissed off at him and yet he could still affect her physically. He made her feel weak, and no one had ever made her weak.

"Lily, I might be a lot of things, I might have made a lot of mistakes in my past, but I could never hurt millions of innocent people, least of all children. You gotta know that about me."

She did know that about him. She'd seen him angry when he was younger. Violently angry and frustrated, so hot with fury that she felt the tension in him without even touching him. But he'd never lashed out, had never deliberately hurt anyone. He'd always held his anger in check.

"I know you couldn't." She had to tell him that, had to let him know she didn't believe he could deliver that virus to anyone who would hurt children, destroy families. This was just so damn frustrating. She wanted to know, had to know what he was going to do with it.

But she couldn't force him to tell her.

He kissed the back of her neck, his murmurs against her skin sending shivers of wicked delight down her spine.

"I know trusting me is a huge issue for you. I know there are things you want me to reveal. Believe me when I tell you there are so many things I want you to know about me. About where I've been the past ten years and what I've done with my life." He turned her so she half faced him, desire and serious intent mixing across his moonlit face. "If and when the time comes that I can reveal it all, I promise to tell you everything. I want you to know."

There were things she wanted him to know about her, too. At least about how she stood on things. "I won't stop trying to figure it out."

His lips curved. "I know."

"And I'll continue to try and take the virus away from you."

"I wouldn't expect any less than your absolute best attempt."

Her lips quirked. He leaned in and kissed her neck again, dissolving the last shred of her anger and frustration. She needed to relax. Nothing was going to be solved tonight. She was still with him and he didn't seem to be in any hurry to get rid of her, which meant that he still held the virus. She knew damn well that as soon as he'd delivered the vial, he would let her go. He was only holding onto her so she wouldn't give him up. She was no fool.

But for now, that was good enough. In the meantime, she'd work on her own theories. By herself.

Later, she'd work on the mystery of Mac Canfield. Right now, there were other, more physical mysteries to uncover. Ties to bind him closer to her, because keeping him close was the objective, wasn't it? Pushing him away was fruitless. Not when she had to get to the virus. She had to keep her emotional confusion at bay, had to remember what she was ultimately here to do.

When Mac moved around and kissed her jaw, then her lips, she didn't object, just opened her lips under his and let him explore.

She sighed into his mouth and joined with him, grateful to let the tension melt away under his expert lips. A soft nibble at the corner of her mouth, the slide of his tongue along her bottom lip, then his probing tongue delved deep into her mouth to sweep along hers, igniting a fire inside her belly that made her whimper.

"Oh I like when you make that sound," he said. "It makes me a little crazy."

"It does, huh?"

"Yeah. Like you're begging for it."

She laughed and crawled onto his lap, facing him. She wrapped her legs around him, drawing closer to the heat of his body.

"You cold?" he asked.

"Yes. Warm me."

"I'll have to get you naked to do that."

She leaned back on her hands, thrusting her breasts out. "Go for it."

"Not easy given your position. I'll have to throw you off me and toss you around a bit."

"Good. Wrestling will heat me up."

"Not if you cooperate."

"Who says I'm going to cooperate?"

Even in the darkness she caught the dark gleam in his eyes. Her pussy quivered at the thought of wrestling with him, fighting him for dominance, for control. In this tiny tent it would be difficult, which made it all the more enticing. Physically, of course, he was stronger, but she had a few moves of her own.

They stayed like that as quiet seconds ticked by, neither of them budging an inch. When Mac pounced, she was ready for him, using her legs to brace herself and push him off. He grabbed for her hands but she kept them out of his reach and tried her best to stay behind him, knowing if he pinned her wrists she was a goner. She tightened her thighs, knowing they were her strongest feature, and wrapped them around his torso, whipping him to the floor as if it were a true wrestling match. He went down with a loud *oof* of surprise.

Lily laughed and jumped on his back, but she knew her attack would only last seconds. Mac bucked her off and immediately jumped on top of her. She rolled away and brought her knees to her chest, then pushed at him with her feet, keeping him away from her arms. He strained, and she enjoyed the play of his muscles as he pushed forward to reach her.

His strength overpowered her though, and she knew he'd been holding back so he didn't hurt her. He dropped off her, rolled to his side, then grabbed her around her waist, lifting her off the floor of the tent and rolling her with him until she was on the bottom on her belly. He pulled her arms out, pinning them with his hands over her wrists.

"Gotcha."

He panted against her neck, his breath hot.

It made her even hotter to know his cock was hard against her ass cheeks. This play was a huge turn-on for him, just as it had been for her. She lifted her hips and ground her ass against the thick ridge pressing down on her.

"Tease," he whispered, surging forward to further torment her with his cock.

"Prick."

"Yeah, a hot, hard one. You want it?"

She bit down on her bottom lip, her panties flooding with moisture. She lifted against him. "Do it. Hurry."

He grabbed her around the waist and hauled her to her knees, reaching underneath to unzip her jeans. She held still while he jerked them down over her hips and legs, leaving them at her knees. She heard the slide of his zipper, then felt his thighs brush hers, his cock making contact with her pussy.

He grabbed for her ponytail, tugging it lightly. "Ask me for it."

She grinned, refusing to speak. Oh, she wanted him inside her in the worst way.

He rubbed the soft crest of his cock against her clit and she closed her eyes against the sparks of intense pleasure, already imagining the feel of it inside her.

"What do you want, Lily?"

He knew damn well what she wanted. Why didn't he just give it to her? She was primed and ready, her pussy wet and throbbing with anticipation. He kept rubbing his cock up and down her slit, making her throb with unanswered need. But she refused to beg him for it.

He tugged on her ponytail again, the sharp sensation shooting straight to her pussy, firing her up even hotter.

"You like that."

He didn't even ask. He knew. So why should she bother to confirm it?

He pulled again, harder this time. "Tell me what you want, Lily, and I'll give it to you."

He rubbed between her legs. Having his hands there was torment as he teased her with expert, merciless strokes, only to pull away when he had her hot and writhing against his hand. He replaced his fingers with his cock, the promise of filling her so close as he teased his thick shaft between her pussy lips.

"I'm going to pump my dick in you and give it to you hard and fast, Lily. You ready for it?"

"Oh, Mac, yes," she finally said, admitting defeat in this game with great reluctance. She couldn't help it. She was tired of waiting.

He leaned forward and licked the side of her neck, sliding his cock against her. Goddamit, she couldn't stand this.

"You win," she groaned. "Fuck me."

With one thrust, he was inside her, pushing in with force. But she hadn't lost, she'd won. He was inside her, stretching her. Lily fisted the blanket underneath her hands at the unexpected thrill. Her pussy tightened around his cock, capturing him like her possession.

"So tight. So hot. And damn, baby, you're wet. You were ready for this, weren't you?"

She didn't answer, couldn't speak. Her only response was to push back against him so he could power more of his cock in. And he did, thrusting so deeply she felt it in her belly. The need spiraled, grabbing hold of her from the inside with every stroke. He knew just how to move to give her the utmost pleasure, sliding his cock upward to brush along her G-spot, rewarding her with tiny pulses that felt like orgasms. She whimpered, wanting more.

"Mac. Mac." She could only say his name as he pushed deeper, taking her where she needed to go. He wrapped his arms around her and moved his hand between her legs, stroking her clit with slow movements that drove her mad. It was perfect. The sensations inside and out splintered her in a million pieces.

"Yeah, baby. Come on me," he whispered against her. "Milk my cock."

The sounds of her cries as she climaxed mixed with the raging band noise. Lost in the sensation and the relentless thrusts of Mac's cock, she rode the vibrations, catapulting again when he gripped her hips and began to shudder against her, groaning as he came in hot torrents within her.

This was the wild life, the madness she'd always wanted, needed with Mac. No one else had ever been able to give it to her. Only Mac could give her what she craved.

Panting, exhausted, she stayed that way while he held her in his tight grip and kissed her neck.

"I'm sweaty," she said, laughing when he responded to that with a lick along the side of her neck.

"I crave salty things."

After they cleaned up as best they could and dressed, he lay on his back and pulled her against him, drawing the blanket over them both.

"You warm?" he asked.

"Yes. Very."

"Good."

She snuggled against him, letting her eyes drift closed as the sounds of the raucous party outside continued. She felt comfortable, warm, and safe.

Though she didn't quite feel settled. Not yet. Not when there were still unanswered questions.

She didn't have resolution with Mac, but for now, at least, there was an uneasy peace. That would have to do.

*   *   *

MAC DIDN'T KNOW WHAT WOKE HIM. MAYBE BECAUSE THE BAND finally stopped playing and the noise had died down. No crowd talk, no footsteps.

The quiet unnerved him. He sat up, letting his eyes adjust to the darkness. He slept light anyway—had to in his line of work, especially considering the package he carried.

Lily slept, his movements not disturbing her. He pulled the blanket around her, tucking it in so she wouldn't catch a chill. He pulled on his boots, zipped up his jacket, and slid the gun into his pocket. Debating whether to leave the virus in the tent or take it with him, he chose the latter. Leaving it in the tent put Lily at risk, and that he wouldn't do. If someone was watching them, they'd probably follow him, not stalk Lily.

He stepped out of the tent and zipped it back up, pulling his collar up against the biting wind. A few all-nighters were still milling around, but almost everyone had bedded down. The drink and food tents were closed and wouldn't reopen until after dawn. The band had packed up and left.

That uneasy sensation settled over him again. His gut told him something was wrong, and he always went with his instincts. Slipping one hand in his pocket, he made sure the safety was off his gun and began to wander behind the tents where the bikes were parked, keeping his gaze peeled for anything or anyone who looked suspicious.

He didn't hear or see anyone who seemed to be lurking around or watching or who didn't belong, but the hairs on the back of his neck raised, and that wasn't good. Someone *was* watching him. He knew it. When he got to his bike, he knew why.

His saddlebags, normally locked, were open. Not an amateur job either—not knifed or ripped or torn, but the locks had been picked. His stomach twisted as he circled the bike. It hadn't been vandalized, it had been searched. Keeping one eye on the area around him, he felt inside the bags. Nothing was missing, which meant this break-in hadn't been about petty theft. He knew exactly what the perpetrator had been after.

The virus. He and Lily had been tailed here. How had he missed that? Then again, in the crowd of bikers heading to the rally, everyone blended in. It could be anyone on a bike, or in one of the many cars that had also come to enjoy the rally. He scanned the trees and rows of tents, but didn't see anyone, nor did he expect someone to make a move right now. Not with the smattering of people still wandering around. Taking him down would call attention to him, would send a crowd running. Bikers supported each other, and Mac knew a lot of people here. Whoever was after him had to be aware of that. They weren't going to do anything at the rally, but Mac had to be on his guard when they left, because once they were out of the safety of the group of bikers, he and Lily would be targeted.

He needed a plan. A good one. A way to slip out of the rally without whoever was tailing them following.

First thing he had to do was wake Lily. Then go find Jessie.

EIGHT

MAC WOKE LILY OUT OF A DEAD SLEEP.

"Something's going on."

Lily bolted upright and grabbed for her boots. "What is it?"

"Someone broke into the bike last night."

Her eyes widened. "Vandals?"

He shook his head. "Professional job on the saddlebag locks."

"So they were looking for the virus."

"I'm pretty sure."

"How did they find us? I don't remember seeing that many cars on our way here."

"There were some. Enough. Could even be someone on a bike. They blend in better. Trust me, someone was obviously on our tail because they searched the bike. And that doesn't mean it was the guy who shot at us at the museum, but I can't take any chances that it was."

"Do you think they're still hanging out around here? Is someone watching us?"

He nodded. "It happened several hours ago. I've been sitting in here waiting for dawn, figuring out a plan."

"Why didn't you wake me?"

He smiled. "You needed the sleep."

"I'm ready. What do you want me to do?"

"We're going to find some friends and have a talk, figure a way out so we're not noticed. When we exit the tent, just hold my hand, smile a lot, act casual, and stay close."

Lily had a million questions, but right now she was thrilled that Mac confided in her, was including her in what was going on. "Got it."

They casually headed over to the food tent and grabbed a cup of coffee and breakfast, moving over toward Jessie and a group of men and women. To anyone watching, it seemed like a bunch of sleepy bikers having a quiet, innocuous conversation. They huddled around a table, heads bent together and whispering.

Mac didn't tell them anything about the virus, only that someone was following them and that he and Lily needed to get out of there without being tailed. She was surprised that these people didn't ask for more details, but they must be tight with Mac because they immediately agreed to help.

Must be a biker code of honor or something.

They had a plan, and as Lily listened to it, she couldn't keep the grin from her face. It was a great idea.

"So we're set?" Mac asked, his voice lowered to a whisper.

The big guy sitting next to Jessie nodded. "Don't worry about it. We've got it covered."

"You do your part, we'll do ours, and we'll meet where we've arranged, okay?" Jessie said.

"I appreciate this, guys," Mac said.

"No problem," one of the other guys said. "Let's do it."

After the others left, Mac straddled the bench and kissed her.

"So, any idea who?" she asked.

"Someone who wants the virus, is my guess."

"Don't you think we should try to figure out who broke into the bike? This is our chance to catch the person. Maybe it's the same person who fired on us at the museum."

"It might be, and then again maybe it isn't. I don't know." He dragged his fingers through his hair, his lips set in a grim line. "My gut tells me this guy picked up our trail and followed us, and that I don't like. And no, this isn't the right place or time to have a showdown with him if it is the same guy. I'm not putting all these people at risk." He turned to her. "We'll have our chance with him. This isn't it."

"You know you're going to see this guy again."

He nodded. "I'm damn sure of it. We'll lose him, but he'll find us again."

That wasn't comforting. "I hope this plan works. You have great friends."

Mac grinned. "I know." They stood, and he pulled her into his arms. "Just follow my lead and do whatever I say without question. This is going to go down fast, which is exactly the way we want it."

"You got it."

LILY PACKED UP WHILE MAC TOOK THE TENT DOWN, HER PULSE racing with excitement. When they made their way to his Harley, Jessie was there, along with the group who'd shared their table.

Lots of bikers wandered around, many packing up and heading out. It was chaotic. Lily grabbed a clue when everyone huddled close. She was grabbed, helmet slammed on and a terse warning from Mac to keep her head down and face covered. Then she was shoved on a bike that wasn't Mac's. She and Mac tore out of there in a hurry. She barely had time to hang on, nor did she even know who got on Mac's bike. They were surrounded by others as they headed out on the main road. Lily kept her head tucked to her chin; her hair was jammed up in her helmet so no one could tell who she was.

They were no longer heading south. More like east, northeast, and the group of bikes traveled with them. No one had broken off yet and they'd traveled about twenty-five miles so far. Lily really wanted to turn around to see if anyone was tailing them, but the best she could do was take an occasional peek over Mac's shoulder to look in his rearview mirror. All she saw were more bikes.

Finally, they reached an intersection that cut off into three other highways. It was then she noticed that all the bikers riding with them had virtually the same bike, and all the riders had women riding with them. And everyone was dressed similarly to her and Mac, in leathers with helmets on. No one tailing them could tell who was who.

What an amazing, tightly knit group. And talk about mass confusion. The bikes all took off in different directions. Lily felt a spark of adrenaline to be part of it, and she really hoped this worked.

They rode with four other bikes for about an hour, then those split off to two other bikes, then finally just her and Mac. Anyone following them wouldn't know which bike to watch for. Even Mac's Harley was similar to hundreds of other bikes at the rally. He turned off a side road and doubled back the way they came. This time Lily did turn around and watch behind them. She didn't see anyone there.

Other than a stop to use the bathroom and grab a quick bite to eat at a convenience store, they kept moving. They rode the entire day. It was dark by the time they met up in a park with ten other bikes. Jessie's was one of them, and Mac's bike was there.

"Anyone follow?" Mac asked as they switched bikes and he reclaimed his. It was then that Lily noticed they'd even swapped license plates. A couple of the guys were putting Mac's license plate back on his bike. Wow. These guys had thought of everything.

Jessie shook her head and grinned. "No one. We're clear."

Mac shook everyone's hand. "I owe you all."

"Hey, nice day for a ride," one of the guys said. "My pleasure."

"Anytime," another said. "You know that, Mac."

She climbed onto the back of Mac's bike and waved to Jessie as they rode off. As soon as the sun went down it was much colder riding. She wrapped her arms around Mac and huddled close to him, grateful for the leather jacket and chaps that kept the cutting wind off her body.

SHE KEPT EXPECTING MAC TO PULL OFF AND STOP SOMEWHERE, but he kept riding. And riding. Until she couldn't feel her toes anymore. Or her fingers, despite the gloves she wore. Eventually she shoved her hands in Mac's coat pockets. She shivered against him.

Okay, he was obviously continuing to ride because he felt a threat, so she was just going to have to buck it up. She thought about warm things. The tropics, the beach, the ocean, lying out in the baking sun until she was drenched in sweat.

Or rolling around naked with Mac until they were both so hot they couldn't breathe. Oooh, that was working. She felt warmer already and scooted closer to Mac, laying her head against him, wishing they were in a room somewhere, stripped of their clothes. Stripped of everything that kept them apart.

She'd really like that. She wanted this invisible wall of distrust to disappear. She would have loved to run into him by accident in a coffee shop, to renew what they once had without the theft, the virus, the what ifs having come between them.

But that wasn't going to happen. He was who he was, and so was she. She couldn't pretend to be someone she wasn't.

With a resigned sigh, she relaxed against him. For the time

being, at least, they were on the same side, keeping whoever was after the virus from getting it. It wasn't the authorities. They would have marched into the middle of the rally and identified themselves with badges. That meant it was someone who had nefarious intent. Mac either didn't know who it was, or he did know and wouldn't tell her. The good thing was, he had at least revealed his plan to her, had admitted to still having the virus, and that was a step in the right direction, a signal that he believed in her. That made her feel a little better. And while they weren't exactly working the same side of the street, it gave her hope. A tiny spark of hope she desperately needed.

Maybe things were starting to turn around.

Now if they could just stop moving for a couple of hours and get inside somewhere. Her back was stiff from so many hours of riding. So much that when Mac finally turned off the main highway and onto a tiny road, she prayed they'd be stopping soon. He pulled up in front of large iron gates and pushed a button. This was private property, obviously, but at least they were someplace that they might get off and rest for a while. She was so grateful she almost cried. She had no idea where they were or how far they'd come, and she didn't care. She wanted off this damn bike. But she did take the time to scan the front area for an address, a name, anything identifying where they might be. Nothing.

They waited a few seconds while a camera above the gates surveyed them, then the gates opened and Mac rode through. Lily turned around and watched the gates close securely behind them. Whoever lived here had some serious security. The long driveway was very well lit. No chance of anyone somehow getting over the high stone wall and skulking their way up to the front door without being seen.

The house itself was a modest two-story frame, built up to avert flooding. Mac pulled past it and along a covered driveway to the back. It was too dark to see beyond the lit screened-in porch, but after Mac shut down the bike's engine Lily heard the sound of water.

"Where are we?" she asked.

"Lake of the Ozarks. A friend of mine lives here. Come on."

THEY CLIMBED THE STAIRS AND MAC OPENED THE SCREEN DOOR leading onto the back porch.

"Shouldn't we knock?" she asked.

"Nah. He knows we're here." He pushed the door open and walked inside, holding it open for her.

They stepped into a cozy kitchen. Neat and tidy, everything put away. Nothing modern or extravagant. Definitely a summer-type home with older appliances and furniture, curtains on the windows and vinyl flooring in a yellow checked pattern.

It felt warm inside. Like being at someone's grandmother's house. Lily instantly felt comfortable, but stayed near Mac's side, not knowing what, or whom, to expect. When a tall man came down the hall and entered the brightly lit kitchen, Mac stepped up to him and shook his hand.

"Tom."

"Mac. So glad you stopped by."

He looked to be in his late forties or so, well built with short-cropped dark hair that was graying at the temples. He had pene-trating eyes that seemed almost black, but his smile was welcoming and friendly.

"And who did you bring with you?" Tom asked.

"This is my friend Lily. I've known her since high school."

While Mac went to retrieve their things from the bike, Tom arched a brow and moved forward, clasping both his hands over hers. "I'm so glad to meet you. I didn't know Mac had any friends from that long ago who still liked him."

Lily snorted. "One or two, I imagine."

"Good to know. Come in and take off your coat. It's a little cool out tonight to be riding, isn't it?"

Understatement. Her fingers were icy.

He led them into the living room. Again, it was cozy, with a striped couch and two matching recliners sitting on a polished hardwood floor. Stacks of books were piled on a couple of end tables as well as scattered across the coffee table. Very simple, nothing fancy. She liked the place.

"Do you live here by yourself?" she asked.

"Yeah. I like the quiet and I love to fish, so this place is perfect for me."

She took a seat in one of the recliners, rubbing her palm over the worn material on the chair arm. It was so real in here. So different from her father's home where furniture was so stiff, formal, unyielding. Like its owner.

She gestured to all his books. "You must like to read."

"Keeps me busy when the weather's too cold to go fishing."

She smiled, realizing that in five minutes she had become instantly comfortable with Tom—and she knew nothing about him.

"How do you know Mac?"

"The Major and I go way back," Mac said, sliding onto the recliner next to hers.

The Major? It was then that Lily noticed the medals in frames along the wall in front of her.

"Oh. You're military."

Tom nodded. "Retired. Marine Corps. It's in the family blood. All the way back to my great-grandfather."

Lily arched a brow and looked at Mac. "Military?"

Mac snorted. "Hardly. Not my thing."

Tom laughed. "No, definitely not your thing."

Confused, Lily said, "Then I don't get it. How did you two meet?"

Mac shot a look at Tom. He stood and said, "I'll bet you two are hungry. Mac, take your things into the spare room and I'll put some food on."

Way to avoid her question. Obviously another mystery for her to try and figure out. And they'd left her alone. Surely Tom had a telephone. She heard Tom in the kitchen and Mac rummaging around upstairs. Perfect opportunity to search for the telephone. It wasn't in the living room, so she moved into the kitchen.

"Need anything?" Tom asked, throwing a glance over his shoulder.

"No. You need help?" She did a quick scan of the kitchen, but didn't see a phone.

"I'm fine here. You just get settled in. Make yourself at home."

"I'll do that. Thanks." She slipped out of the kitchen and hurried down the hall, opening doors along her way. Closets, a bathroom, one bedroom, which must be Tom's. She hated sneaking around, but she wanted a phone.

No telephone. How could he live out in this remote area and not have a telephone in his kitchen or bedroom? She eased the door to his room closed and tiptoed upstairs. There were two bedrooms and one bath up here, but she already knew what she'd find. Or, rather, not find. The first bedroom was empty, the bathroom was useless, and Mac was in the third room.

"No, there are no telephones here," Mac said, obviously reading the frustration on her face.

"How can he live out here and not have a phone?"

Mac grinned. "He has a cell. And he keeps it on him."

Dammit. The fates were clearly conspiring against her. Well, them and the men.

"I'm going to take a shower," Mac said. "Care to join me?"

Lily laughed. "As tempting as that sounds, I don't think so. Not with Tom downstairs cooking a meal for us."

"He'll keep it warm." He took a step forward.

Lily took a step back. "You go first. I'll shower when you're finished. Does Tom have a washer and dryer?"

Mac nodded.

"Good. I need to wash some of our clothes."

"Now you're thinking practical things. I like it when you think about sex, instead."

"You just prefer me distracted so I won't try to find a phone or ask you any questions."

"Well, yeah." He moved forward again, this time pinning her between his body and the wall, leaving her no escape.

A sharp awareness and a swelling heat rushed through her. Just like that, thoughts of laundry and telephones and Tom cooking downstairs were lost. Mac's eyes went dark, his focus only on her. He skimmed his hand across her shoulder, down her arm, moving to her waist.

"Mac. I'm not stupid, you know."

Just being near him was a distraction, and she couldn't deny it.

"Of course you're not stupid. That's why I have to keep distracting you with my dick."

She couldn't help it. She laughed. "Yes, it is quite impressive, but eventually we have to talk. Who is Tom?"

"He's a friend of mine. I met him during my troubled days. He helped me out of a tight spot or two. Kept me from going to jail."

Okay, that was honest. She kept getting little revelations from him, pieces of his past that he fed her bit by bit. At least it was something. "Is he just a friend now, or are you two involved in some professional capacity?" Not that she expected him to tell her if they were.

"Just a friend. His place was close, and he's big into security. I figured we'd be safe here for a couple days. No one gets on Tom's property without him knowing it. If anyone is tracking us and follows us here, we'll know it. Tom's pretty high-tech with surveillance equipment. This is the best place for us to be right now."

"Thank you."

His brows lifted. "For what?"

"For talking to me. For telling me . . . anything at all at this point."

"You're welcome. Now kiss me. My cock is hard and I want you." He leaned in for a kiss and she didn't resist, needing to feel his lips on hers.

Contact with his mouth brought about another blast of heat. Her pussy quivered, moisture pooling and signaling her readiness.

Instantly, she was wet, her nipples tingling, her clit swelling, her body crying out for Mac. No man had ever done this to her, had ever made her feel this instantaneous passion. She threaded her fingers into the soft thickness of his hair and pulled, experiencing a sudden desperation to bring him closer, to draw him inside her.

She heard the zipper on Mac's jeans drawing down, and it was like a fire in her blood. The way he needed her was intoxicating. Was there anything more exhilarating than a man who desperately wanted his woman?

Lily pushed away long enough to shuck her boots and pants. That was as far as she got before Mac slammed her back against the wall again.

"God, Lily. I need this. Hard and fast. You ready for it?"

"Yes." The pain was like an aphrodisiac, enticing her to crave more of it. She spread her legs, and he reached around to grab her buttocks, lifting her and placing her on his cock. She wound her arms around his neck and slid down his shaft, latching onto his mouth with a whimper as he entered her with a forceful thrust.

He kept her back to the wall, using it as leverage while he pumped her with relentless strokes. It was fast, hard, and furious, just the way she wanted it. A sense of urgency enveloped her and she drove her tongue between his lips to dance with his in a primal mating of need and desire.

Whimpers and moans were their communication. That, and him inside her, stroking her, grinding against her with furied intent. Maybe it was because Tom was downstairs, but Lily felt it was more her need for Mac, the strange draw she felt toward him, that made her orgasm approach so quickly. She felt the tightening. He did, too, because he pulled his lips from hers and watched her as she came, his gaze dark and hot. She bit down on her bottom lip to keep from screaming as wave after wave of intense pleasure squeezed her from the inside out.

Mac's fingers dug into her ass cheeks as he pushed into her and shuddered. He still watched her as his orgasm thundered through him, the action so incredibly intimate it was almost unbearable to watch. Yet she did, stroking his hair as his breath caught and held while he stilled against her.

Her legs were shaking when he released them, and she held onto his arms while she caught her balance.

"Guess I'll go take that shower now," she said, slipping away from him to grab a change of clothes.

He grabbed her before she could leave the room, pressing his lips against hers. It was so unlike the hard passion they had just shared. The kiss was tender, a soft sweeping of his lips against hers. It made her ache inside.

"Don't use all the hot water," he whispered against her mouth.

She sighed and closed the bathroom door. She turned on the shower and stepped in, letting the steamy hot water pour over her, wincing as it hit her scraped back. She smiled though, her body still trembling with postcoital bliss. Sometimes things between them were so perfect.

But there was more to a relationship than just great sex. A lot more. Like trust, and communication. Areas where she and Mac were still sadly lacking. They had made some headway, at least. That was promising. But was it enough? Was he going to start opening up to her, confiding in her about what was going on? Granted, a phone was still off-limits, and she actually understood his reasoning for that. It didn't mean she wouldn't try to find and use one, but she did understand why he didn't want her to.

He had to protect himself. If their situations were reversed, she'd do the same thing. She knew she wasn't working for the bad guys, so it was different. She didn't know who he was working for. That was the piece of the puzzle still missing, the integral part he refused to share with her.

And who was Tom? Was he connected at all to the virus, or was he just another stopping point along the way to the drop-off? She had a hard time believing that Mac, if he really was a thief, if he had less than reputable intents for the virus, would trust someone in the military. Maybe Tom really was just an old friend and didn't know a thing about the vial. Maybe Mac was keeping Tom in the dark, too.

Once again, Lily had a ton of questions. And doubts about Mac. She hated her own skepticism, but she wasn't certain if he was telling her the truth, or just feeding her a pack of lies to placate her.

She hoped that wasn't the case, because she needed truth from him more than anything. She'd rather hear silence than lies.

And she wanted to believe him. Her heart needed to know. She didn't want the heartbreak, but she could feel it coming and despite the walls she built up, knew she wouldn't be able to avoid it when they went their separate ways.

But leaving with lies between them, with deception, without knowing the truth and without having a positive outcome to all this—that would be a knife in her heart.

God, she didn't ask for much, did she?

She shook her head and reached for the shampoo.

Maybe she just wanted too much.

nine

LILY WOKE THE NEXT MORNING ALONE IN THE OH-SO-COMFORTABLE bed she and Mac had shared. They'd even managed to sleep. Tom had fed them well, and while she did laundry they'd spent a few hours talking to him about books and his military life. By the time Lily had climbed into bed, it had taken her exactly two-point-two seconds to completely pass out.

She was fairly certain Mac had been even more exhausted than she was. He'd yawned several times, his eyelids had blinked closed, and he'd even fallen asleep in the chair downstairs. She finally booted him upstairs to bed when she finished the laundry. And though he'd acted like he wanted to devour her from head to foot, she knew better. Sometimes sleep was more important than sex.

At least it had been last night. She woke up well rested and eager to find Mac.

She dressed in a hurry and headed downstairs, the aromas of freshly brewed coffee and bacon alluring to her senses.

Tom and Mac were sitting at the kitchen table. When she walked in, conversation stopped.

She hated that. It made her think there were plans being made that she wasn't privy to. Secret plans. Maybe she was becoming paranoid.

Yeah, right. No maybes about it. She was already there, front and center in Paranoid City, and rightly so considering she didn't know a damn thing.

Tom stood and pulled a mug from the cupboard.

"How do you take it?" he asked.

"With cream if you have it. Otherwise, black is just fine. But I can do it myself."

"Have a seat. I made breakfast, you're a guest, and guests get served around here."

She cast a smile in his direction and slid into the chair next to Mac. He cupped the back of her neck and pressed a soft kiss to her lips.

"Morning, sleepy."

"Morning."

The coffee tasted phenomenal and Tom slid a plate of bacon and eggs in front of her that she tried really hard not to devour like a starving animal. But she was hungry.

"I'll be gone two days at the most," Tom said.

Lily paused midbite and laid her fork down. "You're leaving?"

Tom grinned. "Fishing trip."

"When are you going?"

"This morning."

She glanced at Mac. "We should pack, then."

"Why? We're not leaving," Mac said.

"We're not?"

"Hell no. There's no reason the two of you have to go." Tom said. "You stay and enjoy the deck and the water. Temperatures are already warming up. The next couple days are supposed to be great." He stood and put his cup in the sink. "I'm the one who needs to finish packing."

He left the room, and Lily shot a quizzical look at Mac. "Why are we staying?"

"Safety reasons. Tom has a fortress here and I want to ride it out for a few days, see if anyone followed us or picked up our trail. I can monitor the perimeter, keep an eye on the surveillance cameras, and watch the area. Then, if I think we're all clear, we'll head out."

"Okay, that makes sense." Her stomach tumbled at this news. Once again he was communicating with her, sharing information. This was a very good thing, a step in the right direction. Okay, so maybe she was grasping at any straw she could right now, but they were light-years ahead of where they had started in terms of progress in their relationship, and she'd take that as a good sign.

"And like Tom said, we have the place to ourselves. We can make use of the boat dock, do a little swimming, lie around in the sun, and have some fun. Relax a little."

He waggled his eyebrows at her. Lily knew what he meant by relax, but she wasn't sure that was possible. Not with the virus still in his possession and its destination unknown.

Of course *he* knew what he was going to do with it. He knew everything, so it was easy for him to take some downtime. For her? Not so simple.

But the longer she played this game with him, the more he trusted her not to betray him, not to try and run, the more information she could potentially get out of him.

The problem was, every day she spent with Mac, the more accustomed she grew to being with him, to renewing the feelings she'd had for him all those years ago. It was getting harder and harder to keep her professional side at the forefront, to use sex as a bargaining chip to gain his trust and to keep her emotions at bay.

She wasn't that good at this spy stuff. She had a heart and she couldn't keep a wall of ice around it forever.

Maybe he was better at it than she was. Maybe he was able to keep it all about the sex and not get emotionally involved. She really had no idea since they hadn't broached the subject of how they felt about each other. He hadn't brought it up, and she certainly wasn't going to. She wanted him to think what was between them was easy and playful and all about "right now," that it didn't mean anything significant to her beyond just a physical thing. She wanted him to think that when this was over she would walk away without looking back, without any attachment to him.

Which meant it was time to step up the sex, to really have some fun with him, to let him know she was going to let things go for now and enjoy their time together.

She was going to bridge the gap of mistrust between them so he would continue to feed her information, so he would think he could tell her anything.

But when the time came for him to deliver the virus, she was going to snatch it out from under him and take it to the authorities. She had to, no matter what her feelings for Mac were.

Tom walked out with a small bag in one hand and fishing pole in the other.

"I take that to mean you're packed?" Lily asked, eyeing the tiny duffle bag.

"Everything I need," he grinned. He turned to Mac. "You know where everything is, and I have my cell if you need me."

Mac nodded. "Thanks again."

"Anytime. You two enjoy yourselves."

Tom headed out the back door. Within a few minutes, Lily heard the sound of a boat engine firing up, then he was gone, and she and Mac were alone. She got up and washed the breakfast dishes. Mac dried and put them away. Neither of them said anything, and the routine of working side by side with him was nice. Peaceful.

The windows were open and she realized soon that Tom was right. A warm breeze blew through the kitchen window and it smelled like summer. The sun was bright and Lily was ready to get outside.

"Let's go exploring," she suggested.

"Sure. I'll take you down to the dock and show you the lake."

"I don't have shorts or a swimsuit." Which was really too bad, because after last night's chill, she ached to feel the sun on her body.

"That's no problem. Tom's college-aged niece and her boyfriend come to visit a lot. She always leaves some of their stuff here. Check the drawers for a swimsuit and some shorts."

"Okay. She hurried upstairs and rummaged through the dresser drawers, thrilled to find a two-piece swimsuit and a pair of cotton shorts to toss on. Fortunately, they fit fairly well, though the top was a bit small. Her breasts poured over the material, but it would have to do. Besides, it would just be her and Mac, and he'd seen it all already.

She was glad to have the suit to wear, since as soon as they stepped outside she couldn't believe how hot it was. The sun beat down on them as they walked the smooth path from the back porch to the boat dock. She was barefoot and the wooden-planked walkway was warm under her feet.

It felt so good. Some of her stress was already melting away in the heat.

The dock was incredible and much more than just a spot to anchor Tom's boat. It was huge, with lawn chairs and tables with sun awnings to block the rays and a couple of lounge chairs for tanning. There was even a small boathouse next to the deck with a private changing room and bathroom so you didn't have to walk back up to the house. She could spend an entire day sprawled out near the water's edge and be perfectly content.

And the view—awe inspiring didn't begin to describe it. The sun cast rays down upon the water, rendering it smooth, shiny glass. Beyond were miles and miles of waterway, broken up only by shoreline and rising trees, so dense they looked like one giant mass of green hill, instead of thousands of hickory and oak. It was breathtaking. She sat at the edge of the dock and slipped her feet in the water.

"Yikes, that's cold," she said.

Mac stood next to her, looking out over the water. "Yeah, the days have been warm, but the sun hasn't heated the water enough to take a dip yet. If you get hot enough lying around out here, though, a quick swim will feel pretty good."

"We'll see about that." It felt frigid to her at the moment. She'd have to be pretty damn hot to plunge into the icy lake. But the view was spectacular, it was quiet here, and she was actually relaxing. She scanned the area. Other homes sat off in the distance, their docks bobbing up and down in the water. Some had boats tethered to them. So far she hadn't seen any people. With the thick trees and bushes, it would be easy for someone to hide, either on this side or the other side of the lake.

Someone could be watching them right now. Targeting Mac. She realized she wasn't at all worried about herself, didn't see herself as the target. He was the one with the virus. Somehow she figured the bad guys knew that.

"We're safe here, Lily. Properties in this area are well secure. If there was a problem, we'd know it."

Mac had changed into shorts and a T-shirt with cutoff sleeves. She liked the look. It gave her an opportunity to ogle his muscles.

"Are you going to sit?" she asked.

"I'm not much for lounging. Thought I might scrub the deck for Tom."

She rose and wiped her hands on her shorts. "I'll help you."

He cocked his head to the side. "You don't have to."

"I want to. I've been doing a lot of sitting around the past few days. I like being active."

"Okay."

He gathered materials and they got to work doing some serious cleaning.

The day grew hotter, but it felt good. No, it actually felt great
to be outside, to feel the heat on her skin and to simply enjoy
working and playing alongside Mac. Every time the sweat would
really start pouring off her, he'd squirt her with the hose and cool
her down. Which would require her to jump up and wrestle him
for it, and they'd both end up wet, which both cooled and heated
her.

It was light and playful and the hours passed quickly. Before
she knew it the deck was clean. She went into the house and fixed
them sandwiches. They ate at one the shaded tables on the deck.

"This reminds me of lunch on the quad in high school," she
said. "Do you remember?"

"Not really."

"Oh, that's right. You were too cool to join the masses."

He snorted. "I was out smoking in the parking lot during lunch
hour."

"Tsk tsk. Such a bad boy."

His grin was devastating, making her heart skip a beat.

"That's what turned you on, if I remember right. That bad boy
streak in me. The thrill of the forbidden."

He was so right. At first, anyway. She remembered running out
to her car one day at lunch because she'd left a book she'd need
for an afternoon class there. Mac had been in the parking lot with
a group of other guys. Some of the guys spotted her, came up to
her and started teasing her, cornered her. She'd been scared to
death, wondering what they were going to do. Mac had sauntered
into the middle of the group and told the guys to get lost, that
Lily was a friend of his and she was cool. The guys had shrugged
and walked away.

Lily had been stunned Mac had come to her rescue, especially since she didn't know him at all. She'd thanked him, but he blew her off, said no big deal and left her standing there by her car.

To her it had been a big deal, and she'd made it a point to find him again, to figure out who he was.

"You were my knight in shining armor," she said.

His brows lifted. "Is that right?"

"Or maybe a bad boy in shining leather?"

He grinned. "Sounds more like me."

They finished their sandwiches and spent an hour after that just lazing away in the shade, cooling down their bodies and relaxing.

"Your face is getting sunburned," Mac said.

"It is?"

"Yeah." He reached out and brushed his thumb across the tip of her nose. "You look like Rudolph the red-nosed reindeer."

She pushed his thumb away. "I do not."

"Your cheeks are red, too. Are you blushing?"

She snorted. "Hardly. After what we've been through together, you can't make me blush."

He arched a brow. "Wanna bet?"

The challenge in his gaze warmed her more than the sun had. She took a long swallow of water and shook her head. "Not a chance. I don't want to take your money."

He braced his elbows on the table and leaned closer. "Baby, I can definitely make you blush. All over, in fact."

Lily didn't even want to think about all the ways he could do that. Then again, maybe that's exactly what she wanted.

"Prove it," she challenged.

Without a word, he pushed his chair back and stood, then came around to her side of the table.

"Stand up," he said.

Curious and excited, she stood and turned to face him.

"Now turn around."

She quirked a brow. "Huh?"

He grasped her shoulders and turned her so her back was to him and she faced the water. His chest brushed her back; his hips nestled against her buttocks. When he wrapped his arm around her middle and pulled her in to him, she resisted the urge to let out a purr of delight. It always felt so good to be held against him.

"Ever make love outside, Lily?" he whispered against her neck. Tremors of sensation shuddered through her nerve endings at the dark promise in his voice.

"No."

"You're going to."

Her eyes widened. "Here?" Her gaze darted toward the trees and coves nearby. No boats had cruised by them, but there were other properties, other houses. People could see. "Mac, that's not a good idea."

"I don't care. I want you, and I'm going to fuck you right here."

His cock was already hardening against her, the firm ridge of his shaft pressing insistently against her buttocks. Despite her shock at what he proposed, her nipples tightened and her pussy quivered. The thought of him touching her out here, making love to her in such a public place, excited her.

"Everyone has a little of the exhibitionist in them, baby," he said, sliding his hand over the plane of her stomach. Her belly did somersaults in response. "Knowing that someone could be watching, could be getting off on seeing you and me together . . . doesn't that turn you on just a little?"

She didn't want to admit that it did, but she couldn't help herself. "Yes."

He moved his hand upward, his fingers widening as he splayed them over her rib cage, coming to rest just underneath her bikini top. Her heart pounded against his palm.

"Are you scared?"

"No." Excited, yes. But she wasn't frightened. Mac would look out for her. He always had.

"Your heart is beating fast. I'll bet you're creaming in your bikini bottoms, too."

He was right. She was wet, her pussy throbbing in anticipation of his touch, his mouth on her clit, licking her and giving her the orgasm she craved.

"You're going to have to learn to tell me what you're thinking, to voice those nasty little thoughts rolling around in your mind. I want to hear them. They make my dick hard."

"I'm wondering when you're going to touch me."

"I am touching you." He moved his hand across to the other side of her rib cage, teasing her with his fingers, but not touching her breasts.

"Touch me more."

"How?"

She wanted him to rip off her top, pluck her nipples, suck on them. She needed so much more than what he was giving her. "Touch my breasts."

He moved both hands up and covered her breasts. Oh, no, that wasn't right. He'd left her top on.

"No, not like that." Her breathing had become labored, her voice low.

"Tell me what you want."

"I want your hands on my skin."

"You want me to take your top off? Out here, where someone might see?"

Damn him for teasing her like this. "Yes, take it off." She didn't care. She needed his hands molded to her skin, touching her nipples. She wanted to feel that sensation between her legs, firing up her arousal.

He untied the top and it fell forward, releasing her breasts. When his hands covered the mounds, she let out a whimper that was a mixture of relief and agony. She focused on the sensations his hands created, but couldn't help scanning the area. Her breasts were exposed. Could someone see? And if they did, what would they think?

The thought excited her.

"I think you like this," Mac said, sliding his thumbs over her nipples.

She gasped, and he rolled the buds between his fingers, pulling a little harder. He rocked his hips against her, his cock fully hard now, his breath hot on her neck. He placed light nibbles on the tender spot between her neck and shoulder, and she shivered in response.

This was absolutely wicked. She felt so bare. Even though she was half-shaded under the canopy, anyone really looking could spot them. She never knew being an exhibitionist could be so arousing. And the strange thing was, she really didn't care who was watching, especially when Mac's fingers crept down her stomach, then lower, skimming the edge of her shorts.

She knew where he was going, and she was desperate for him to touch her there, to feel his hand cupping her sex, his fingers dipping inside her. And she wanted him to do it right here.

He paused, his fingers teasing the top edge of her bikini. She shivered at the sensation.

"Are you wet, Lily? Do you want me to touch your pussy?"

"Yes."

"Do you want my fingers inside you?"

"Oh, God. Yes, you know I do." Her pussy quivered.

"Pumping deep, then drawing all that sweet pussy juice out to coat your clit. Is that what you want me to do?"

He was making her crazy. He was doing this deliberately, toying with the edges of her bikini, but not touching her where she needed it the most.

"Yes," she said, tilting her head back to rest on his shoulder. "Make me come, Mac. Hurry."

He slipped his hand inside her shorts, pulled the ties on the sides of her bikini and jerked it free, tossing it on the table.

"That was in my way," he said, his voice a low growl against her ear.

The tension in his voice was evident. He was as taut with need as she was. She barely caught her breath from his removal of her bikini bottom before his hand covered her pussy. The heat of his palm was like stoking an already raging bonfire. She arched against his hand, curling into that singeing contact.

Then he began to stroke her, with soft, silky movements, coating his hand with the cream spilling from her pussy. Now wet, his hand glided over her in a smooth rhythm, and each time he brushed her clit she felt a stroke of lightning deep in her core. It was like a shock wave of electricity, the most pleasurable kind imaginable.

"Damn, baby, you *are* wet." He dipped the tip of one finger between her folds, teasing her with what could be. It was sheer torment, because he removed it, continuing the slow torture of his caresses.

"Please," she begged, not caring how it sounded. Mac was in control of this, of her. She needed what he could give, and she'd do anything to get it. She wanted this exposure, to feel the sunshine warming her pussy while his mouth covered her aching clit.

"Tell me what you want, Lily."

"Lick me."

His tongue lashed out against her earlobe. "Like this?"

She shivered, goose bumps breaking out over her heated body. "No."

"Where do you want it?"

"I want your mouth on my pussy."

He withdrew his hand and dragged her to the picnic table across the deck. No canopy there, only bright sunlight and open to the water.

"Lie down on the table."

She lay on her back, her legs dangling over the edge of the table. His eyes were so dark with passion . . . she felt drugged looking at him. No smile creased the lines alongside his eyes. Only concentration and deep need—so serious, so intense. Her heart slammed against her ribs and she found it hard to breathe.

"Lift," he commanded.

When she did, he grasped the top of her shorts and dragged them down her thighs. When he pulled them off, he widened her legs and stepped between them. She arched up to reach for him, but he splayed his hand over her chest to keep her in place.

"Uh-uh. Stay put. You're mine."

His. Was she really? For the moment, yes, and that's all she cared about. This moment, and what he was going to do to her. She relaxed and shielded her eyes from the sun, keeping her head tilted up so she could watch Mac pull up the bench and sit between her legs. He shot a quick glance at her, his lips curving into a devilish grin before he dragged her down along the smooth table, her pussy balancing just at the edge.

His mouth covered her sex, and she let out a shriek she had no hope of holding in, because his lips were warm, his mouth wet, his tongue circling her clit with soft, slow strokes meant to tease and torment. She couldn't bear it, she was already so close to orgasm. She jerked upward, grinding against his face in desperation. He slid his hands underneath her buttocks and held her while he feasted on her pussy, licking her up and down as if she were a fast-melting ice-cream cone and he wanted to slurp every last drop before it spilled.

She was spilling, all right. Her climax rushed at her like a fast-breaking ocean wave, and she held tight to the edge of the table as it rocked her senseless. The hot rush of liquid seeped down the crack of her ass as she flooded his face with come. She shook in uncontrollable spasms. Mac, utterly relentless, licked her, sliding his tongue inside her pussy to lap up every drop until she lay limp and panting.

If she thought she'd have time to recover, she was wrong. He stood and lifted his shirt over his head. So overwhelmed by her orgasm, she lay there, staring at his chiseled body while he dropped his shorts and took his cock in his hands. He stroked it for her, fisting it in a tight grip and using slow, deliberate motions from base to tip. Pearly drops formed at the head, and she licked her lips, eager to taste him.

"Don't even think about moving," he warned, continuing to thrust his cock into his tightly fisted grip. "I'm going to fuck you right there. Plant your feet on the table."

Renewed desire sparked within her as she watched him masturbate. She bent her knees and flattened her feet on the edge of the table. Mac moved forward between her legs and slid inside her with a firm push. She tilted her head back and closed her eyes, exhaling in a moan that signaled the sweet pleasure she felt at his entry. He stretched the walls of her vagina, striking nerve endings that no man had ever hit. Maybe it was a psychological thing. Surely one penis was just as good as another, wasn't it?

Then again, maybe not, because no man ever touched her inside like Mac did.

He withdrew and surged forward again. Lily gasped as sensation exploded inside her. She lifted her hips to drive more of his cock inside her.

"Look at me."

She opened her eyes and her breath caught, the explosion catapulting her and rocking her senses. What really drove her pleasure was his eyes, the way he looked at her. He wasn't centered on her pussy, he wasn't getting off on watching where they were joined; he was watching her face. With every thrust, he looked in her eyes for her reaction.

He was watching her. The whole woman, not just the body. He was searching beyond the physical, reaching for all of her.

Oh, God. She felt it, and she didn't want to. The emotional connection. *Goddamit.* Even outside, during this naughty little experiment of hot, wicked exhibitionism, what should have been harmless fun and games shattered her inside when she looked at him.

He wasn't fucking her. He was loving her. Not just with his cock, but with all of him. Oh, he hadn't said a damn thing. She didn't need words spoken to know it. She read it in his eyes, felt it in the sweeping caress of his hand along the side of her face as he bent over the table and with his eyes still fixed on her, pressed an intimate kiss to her lips.

Yes, it was hot and it was sexy and she gripped him from the inside out, claiming him at the most primal level.

At the same time he smashed the wall around her heart and claimed it.

Tears pooled and fell from the corners of her eyes, streaming down her cheeks. The funny thing was, they only increased her pleasure, not in any way diminishing it.

The knowledge that no matter what kind of game she played with her own mind, no matter what she said to try and convince herself that it wasn't true, this wasn't just a job. She always had been and always would be in love with Mac.

Ten

LILY WAS CRYING. MAC WAS INSIDE HER, AND IT FELT SO DAMN good, but tears fell from her eyes and he didn't understand what was happening. He stilled and leaned over her, using his thumb to wipe away a tear rolling down her face.

"Baby, what's wrong?"

She shook her head and grabbed his wrists, pulling him toward her. "Nothing's wrong. Don't stop."

Her voice was a breathy whisper, her face tight with passion. Her body blushed all over. A fine sheet of perspiration from the sun, from their lovemaking, cast her in the role of a golden goddess spread out before him. He moved inside her and his thought process was lost. If she was okay, then he was okay.

Some women got emotional during sex, or so he'd heard. He'd never had a woman cry when he fucked her. Then again, Lily wasn't like any other woman he'd ever been with before. He'd never felt a woman so completely when he was inside her like he did with Lily. The way they seemed to fit so perfectly, the way she responded to him and gave herself to him—all of these things ratcheted up his pleasure in the moment. How could he think of anything else but how she felt wrapped around his cock, hot and wet and squeezing him with soft pulses meant to make him crazy.

She whimpered, but this time it wasn't distress. She lifted, trying to get more of him. He gave her what she wanted, thrusting deeper, grabbing her legs so they hung in his arms. Her ass was off the table and the position gave him the best damn view of her pussy. Now he could watch where they were connected, see the way the puffy lips of her cunt grabbed his dick whenever he withdrew. The sight was erotic as hell and any guy would be riveted on it.

But what he really liked focusing on was her face, the way it contorted with an almost painful pleasure whenever he pulled back, then powered forward again. There was nothing more arousing than a woman completely invested in lovemaking, so connected in body and spirit that she could look into her man's eyes and not feel embarrassed.

Lily made eye contact. God, that was so hot, knowing she wasn't afraid to look at him while he fucked her. The way her eyes got glassy, the way she seemed to be able to see inside his mind, read his thoughts, the way he felt connected to her in the most primal of ways, made his balls knot up. Her slick heat was like a torture chamber, and it was the best torment he could ever ask for. He was hot and sweaty and didn't want to stop. She was beautiful, his little wildcat. The way she looked was mesmerizing. He could stare at her the rest of the day, except he felt a tightening at the base of his spine, the pleasure spiraling up inside him, and he wanted to come in her. It was tunneling through him like a runaway train and he fought to hold it back.

Lily was going to go first. He released her legs, then slid his hands under her back and pulled her up, doing a complete turnaround so that he lay on the table on his back. Without breaking stride, he settled her on top of him.

"Now finish us off, baby."

Her eyes gleamed with delight as she straddled him and surged forward, then tilted her head back and rode him hard. She seated herself fully on top of him, which buried him to the hilt inside her. He paused, feeling the tight walls of her pussy pulse around him. Then he gripped her hips and lifted her, letting her slide down again, watching every inch of his shaft disappear inside her. Her cunt squeezed a welcome as he invaded her, gripping him in a tight vise. Watching what his cock was feeling was a heady sensation. Seeing her reaction to it was even better.

Her breasts tipped forward as she palmed his chest, the rosy tips tantalizing him. He cupped the mounds and teased her nipples with his fingers.

"I like that," she said.

He liked her voice when she was deep into sex. He liked her mentality even better—wild and uninhibited.

"How much do you like it?" He tugged at her nipples, and her pussy clenched around his cock. "That much, huh?" This time, he gave them a light pinch, and she squeezed her thighs against him.

"More."

When she reached between her legs and began to rub her clit, he knew she was too far gone, that this was going to be over soon. He tugged at her nipples, harder this time, concentrating on Lily and trying to force a halt to the contractions threatening to let loose the floodgates of his orgasm. *Not yet, dammit.*

"Make yourself come for me, Lily. Let me see it. I want to feel it."

Ripples of sensation rolled over him, both from her and from within himself. Sweat poured from him at the effort it took to sustain his hold, but he refused to yield. His gaze swept from rapid movements of her hand strumming her clit to the look of utter rapture on her face. He felt what she felt—the sweeping waves of her orgasm as her lips parted and soft cries escaped. Her eyes widened as she came and she once again locked her gaze on him, digging her nails into his chest.

The eruption was powerful, blinding him in its intensity. He bucked up against her as the force of it lifted his hips off the table. Lily held on as he rocketed inside her, shuddering out a loud groan, then collapsing after he had emptied all he had. Panting, he held onto her hips and just stared into her beautiful eyes. And still she kept eye contact, never once looking away.

She smiled down at him, his vixen suddenly turned angel.

"Your skin is going to fry out here in the sun. Let's get inside."

"I'm on top and I'm in charge here now," she said with a sassy grin.

"Is that right?" In an instant he was upright, still inside her, and walking toward the house. She wrapped her legs around his waist, her arms around his neck, but didn't fight him.

"You just think you're so tough, don't you?"

If he was tough, he wouldn't be doing this with her. She really had no idea how much of a freakin' marshmallow he was where she was concerned. "You bet I am."

"Hmph. I know martial arts. I could take you down right now if I wanted to."

He paused and looked at her, their noses practically touching. "And do you want to?"

She shrugged. "Not particularly. I'm hot, I'm sweaty, and my muscles ache. And I need a shower. I'll kick your ass later, after I've had a chance to cool off, clean up, and rest a little."

He tilted his head back and laughed. "That's my practical girl."

He carried her into the house and didn't let her go until he had deposited her in the upstairs bathroom, turned on the shower, then dragged her under the water with him. She laughed when he pulled her beneath the wide spray.

After she was wet, he grabbed her shampoo and poured it over her head.

"What are you doing?"

"Washing your hair."

"Oh."

He massaged her scalp, loving the way the silky strands felt in his fingers. His buddies would laugh at him for doing this. Not quite manly, but anything he could do to put his hands on Lily was fun for him. He didn't really care whether it was a *guy* thing or not, and the rewards for doing it were substantial. She sighed, made moaning sounds, and was utter putty in his hands. He tilted her head slightly back to rinse her hair, then applied the conditioner that women seemed to think was necessary after shampooing.

After he was finished rinsing that out of her hair, he picked up the bottle of body wash and poured it into his hands, rubbing his palms together to make a lather. He spread it over her back in slow circles.

"Mac."

"Yeah."

"That feels . . ."

He waited, but she didn't continue. "That feels what?"

"No one's ever bathed me before."

Her voice was so soft it was almost a whisper. He shook his head, unable to believe no man had ever catered to Lily. She deserved more than this—more than he could ever give her, that was for sure. A woman like her needed pampering by some rich guy who could give her luxuries, entire days at the spa. A maid, servants to cook and clean for her. He smiled, thinking how easily she could slip into that lifestyle. Hell, she'd grown up in it—it suited her. Not hiding out, being shot at and constantly on the run. That was his life, not hers.

He moved his hands down the curve of her back, slipping his soapy fingers between the crack of her ass. She shivered, then bent forward, casting him one hell of a hot look over her shoulder, one filled with promise.

One part rich girl, the other part biker babe. She was a mix of contradictions, and the only woman he'd ever really wanted. The only one who'd gotten under his skin and hadn't let loose. How was he ever going to let her go? How could he not? His life wasn't for her, and the best thing he could ever do for her was cut her loose.

Which was going to happen soon, if all worked out according to plan.

That wasn't what he wanted to think about right now. Now he was sliding his hand between the sweet cheeks of Lily's ass, and she wasn't pulling away—she shuddered and clenched her butt in a way that made his dick twitch. So he kept his fingers there, skimming up and down the little hole.

"Mac."

He leaned against the shower wall, sweeping aside the wet tendrils of her hair to nibble on her neck. "Yeah, baby." He continued to play with her anus, letting her grow accustomed to his touch.

"That feels so . . . incredible."

He smiled and played with her a little more, cupping her sex with one hand while he continued to tease her ass. He wanted her focused on sensation, on pleasure. He wanted her relaxed so she could enjoy this play. He toyed with her clit, patting it, giving her teasing caresses and ratcheting up her need. Her panting breaths, puckered nipples, and the way she kept backing into his finger, then thrusting forward against his hand told him everything he needed to know. She liked what he was doing at both ends.

She was making his dick rock hard. Damn, after the rousing

session they'd just had outside, he couldn't believe he was hard and aching for her again already.

He took it further now, coaxing his finger just past the barrier of her tight-muscled entrance. She gasped as he pushed through, then she moaned as he slid his finger in farther and pulled it almost all the way out.

"Yeah. Just like being fucked," he whispered.

"Oh. Oh, God."

She wasn't looking at him now. Her eyes were closed, her head against the wall and her palms flat against it. He watched her hips thrust forward and back against both his hands. She was lost in it now.

Christ, he wanted inside her, wanted to share that sensation with her.

"Have you ever had anal sex, Lily?"

She turned her head and opened her eyes, sucking in her bottom lip. She shook her head.

"Do you want to?" Because this had to be her call, her choice.

"Yes."

No hesitation whatsoever. She wanted it. With him. *Goddamn*.

And that look. Innocence, curiosity . . . and sexual heat. His cock twitched and he leaned against her hip, pinning his throbbing shaft between himself and her soft flesh as he continued to prime her. He wanted all of Lily, wanted to be inside every part of her, especially where no other man had been. The thought of sliding his cock inside her tight, hot hole made his balls quiver.

But he had to ease her through this first time, wanted to make it pleasurable for her. He didn't want to break this moment, but he sure as hell wasn't going in her this way.

"Don't move." He withdrew and washed his hands, then hurried out of the shower, opening and closing drawers and cabinets in the bathroom, praying Tom had something, anything useful. He almost rejoiced with a loud whoop when he found a bottle of lube. Thank God Tom had a sex life. The he grabbed a condom from his room.

He stepped back in the shower to find Lily leaning with her back against the shower wall, two fingers inside her pussy. Her hot stare shattered him.

"Damn, baby."

"I need you, Mac. Hurry."

He placed the lube on the shelf and planted his hands on the wall on either side of her shoulders, then kissed her with the ravaging hunger eating him up inside. Her tongue thrust into his mouth and met his with wild abandon, her fingers tearing into his hair, pulling with hard yanks. He didn't care. He liked his woman wild and needy. He stroked her breasts, plucking at her nipples until she whimpered against his lips.

When he couldn't stand it anymore, he removed his mouth from hers and flipped her around so her face was to the shower wall.

"Spread your legs and push your ass out at me."

She did, but he wasn't ready to plunge inside her ass yet. He wanted her screaming first, crying out and begging him to fuck her. As soon as she was in position, he knelt and spread her ass cheeks, smoothing his fingers along the soft crack. Even here, she was beautiful. Pink and tiny, her pussy lips swollen and visible underneath. He leaned in and buried his face between her checks, snaking his tongue out to lick around the puckered hole.

"Oh, my God, Mac!"

Lily tensed, but Mac caressed her buttocks, leaning back a bit. "Relax, baby, Let me lick you."

She shuddered when he forced her cheeks apart, then dove in again, licking around the rim with soft strokes. He slipped his hand around her to massage her pussy, wanting her concentrating on pleasure only. He licked her with alternating strokes—fast, then slow, long laps, continuing to play with her clit and pussy lips until she was writhing against him. Any hesitation she had soon disappeared and she was shoving her ass in his face.

Oh, yeah. Just where he wanted her. Wild and out of control. He stood and grabbed the lube, coating his finger and pouring it over the crack of her ass. He penetrated her with one finger, still using his other hand to maintain his rhythm on her clit, moving to her side now so he could maintain a rhythm, fucking her ass with his finger, embedding it deep inside her now. Her tight ass pulsed, growing accustomed to the invasion. This was just the start. There was much more to come.

First, he wanted Lily to climax, then he was going to bury his cock deep in her tiny hole and take her virgin ass.

His cock twitched in anticipation. He could so easily take her right now, before she got off, but he forced himself to wait. He wanted her primed, wanted her pussy dripping wet, pulsing from orgasm. Then it would be his turn.

"Does it feel good?" he asked, tunneling his finger in and out of her in a slow, deep rhythm.

"Yes. Oh, yes. Give me more."

"You like having your ass fucked."

Her nails scraped the wall. "Quit. Quit talking. Make me come."

He grinned at her irritation, but continued to tease around her clit, knowing it wasn't going to take much to push her over the edge. "You want me to rub your clit for you baby?"

"Fuck you, Mac. Do it."

"Oooh, you're a little cranky when you're horny, aren't you?"

She grabbed his wrist and planted his hand firmly over her sex, holding it there, setting the pace and exact location she wanted. She turned her head, her eyes glassy and unfocused as she glared at him. "Shove your finger in my ass hard and make me come. Now."

"Yes, ma'am," he said with a wink, though he doubted she

even saw the gesture. He pressed his palm down hard over her clit, and he felt the contractions as she climaxed. She tilted her head back, closed her eyes, and let out a low moan. The muscles of her ass latched onto his finger and squeezed and he knew then just how damn good it was going to be when his dick was inside her. He held still, letting her ride the wave. He withdrew his finger, washed up a bit, then poured more lube over her ass.

He applied the condom, positioned himself behind her, kicked her legs apart a little more, and coated his cock fully with lube. He leaned over her, kissed the back of her neck, and said, "Now I'm going to really fuck your ass."

Her shoulders hunched with her hard breaths. "Do it."

She bent over even farther, presenting her sweet buttocks to him. He held onto his shaft and pushed the soft head through the tight entrance, holding still while she hissed.

"You tell me to stop if it hurts."

"I'm fine," she said, pushing back against him, which allowed him to slide farther inside her. He stilled, letting her body adjust to his thickness, letting her breathe through the burn. When she moved again, so did he, pushing forward inch by inch until he was fully seated inside her. When she was accustomed to him, he began to move, with gentle ease at first; then, when he sensed her need, a little harder.

"More," she said.

He thrust with determination this time, and she groaned, tossing her head back, spraying him with water that flew from the ends of her hair. It was wild, untamed, as she bucked against him, pushing her ass onto his cock. She was like a vise inside. A hot, melting torture chamber, the tightest thing he'd ever felt. He turned the water temperature down because he was dying, inside and out. He closed his eyes and focused on the sensation of being surrounded by all of that heat, of being inside Lily's ass, of being so intimately connected to her in this way. This was such a gift, and he wanted to make it special for her. He wanted her to orgasm again, to feel her squeeze the come right out of his dick.

He watched her movements, heard the sweet sounds she made when she rubbed her pussy. *So hot.* He felt the end result in the tightening around his shaft. She was going to go off, soon. So was he. It was burning him up inside, the storm swirling around his spine and getting ready to explode. Each time he pulled back and shoved inside her, it was more difficult to maintain control.

"Mac," she said, her voice shaky. "Mac, I need to come again."

It was a desperate plea, and one he was all too happy to help her with.

"Yeah, baby. Come for me."

This time, it wasn't a little moan. It was a loud, rip-roaring scream, accompanied by a tight squeezing around his cock as she climaxed. He went at the same time, his orgasm rushing through him with such a powerful force he had to hold onto the shower door as it ripped him from the inside out. He emptied with several hard thrusts, then he pulled out in a hurry, holding onto her as they both panted and gasped. Lily's heart beat so fast, mirroring his own jackhammering beats. It was a wonder he could even stand.

No woman had ever done that to him.

No woman was like Lily.

He washed them both thoroughly, taking his time to stroke her gently as he cleansed her. She smiled up at him.

"Are you okay?"

"Perfect," she said with a knowing smile.

He traced her bottom lip with his thumb. "Yeah. It was."

Too damn perfect.

Things were about to change. God, he really hated his job. Okay, not true. He loved his job.

But not lately.

They dried off and dressed.

"Are you hungry?" Lily asked.

"A little."

"I'm starving. Let's go see what's in the refrigerator to eat."

They decided on hamburgers, so while Lily got out the meat and started peeling potatoes to make homemade fries, Mac went outside to start the grill. Perfect opportunity to make a call and check on Tom. He answered on the first ring.

"How are you two doing?" Tom asked.

"We're fine."

"How about your tail?"

"No sign of anyone lurking. I've scanned the surveillance equipment and nothing's been picked up, so I think we're in the clear. We lost him."

"Great news. When are you planning on hightailing it out of there?"

"First light."

"About the same time I'll be back. If I don't meet up with you before you leave, I'll be back inside the house shortly thereafter, so the virus won't be left alone."

Mac lit the fluid on the charcoal and stepped back as flames poured up from the grill. "Good. I don't like the idea of the virus being left here without anyone watching over it, though your security is pretty damn tight."

"Yeah, you don't need to worry about that. I'll try to get out of these meetings sooner so I can make my way back there before you leave."

"I'd feel better about it if you were back before we flew out of here." He'd held tight to the vial since he'd grabbed it out of the museum. He wanted to make sure it was safely handed off before he left it in someone else's care. He trusted Tom, but he didn't trust that someone wouldn't be after it.

"I'll do my best. Is my baby still tucked in and locked up?"

Mac grinned. "You bet. Are your plans to deliver the virus all set?"

"Yeah. Contact is in place. Don't worry. This will go off without a hitch."

"Good. The sooner I off-load the virus and finish this assignment, the better. I'm ready to go home and get off the road for a while."

eleven

LILY'S HEART BEAT SO HARD SHE COULD ALMOST HEAR IT. SHE fought to swallow, but couldn't. The world crashed down around her and she couldn't think straight. It was like trying to drive through a blinding rainstorm—she couldn't see. She did the only thing she could think to do. She leaned her back against the rock of the basement wall and struggled to breathe, to regroup and put everything in place in her mind. The cool darkness helped. She needed this right now—the isolation, the blackness all around her. It would help her focus.

Mac was still talking on his phone, so she had some time. He couldn't find her like this. Then he'd know she'd heard, and she didn't want him to know.

She'd come downstairs to find some canned goods, and heard voices. The small window at the back of the basement near the door was open. She could even see Mac's boots. He'd been talking to someone, so she thought maybe Tom was back, but she didn't see anyone else. As she rummaged through the basement pantry, she realized it was only Mac's voice she heard, which meant he was on the phone. The more she heard of his one-sided conversation, the more nauseous she became.

It didn't take long before she had it figured out. Tom was his contact for the virus, and Mac was off-loading it here. And he hadn't told her anything about it.

All this time she'd thought they were moving forward, that he was trusting her, telling her things.

One step forward, ten steps back.

Secrets and lies, as usual. The hallmark of their relationship. She wrapped her arms around her middle and fought back the rush of tears.

No. She was *not* going to fall apart, was not going to let emotion rule her. Not in this, and not over Mac.

She had a job to do, and she'd conveniently let her heart get in the way and overrule her common sense. She'd accused him of using sex to distract her. She'd been right, and she'd fallen for it so easily. How stupid he must think she was.

That stopped now. It was time to think clearly and logically about what to do next.

First, she had to push emotion to the background, bury it deep and not let it surface. Letting her heart rule her actions could mean the difference between a successful outcome and a critical error. This time, she intended to win.

That meant logic. Perhaps Mac just hadn't told her yet. It was possible he and Tom had just now settled on this plan while they were talking on the phone, and Mac was going to let her in on the details tonight. She'd allow him that much and give him the benefit of the doubt. Give him time and see if he'd reveal the plan. He told her to trust him, right? So she would. She'd give him the chance to tell her. If he did, great. If he didn't, she'd have to come up with a plan on her own.

Which meant she'd need to tear this place apart and find out

where the virus was, then figure out how to put Mac out of com-
mission so she could sneak it out of there before Tom returned.

She hoped it wouldn't come to that, prayed that Mac would
come clean with her and tell her what was going on.

Sucking in a deep breath, she gathered her composure, grabbed
a can of green beans, and headed upstairs. Mac was standing in the
kitchen.

"Hey, there you are. I was wondering where you'd disappeared
to," he said.

She plastered on an Academy Award–winning smile. "No
canned goods up here so I went downstairs to see if Tom kept any
spares in the pantry there. I was right." She held up the can.

He grinned and kissed her. "Great investigative work."

She skirted around him and started to make patties out of the
hamburger. "Hey, it's my job, you know."

"Yes, I know. Anything you need me to do?"

"Just cook the burgers. I've got everything else covered." She
finished the patties and handed the plate to him.

"You got it."

As soon as the door closed, she exhaled, moving about the
kitchen like a robot. She finished the potatoes and put them in
the oil, then opened the can of beans and put them in a pot. Taking a quick peek outside to make sure Mac was occupied with the
burgers, she made a mad dash around the house, opening drawers and closets, looking for any place where Mac and Tom could
have possibly hid the virus. She didn't make much headway since
she had to keep running into the kitchen to turn the potatoes
and check on Mac, but she did find one thing in Tom's medicine
cabinet—prescription sleeping pills.

Those might come in handy later. She opened the bottle and
slipped two of them into the pocket of her shorts, hoping like
hell she wouldn't have to use them. She'd find out soon enough,

because she intended to give Mac every reason in the world to tell her the truth.

By the time Mac brought in the burgers, she had everything else on the table. Though she wasn't at all hungry, she made an effort to appear relaxed, ate a little of her food, and tried to figure out how to broach the subject at the forefront of her mind.

"I thought I heard you talking to someone outside a little while ago," she said. "I got really worried, wondering if someone had breached security."

Mac swallowed and took a drink of soda. "No, there was no one around. I was talking to Tom on my cell."

At his admission, hope sprang to life. Was he going to tell her about the phone call with Tom? Her stomach tightened. "Oh yeah? Everything okay with him?"

"Yeah. He's fine. He just called to tell me about a bass he caught this morning." Mac laughed. "Big sucker, too. Too bad we won't be around to see it."

"We won't?"

"No. I think we've stayed long enough. I took a look at the perimeter security tapes. No one's been skulking about. I think we did a good job giving them the slip at the rally, so since it looks like we're in the clear, it's time to take off."

"Really." She tried to keep her hand from shaking as she lifted the fork to her lips. "When?"

"I figure we'll head out first thing in the morning. Tom said he'd be back home sometime later tomorrow, but we need to get moving."

"Have to deliver that virus to . . . whoever, right?"

At least he had the decency to look away for a second. Then he made eye contact with her again. "Yeah. I have work to do and I'm on a tight deadline."

"Okay, then. Tomorrow it is." And just like that, her hope crashed. She didn't need to nudge him or ask leading questions.

She already knew he wasn't going to tell her anything about the virus or the fact he was leaving it with Tom. His plan was to keep her unaware, to let her believe he still had it.

They'd be heading out tomorrow, but without the virus. And as soon as he knew they were safe, he was going to dump her.

Fury boiled inside her, an anger the likes of which she'd never felt before.

Ten years ago when he used her and left her, she'd been crushed. Heartbroken and miserable, because she'd loved him. Now the cold realization smacked her across the face—she'd been in love with a man who had never loved her back: a man who was wholly incapable of the emotion. No man who claimed to love her could treat her with such utter disrespect, could touch her and take her to such heights of passion, could promise to be truthful to her, and then in the next instant lie to her with the clear intent of severing all ties with her.

Her days of heartbreak over Mac Canfield were over. It was time for her to do the right thing, to do her job. That focus kept her from crumbling, gave her the direction she needed.

"You're kind of quiet."

She looked at Mac. "Sorry. Just a little tired I think. All that sunshine and . . . activity today." She batted her lashes and smiled; at the same time her stomach knotted with pain.

His lips curved and he reached for her hand. "So does that mean you're too tired for another round tonight?"

Surprisingly, the thought of making love with him again didn't repulse her. Which didn't say much for her character, did it? She hated that he lied to her, but she still wanted him. She would always have a physical response to Mac. Normal, right? Besides, she'd already vowed to do whatever necessary to make sure he trusted her, so when the time came, she could turn the tables on him. It was payback time, and in a big way.

Offering a teasing smile, she said, "I'm never too tired."

After they ate, she did the dishes while Mac cleaned up outside. They settled into the living room and watched some television. Anxiety itched in her veins, making it difficult to sit still, but she maintained the façade so Mac wouldn't become suspicious.

"You're fidgety," he said, adjusting her in his arms.

Damn. "I know. I'm tired, but a little pent up, too."

He ran his fingers through her hair. "I know what will relax you."

She palmed his chest, pushing him away with a laugh. "That's what got me pent up in the first place."

"So sex with me isn't relaxing?" He feigned a hurt expression.

"Please," she said, rolling her eyes. She stood and grabbed his glass. "Refill on your soda?"

"Sure, if you're headed that way." He propped his feet on the coffee table and leaned back to watch TV.

Perfect. She went into the kitchen and poured him a tall glass, then pulled the sleeping pills out of her pocket. One or two? She didn't really know how strong these were, but the directions on Tom's prescription bottle said one to two pills as a sleep aid. Two certainly wouldn't kill him, and Lily wanted to make certain Mac would be out cold so she could make her escape.

As she dropped the pills into his soda and watched them dissolve, she felt a pang of guilt, then quickly pushed it aside. He'd lied to her, and God only knew what his plans were for the virus. She had to intercede and take it away from him before Tom returned tomorrow. This was her last chance. The virus was deadly. In the wrong hands, it could be devastating. She refused to allow that to happen.

She found some chips and dip, fixed a tray, and brought that into the living room along with their drinks, making sure she knew exactly which drink was Mac's. She handed it to him.

"Oooh, snacks," he said, digging into the salty chips. "You think of everything."

Lily smiled at him. Chips would make him thirsty. Exactly what she wanted. She sipped her cola and nibbled on the snacks, pretending to watch television but casting quick glances at him out of the corner of her eye. He was munching, and guzzling down his soda. Now all she had to do was wait.

It didn't take long. He started to blink a few times, then yawn. She snuggled closer to him and yawned, too, then laid her head on his chest, her palm over his heart.

"This feels normal," he said. "You and me, kicked back and watching television. It feels good."

"Yeah, it does." Saying it hurt, because having his arm around her, feeling this comfort, was a lie.

"I'd like to have a life like this someday."

"A life like what?"

"You and me, a place by the lake. Maybe a couple kids."

Lies! She refused to let her heart believe what he was telling her was truth. "Yeah, that would be nice, wouldn't it?" She fought back tears.

"Damn perfect. I could . . . I could stay here . . . jus like this all nigh . . ."

He didn't finish, his last words slurring as if he'd had too much to drink. Lily didn't move, just stayed there in his embrace. When his arm dropped from around her shoulders, she pulled away and sat up.

"Mac?"

No response.

"Mac." She pushed at him, but he didn't budge. "Hey, Mac. Wake up."

She pinched him, waiting for him to flinch, but he didn't. His pulse was normal and steady. So was his breathing. She got up and banged around a little, making as much noise as she could to see if he'd stir.

No way. He was utterly out cold.

This was her chance. With methodical precision, she started her search around Tom's house, looking for the virus. The first place she looked was in the room she shared with Mac, figuring he'd still have possession of it. She looked in his bags, in every drawer and in the closet, but didn't find a thing. Okay, that sort of made sense. He'd probably handed over the vial to Tom already, who had it hidden.

But where?

She went downstairs and searched Tom's bedroom next, tearing off his blankets, flipping the mattress and box spring off his bed and leaving nothing unchecked. She searched underneath and behind his nightstand and his dresser, pulled all the clothes out of every drawer to search for false bottoms, but came up empty.

Next she searched his bathroom, tearing apart his medicine cabinet. She pulled all the mirrored shelves out, pushing on the back of it, but it was secure. Scrunching her nose, she attacked the linen closet. By the time she had it completely torn apart and had moved into several other rooms and found no luck there either, she was starting to feel disheartened, wondering where the hell Tom had the virus hidden.

Basement, maybe? The last time she'd been down there she hadn't really done any investigating, just headed straight for the pantry, then got sidetracked by Mac's phone conversation with Tom.

First she checked on Mac, who still hadn't moved. She nudged him, but got nothing, not even a smidgeon of movement. He was even snoring. *Good.* She hurried downstairs and flipped on all the lights in the basement, then stood in the middle and looked around.

Lots of good hiding places down here. A couple of locked storage cabinets. She'd start there. First she had to break the locks.

She searched every single corner and pile of tools until she found bolt cutters. *Perfect.* Having been a cop meant she knew how to get into things like locks. With a little effort and muscle, she snapped the lock on the first storage cabinet, this one large enough to walk in. There was a hanging light overhead, so she grabbed the string and flicked it on. Boxes of old papers and nothing more, but she opened each box to check the contents just to be sure.

No luck there, so she moved onto the next cabinet, this one small and compact, sitting on a workbench in the corner of the basement. She worked the lock until she snapped it in two, then pried the metal door open.

It was completely empty. *Well, damn.* She'd been so certain she'd found his hiding place.

She searched the rest of the basement, including inside his washer and dryer, leaving nothing unchecked.

It wasn't down here.

Frustrated, she moved back upstairs. Mac was still sleeping, but she couldn't wait forever. She had to find the virus. She stood in the center of the living room, her heart pounding, hands on her hips as she turned in a circle. Where the hell was it?

Her gaze hit the wall where Tom's medals were, and she sent him a ton of mental curses.

Damn both of them.

Then she frowned and moved toward the wall. Could she really be that lucky? She lifted one set of medals off.

Nothing but wall. Okay, maybe she was grasping at straws. But when she moved to the other, it didn't lift off—it pulled open. Underneath was a locked cabinet built inside the wall.

Excitement thrummed inside her. She took a quick glance over her shoulder at Mac, then turned back to the vault. Okay, it needed a key, and she'd just bet Tom had it. Which meant she would have to jimmy the lock.

She ran down to the basement and found Tom's toolbox, rummaging through it until she found what she was looking for—a tiny pick, the barrel slim enough to fit into the lock. She hurried back up, once again taking a quick look at Mac. He hadn't even moved positions.

She slid the pick into the lock, put her ear against it, then started wiggling it, turning it this way and that, listening to the sound of the tumblers. She worked it for about ten minutes, keeping the palm of her other hand wrapped around the handle. Every once in a while she'd turn the handle, hoping she'd managed to undo the lock.

Finally, it clicked. She prayed, and turned the handle.

Bingo! The handle shifted down and she pulled the door open. Inside the vault was the virus.

If she wasn't afraid she'd wake Mac, she'd shout for joy. Her heart accelerated to breakneck speed and she had to take a step back and rest her palms on her knees to catch her breath. Finally, it was hers, and no way in hell was she going to let anyone take it away from her. Using both hands, she cradled it in her palms and lifted it out of the cabinet, heading out of the room. She deposited it on the kitchen table and stood there, staring at it.

Okay, she'd found the virus. Now she had to get out of here. Which meant she needed transportation. Sadly, Mac's bike was out of the question since she didn't know how to ride. *Damn.* She should have asked him for lessons, though she was pretty sure he wouldn't have given them to her.

There was a garage on the side of the house. She stepped outside and headed toward the small wooden building, wondering if her luck would hold out.

The door was locked, but there was a window next to it. Though it was dark inside, she made out the shape of a car. *Yes!* She resisted the urge to whoop out loud with sheer exhilaration. Next step was to get inside the garage and figure out if there were keys.

She hightailed it back inside the house and into Tom's room. She remembered seeing a set of keys in the top drawer of his dresser before she upended everything, so she crouched down on the floor and rummaged through the scattered contents of his drawers until she found the key ring, then clutched it in her hand. She paused, looked at the keys, and rolled her eyes, wondering if any of these keys would have opened the safe in the living room.

Goddamit, she was stressed. She couldn't think of everything, could she?

On her way through the kitchen, she grabbed three thick towels and marched back out to the garage, just in case she had to break into the garage through the window. She hoped one of the keys on the ring would unlock the garage door.

It did. With a satisfied grin, she flipped on the light and moved toward the car. It was unlocked and she slid inside the driver's seat and looked at all the keys on the ring. There was only one Chevy key. She slipped the key into the ignition. It fit. She closed her eyes and held her breath.

When the engine turned over and roared to life, she almost cried. She had a way out. She had the virus, and she had a means to escape. It was almost too good to be true. She beat her hands on the steering wheel, let out a mini squeal of victory, then turned the ignition off and got out of the car, pocketing the keys.

She ran into the house and grabbed her bag, then tossed on a pair of jeans and ran downstairs, checking on Mac one more time.

He was still asleep. She leaned over him and felt his pulse. Still regular.

God, he looked so beautiful when he slept. His lips full, his lashes thick and inky black, a stark contrast against the top of his cheeks. She let her palm linger on his face, felt his warmth, his breath against her hand.

She hesitated, knowing this was the last time she was going to see him.

Why? Why did she feel this regret? Would Mac feel remorse

when he left her at some rest stop or restaurant or hotel? Would he feel this jabbing pain in the pit of his stomach at the thought of never seeing her again?

Get over yourself, Lily. He's not the man you want him to be. He never was, and he never will be. Get the virus and get out.

Still, she couldn't help herself. She pressed a soft kiss to his lips.

"Good-bye, Mac."

He didn't move at all. She sighed and moved out of the room.

She'd gone with Mac into Tom's office to view the surveillance equipment, and knew the front gates were electronically operated. It had to be opened from in there. She went into Tom's office and pressed the button, watching on the monitor as the iron gates slowly opened. Then she went into the kitchen, grabbed the vial, and tucked it into her bag. She closed the back door, hurrying down the stairs and to the garage. The garage door was heavy, but she pulled it open, then started the car, resisting the urge to floor it down the long driveway. As soon as she pulled past the gates, she hit the button on the visor, which closed them behind her.

Only then did she jam the gas pedal hard and peel away in a hurry.

She was free. Finally free, with the virus. But without Mac.

She'd done what she had to do.

So why did she feel like hell?

MAC BLINKED HIS EYES OPEN. GODDAMN, HE WAS TIRED. AND HIS mouth felt like someone stuffed cotton in there.

He heard a car. Was Tom back already? Dizziness hit him when he bolted upright and clutched his head. What the hell was going on? This time he took it slower, easing to a standing position and moving with careful steps to the window. It was dark outside. Where was Lily?

He walked toward the kitchen. Empty, stuff scattered every-where. Dread fell like a boulder in his stomach. He quickened his pace down the hall and into Tom's room, which was a shambles.

Jesus Christ. The house was a mess. Panic cleared his head in an instant.

"Lily?"

He did hear a car. He wasn't dreaming it. He ran to the side window in time to see Tom's car pulling down the driveway, the gate closing behind it.

The grogginess, the disorientation . . .

His gaze shifted to the empty glass on the coffee table, his mind a whirl as he tried to piece together what had happened be-fore he seemingly fell into a coma.

Lily.

She wouldn't . . . would she? And why?

Unless she had somehow found out . . .

Son of a bitch!

His gaze shot to the open vault, confirming his worst fears. The cabinet was torn open, the vial containing the virus gone.

Fuck! He'd completely underestimated her. His mind processed a mile a minute as he paced the center of the room and dragged his fingers through his hair. Okay, he had to think and do it damn fast. He had to get to Lily.

He slid his hands in his pocket and breathed a sigh of relief. His bike keys were still there. The first thing he did was grab an energy drink out of the fridge and guzzle it down, hoping the caffeine jolt would countereffect the drug and help wake him up in a hurry.

After hitting the button to open the gate at the end of the driveway, he ran out the door and jumped on the bike, weaving a little as he started it up. Blinking to clear the persistent fog in his head, he tore down the driveway, stopping only to push the code on the box by the gates to close them.

He had seen Lily turn right and head west. He took off at high speed after her, hoping she hadn't gotten too far, and that she wasn't speeding like he was. If he was lucky, no cops would be meandering down this deserted stretch of road tonight.

The cool night air helped clear his head a little, but he still felt the effects of whatever Lily had drugged him with. Damn, he couldn't believe she'd done that to him. And why now? She must have figured out Tom was the drop point for the virus, but how?

Not that it mattered. If he didn't find her and get the vial back, he was screwed. And Lily could be in serious danger.

He took a curve at a breakneck speed he wouldn't recommend for an inexperienced biker—or one under the influence of God-only-knew what. But he managed. Finally, he caught taillights up ahead. Could that be Lily? *Please let it be her.* The back of the car looked familiar. He pushed the bike harder, and whoever was driving sped up. That meant it had to be Lily and she'd spotted his bike.

Relief washed over him when he realized it was Tom's car. Lily didn't seem to be slowing down, which meant he was going to have to find a way to stop her. He pushed the bike hard, traveling at a dangerous speed. Eventually, he pulled up alongside her, waving at her to get her attention. She took a glance out the window, shook her head, and sped up.

Oh, no, baby. You're not getting away. He revved the bike and passed her, hoping like hell he didn't wreck. Now was where he had to gamble, because if he knew Lily like he thought he did, she wouldn't jeopardize his life to lose him. He flew around curves, grateful to hit a straightaway where he could really punch the speed. Finally, he was far enough ahead of her so she'd have time to stop, then he pulled the bike around in front of her. The road was narrow. He left the bike in her lane, then stood in the other. She had nowhere to pass around him without either hitting his bike or running him over. Mac was betting that he knew Lily, that he could predict what she'd do.

He hoped he wasn't wrong.

In seconds, she was on him, bright lights approaching and drawing dangerously close. Self-preservation kicked in and the urge to get the hell out of the way came with it, but he stood firm.

True to form, she hit the brakes, tires screeching as the car skidded, then fishtailed. She swerved off the road and into the ditch, the front end slamming into a clump of thick brush.

Shit! That's not what he wanted. He pulled his bike to the side of the road, then went running down the ditch. Smoke poured from the engine, but Lily was already climbing out of the car and glaring daggers at him.

"Are you out of your goddamned mind?" she screamed, advancing on him. "You could have been killed."

He grasped her arms, looking her over for injury. "Are you all right?"

She wrenched away from his hold. "I'm fine, you idiot. What were you thinking, Mac?"

He shrugged. "I needed you to stop."

"Screw you." She turned away and started back to the road.

From the way she was moving, twisting and turning as she climbed up the side of the ditch, she seemed to be fine. Despite the darkness, he didn't see any blood on her. He followed after her, lifting the bag off her shoulder as they reached the side of the road. "I was thinking that I needed to get the virus."

She grabbed for her bag. "Give that back!"

He shook his head. "Not a chance. Goddamit, Lily, I trusted you. How could you drug me?"

Her glare was mutinous. "Oh, that's rich, coming from you. *Trust* isn't a word in your vocabulary. *Lies?* Now that's a word you live by, isn't it?"

"I don't want to talk about this here. Let's go back to the house." He reached for her arm, but she pulled away and took two steps back.

"I'm not going anywhere with a thief who would sell a virus to terrorists."

He arched a brow. "You're making a lot of assumptions about me."

She snorted. "I've had to assume a lot since you've refused to tell me anything."

"I already explained that there were things I couldn't tell you right away."

"No. What you mean is that there are things you will *never* tell me, because you don't want me to know what you're up to. Or what you and Tom are up to. God, Mac. How deep are you in this?"

Between the drug still affecting him and being worn out from the chase, Mac was exhausted. He let out a breath of frustration. "It's not what you think, Lily. Now get on the goddamn bike and let's get out of here and back to the house where it's safe."

"I'm not going with you."

"You are." He wasn't going to stand there and argue with her for an hour. He latched onto her wrist and started dragging her toward the bike.

"I will not go with you," she said, her voice low and filled with anger.

He was getting pretty damned pissed off himself, too tired to talk anymore. He picked her up and placed her on the back of his bike, but before he could get on, she was scrambling off.

"What part of *no* don't you get, Mac?"

"What are you going to do, Lily? Walk a deserted road in the middle of the night and hope a nice guy picks you up?"

She crossed her arms. "I can take care of myself. I'll take my chances alone."

"I'm not leaving you here."

"And I'm not going with you."

He dragged his hand through his hair. He was so damn tired. So much, in fact, that when Lily barreled into him and grabbed the bag, she was able to knock him down. *Shit!* Hitting that asphalt hurt. He held onto her as she jumped on top of him and wrestled him for control of her bag.

He couldn't push her off without hurting her, so he rolled her over, trying to do it as gently as possible, which wasn't easy considering she was a pretty tough fighter and he was still fairly drugged up. He got her on her back and effectively pinned, holding down her wrists and sitting on her hips.

"Stop!" he said, but she continued to struggle, kicking up at him.

"Let me go, Mac. You don't need me anymore."

"I can't."

Tears glistened in her eyes. Goddamn, he hated doing this to her, seeing the mistrust and the beginning of hate in her expression.

Fuck this. He lifted off her and pulled her to her feet.

"I'm not a bad guy, Lily."

"You're full of shit. You're dirty. That's why all the secrecy and lies. If there was anything honest in what you were doing, you'd have told me. Now give me my bag."

She launched after him again, but he held her off with the only weapon that would halt her in her tracks—the truth.

"Lily, I work for the goddamn United States government!"

TWELVE

LILY STOPPED MIDWAY IN HER LUNGE FOR THE BAG, UNABLE TO fathom what Mac had just said. Every part of her hung suspended, as if she were dangling in midair.

"What?"

"I work for the government."

"But you stole that virus."

"Yes. That's my job."

She blinked, then frowned. "Your job for the government is as a thief?"

"Yeah. I steal back what's been stolen from them. What can't be recovered through . . . normal channels."

Lily felt dizzy, trying to grasp what he'd said. Could it be true? "I need more. I need explanations."

He nodded. "I'll give them to you, but we need to get back to Tom's now, while I'm still awake and can manage to maneuver the bike."

"Right, yeah." Then his words sank in. She really looked at him now, the drooping eyelids, the way he was weaving. Of course he'd still have the sleeping pills in his system. God, the way he was riding that bike—she shuddered just thinking what could have happened to him out here.

She stepped up to him and he moved back. "Oh. Mac, I'm sorry. Let's get out of here before you pass out."

He'd ridden that bike like a madman, and while under the influence of sleeping pills. Pills she'd slipped into his soda. Obviously, he'd wanted the virus back in a big way—enough to jeopardize his life to get it.

"Drive slow," she said as she climbed on the back. "I'll shout incessantly in your ear to keep you awake."

At least she got a half grin out of him with that comment.

He started the bike, and as she requested, drove deliberate and easy. From the looks of him, he was going down and fast. She had to keep him awake on the ride back to Tom's, because she couldn't ride the bike without him. So she chattered in his ear the entire way. She knew he could hear her, because he nodded, though he probably couldn't discern exactly what she was saying.

She kept touching him, running her hands over his back and thighs, feeling his muscles tighten under her hands. Even near unconsciousness, he still responded to her touch. She thought about leaning as far forward as possible so she could rub his cock, but didn't want to tempt fate and a possible bike wreck.

Anyway, it worked. Her conversation and touch kept his blood churning and maintained his state of alertness long enough to crawl the bike back through Tom's security gates and down the driveway. By the time he shut off the engine and climbed off the bike, he was done for, staggering as he started toward the house. Lily put his arm around her shoulders so he'd lean into her a little as they climbed up the back stairs and into the house.

"This place is a wreck," he said.

He was starting to slur his words. She had to get him into bed.

"Uh-huh. Let's get you upstairs."

He made it to the bedroom, though not without a lot of wobbling. He fell across the bed, taking Lily with him, his body half covering hers. She wriggled out from under him, intending to let him finally pass out, but he grabbed her hand and held tight to her fingers.

"Don't leave," he said.

She didn't say anything.

"What I . . . told you. It's the truth. Trust your instincts."

She didn't know how to respond.

"Stay. Please." His hand dropped to the bed and his eyes drifted shut. He was out.

She walked from the room, too keyed up to even think about sleeping. She spent the next several hours righting the mess she'd made out of Tom's house, putting drawers back and clothes back in them, sweeping and tidying. By the time she was in a full sweat, she had the place looking normal again. After she showered and threw on one of Mac's T-shirts, she sat on the edge of the bed and looked at him.

Now what? She had so many questions.

When hadn't she had questions? But this time, he'd given her a bone, and dammit, she wanted answers.

Since he'd passed out belly down, she caught sight of his phone sticking out of his back pocket. She slid it out and held it in her hand. It would be so easy to call her boss or her client, to grab the vial and Mac's phone and get out of there. She could even call the police or the FBI if she wanted to, could turn over the virus to the government, so at least it would be safe.

Could she even be certain what he said what true? Did he really work for the government, or had that been just another in the string of lies he'd told her?

Mac had asked her to trust her instincts. Wasn't that what she'd *been* doing all this time, why she'd agreed to stay with him? Because of her inherent belief that he couldn't possibly be doing something that could potentially harm millions of innocents?

Instinct was screaming at her to trust him, to wait this out until he woke up so she could finally hear the truth.

She needed to hear the truth about this government thing.

She bent down and pulled off his boots, then pushed at Mac to roll him over. He groaned, but cooperated, flipping onto his back.

"Let's get you undressed," she said, not sure if he even heard her. She worked on his jeans, undoing them and struggling to drag them off his legs. The rest was easier. When she had him naked, he climbed onto the pillow without a word or waking.

With a sigh, Lily pulled off the T-shirt and climbed into bed, shut off the bedside lamp, and scooted next to Mac. He wrapped an arm around her and pulled her against him.

The answers she sought could wait until morning. She snuggled closer to Mac and closed her eyes.

MAC DIDN'T WANT TO WAKE UP. LILY'S WARM BODY WAS NESTLED against him. The sun wasn't shining through the windows yet, which meant it was early—too damn early to be awake.

Yet he was awake. His mouth felt like cotton, and his head hurt. Goddamn, what truck ran over him last night? He lay there trying to find his brain cells, because he couldn't remember a thing. Maybe he'd just go back to sleep for a while longer. He inched closer to Lily, burying his nose in her hair and inhaling her sweet scent. He could so easily drift off again. God, he felt drugged.

He blinked his eyes open. *Drugged.* Recall inched its way through the fog. *Oh, yeah.* Last night, Lily drugged his soda and ran off with the virus, and he chased her on the bike. It was all there, on the fringes and a little fuzzy, but he remembered now.

He must have been insane to chase her on his bike while he

was as drugged up as he'd been. Then again, he hadn't really had much choice, had he? He'd needed to get the virus back.

He'd needed to get Lily back.

The important thing was, she was still there with him. She'd stayed. He did remember asking her to trust him, to give him a chance to explain it all. How many times had he asked that of her? It was so unfair. He'd been unfair to her this entire time. He should have come clean right away, instead of waiting so long to tell her.

He would have to tell her the whole story today. The secret was out now.

But not yet. Not when it was still warm in bed, and even warmer pressed up against her sleeping body. They were spooned together, her butt nestled in his crotch. His hand rested between her breasts. He smiled at the thought of waking up this way, with his nose buried in her neck, knowing the first thing he was going to smell in the morning was Lily's sweet skin. Just breathing her in turned him on. Waking up with her ass against his cock was better than any alarm clock, making him rise to life in an instant. The blood rushed south and his shaft finally started paying attention to where it was—nestled between the legs of a very hot woman.

He leaned up on one elbow so he could see over her shoulder, then dragged the sheet down to her waist, uncovering her breasts. Like the rest of her, they were perfection—round, with pink nipples that perked up when he moved his palm over them. He cupped one, teasing the pink crest with his thumb by drawing slow, lazy circles around it until it puckered.

Lily moaned and arched, but her eyes stayed closed. He continued to toy with her nipple, captivated by the way it hardened as he rolled it between his fingers. Even better was her response, the way she wriggled her ass against his cock.

Oh, she was awake, of that there was no doubt, because she was moving against him now, but not in any kind of frenzy. It was more of a slow awakening, and he enjoyed these little sounds she made. Moans and sighs that signaled she was still waking up and enjoying his touch.

He slipped his cock between her legs. She was wet, her slick folds hot and welcoming as he surged between them. Though eager to be inside her, he liked this lazy morning lovemaking and didn't want to get too wild and crazy. Not yet, anyway.

Just having this intimate contact with Lily was enough. He positioned his cock at the entrance to her pussy and entered her with care, not penetrating with a hard thrust. Instead, he eased inside her inch by inch, feeling her melt around him in greeting as she pulled him inside.

Sex with Lily was usually so wild. Making love to her this way, being able to listen to every sound she made, every breath she took as he thrust with slow precision, was a nice change. He felt everything, from the way she pulsed around him, to the way their bodies seemed to fit perfectly together—from his chest against her back to her thighs tucked against his.

He should have known it wouldn't last. Not when the passion they shared kicked up a notch. He tried to hold back, to take things light and gentle. But Lily pushed her ass against him, widening her legs to give him better access and gripping the sheets for leverage so she could push off, move forward, then grind back against his cock. Her light breathing and delicate whimpers had turned into deeper, needier moans. She wanted more.

So much for slow and easy. If she wanted to pick up the pace, he'd be more than happy to oblige her.

"On your stomach," he said, pulling out and tossing a pillow in the center of the bed.

She rolled over, situating her lower belly on the pillow, which lifted her ass high in the air.

"Mmmm," was her only reply.

Palms braced on either side of her shoulders, he dropped down on top of her, sliding his body against hers to feel that skin to skin contact. She moaned, lifting her ass against him. He positioned his cock at the entrance to her pussy and drove inside. Her tight walls grabbed onto him and sucked him in, squeezing and quivering around him.

Oh, yeah. But he wanted deeper penetration.

"Come on, baby. Up on your hands and knees." He swept his arm underneath and helped to lift her. She flattened her palms onto the mattress and spread her legs, bending down and lifting her ass in the air. She cast him a sexy look over her shoulder as he slid inside her pussy.

He started slow, but Lily wanted more, backing up against him, fucking his cock with deep, forceful thrusts.

His woman was awake, and she was hungry. He gripped her hips and plunged hard. She tilted her head back and let out a groan of pure delight, her fingers grasping the covers in a tight hold. She arched her back and held on while he gave her exactly what she'd asked for.

Juices poured over his cock as she grew wetter with every thrust. He bent over so he could reach her clit—she was so wet, so hot, and he could barely hang on as her walls tightened around him.

He surged forward, rubbing her clit as he did. "Come on, baby," he whispered against her ear. "Let go."

She groaned, pushing back against him with wild abandon, shaking her head from side to side. "Mac."

"Yeah, I'm right there with you. Now let go for me."

He felt it before she cried out—that sweet spasm that let him know she was coming. He went at the same time, jettisoning come inside her, planting his hips against her ass while she shuddered against him in ecstasy. She was shaking as she came, her whole body one giant vibration from the inside out, rocketing him, too.

Panting, he held onto her middle, pulling her upright so her back pressed against his chest. They were both wet with perspiration from their efforts, Lily's heart beating wild and fast against the palm of his hand.

He pressed a soft kiss against her neck. "Good morning."

"Good morning," she said back. "I need a shower."

"Me, too."

They showered together, and Lily got out first. She dried off and dressed, then said she was going downstairs to start breakfast. While he dried himself, she said, "After breakfast, I want some answers."

He nodded, realizing he was going to have to give them to her.

Grange was going to have his hide. He was going to be in deep shit for telling Lily the truth, but at the time he'd had no choice. Maybe he could blame the drugs.

Screw it, he thought as he climbed into his jeans and pulled a T-shirt over his head. He trusted Lily.

He went downstairs. She already had breakfast going, so he grabbed a cup of coffee for fortitude.

"Need any help?"

She shook her head. "I've got it covered. You can pour us some juice."

By the time breakfast was on the table, he had a pretty good idea what he was going to tell her—everything. He owed it to her after jerking her chain this entire time. And she'd stayed with him last night instead of running off again. She'd had access to his phone and she could have called in the cops, or her boss, or anyone she'd wanted to. Instead, he woke up this morning to find her snuggled up asleep next to him.

She'd trusted him enough to stay, and that meant he owed her the truth about the whole deal. But first he wanted to get this meal down. He was starving.

Lily didn't press Mac for the details, opting to stay quiet and eat her breakfast, and let him do the same. She felt guilty enough over the whole drugging thing last night, and wanted to make sure he had some caffeine and food in his system to clear the last of the sleeping pills out.

Inside she was hopping up and down and dying to know if Mac was really going to tell her the truth, so his first words came as a shock to her.

"I got into some serious trouble while you were away at college."

She gave one nod of encouragement and let him talk.

"I was twenty-one, working dead-end jobs and stealing on the side. I was damn good at it, too. But not good enough. Got mixed up with the wrong people, and ended up involved in this grand theft auto ring. I didn't really know what I was getting myself into, and once in, had no idea how to get out. I got caught. Cops hauled me in and I was looking at some serious jail time. With no family and no money to back me up, I was screwed and going down fast. My life was over."

Lily's heart broke for him. Mac never could catch a break.

"But it was my own damn fault. I could have straightened up, and I didn't. I chose the wrong path and had no one to blame but myself for screwing up. So I stood up and took it like a man, told the public defender I wanted to plead guilty and accept the consequences of my actions. He told me I was insane."

Lily was about to say the same thing.

"Then a miracle happened. A guy by the name of Grange Lee walked into my life and changed it forever. A tough ex-military general, he made me an offer that seemed too good to be true."

"What kind of offer?" she asked.

"General Lee was putting together a crack team of specialists, sworn to secrecy and bound to work for the United States government, a department within the Department of Justice. In exchange for wiping out all the charges against me, I could work for him."

"Doing what?"

"The United States government is stolen from all the time. Things that they can't recover. Things that the government tries to retrieve by conventional means, but for some reason can't get back because either the court system is flawed or the bad guys have really good lawyers. Some things they just can't confiscate the legal way."

Lily snorted. "As both a cop and a PI, I've seen that happen all too often. And it's frustrating as hell."

He nodded. "Tell me about it. Anyway, Grange laid it all out for me. Told me what I'd be doing . . . what we'd all be doing. No one outside a single branch of the government even knows we exist. It was risky and it was dangerous and if we were caught at it, the government, and he, would deny our existence."

"In other words, you had to be really good at what you did, because if you got caught in these thefts, you would go to jail and they wouldn't be able to bail you out this time," she said.

"Right. But hell, it was worth the risk. I wanted a chance to turn my life around, to do something right for a change instead of fucking up like I had been."

"So you said yes."

He smiled. "I said hell yes. Grange made the arrangements, the charges disappeared, and I left with him."

"Sounds so simple."

"It wasn't. He worked me . . . all of us. He's one tough son of a bitch. He knew he had a half dozen lazy, young, good-for-nothing criminals on his hands. So he had to show us the way. It was like boot camp. We got up at dawn, did physical conditioning, had rules and regulations. There was no partying, no drinking, no smoking, no women—"

"Shocking. How did you survive?" she asked tongue in cheek.

"Nearly died the first month," he teased back. "It was awful. You never heard a bunch of grown men whine like babies more than we did. But little by little he turned us into the men we were supposed to be—the men he knew we could be. He broke us down, then he built us up again. He taught us that we weren't worthless, that we did have something of value to offer. He made us stronger, mentally and physically. There wasn't one among us who wasn't whip smart to begin with, so he made us take classes. The ones who didn't have their high school diplomas got them in a hurry or else. Some of these guys should have gone on to college." He ran his fingers through his hair. "I wish you could meet them, Lily. I've never had brothers, until I joined Wild Riders. I've never been closer to a group of guys before."

"Wild Riders?"

He cocked his head to the side and cast her a half smile that she'd always found boyish and charming. It reminded her of the old Mac, the one who could make her toes curl. "That's the name of the organization. We're into cars and bikes. We all ride together."

"So you're all bikers?"

"Yeah. Grange made sure to choose guys who were familiar with bikes and cars and were comfortable riding them."

"And stealing them?"

Mac let out a laugh. "Yeah, you could say that we all had that kind of history in our backgrounds."

"So do you all ride bikes? Certain kinds? Harleys, crotch rockets, or what?"

"One bike is pretty much the same as another, Lily. We can ride anything. But mostly we're all Harley riders. Each guy has his own preference as to the type of Harley he runs with. And muscle cars, too. Just like the ones I used to work on when we first met. We're all around the same age, too."

"Are all you from Dallas?"

He shook his head. "No. Wild Riders headquarters is in Dallas. Convenient for me since that's where I grew up. But the other guys are from all over."

"So you live at this headquarters?"

"A few of the guys hang out there a lot because they don't have permanent places and travel a lot. Some have apartments in other cities. Grange and I do live at Wild Riders headquarters, though. Easy for me to stay there instead of paying rent at another place. We all meet there when we have an assignment or when Grange wants to run through some kind of operation, like doing tech stuff or working on the bikes and cars."

"All the bikes and cars are stored there?"

"The ones we use for ops, yeah."

"I see. I guess you have a lot to tell me, don't you?"

"About Wild Riders?"

She shook her head. "No, about how you became one."

He nodded. "Okay."

Mac's eyes lit up as he told the story of his transformation. She felt the pride emanating from him. "You're an amazing man, Mac."

He shook his head. "Nah. Grange is the one who did it all. I just went along for the ride. He took a bunch of worthless losers and made us into something."

She reached for his hand. "You were never worthless or a loser. I never thought so anyway."

He put his other hand over hers. "Then you're about the only one who didn't think it. Most everyone else did."

"I always believed in you, Mac. I still do. That's why I'm still here."

"And waiting for answers on the virus."

She nodded.

He dragged his hand through his hair. "We were hired to retrieve an artifact from a traveling exhibit, already knowing it contained the vial with the virus inside. The virus was stolen from a government lab—an inside job, it was assumed, though they don't know who did it. A major fuckup and one that our government,

obviously, didn't want anyone to know about. Their own opera-
tives have been involved and searching worldwide for it. Word was
that it could have been located in multiple places. We had a lead
that it was sold to a private party and was making its way across the
country. Since they couldn't bring in the FBI or any government
resources without calling attention to what was going on, our job
was to search the museum artifact."

"So you weren't certain the virus was even inside the artifact?"

"No. It was just one of about a dozen leads. We got lucky."

"Lucky, huh?"

"Yeah. Of course, getting shot at wasn't in the plan. We didn't
count on anyone else being there to intercept, but there was always going to be the possibility that someone else would be after
the virus, too."

"Any idea who?"

"No clue. I was supposed to retrieve the artifact, and if the vial
was there, run it down here to Tom, who would turn it over to his
government contact. Which is still the plan."

The plan she'd almost ruined by running off with the virus. No
wonder Mac risked his life coming after her on the bike. "I didn't
know."

"Of course you didn't. I should have been honest with you earlier. But we swear an oath, Lily, never to reveal information about
the Wild Riders. Anyone who tells an outsider about it is out."

In other words, Mac's career was in serious danger because
he'd told her. "I understand. And I won't tell a soul, Mac. You
can trust me."

"I know that, too. And I'm sorry you got caught in the cross
fire and in all this. I didn't intend for this to happen, but when the
artifact broke and you saw the virus, I had to make a snap decision.
I couldn't let you go knowing what you did, and I couldn't tell
you the truth. Not then, anyway."

She nodded. "I understand. So now what?"

"Now we—"

He started to say something, but his cell phone went off and he grabbed it out of his pocket. Lily knew something was wrong right away when Mac frowned.

"What happened?" he asked. "How bad is it?"

Lily froze, knowing whatever was going on wasn't good.

"Get yourself to a safe place in a hurry. We're out of here." He closed the phone and looked at Lily.

"What?" she asked.

"Tom was ambushed on his way back here."

"Is he all right?"

"He's been shot."

"Oh, God."

"Our cover is blown. Tom's certain whoever hit him is heading this way. We've got to take the virus and get the hell out, now."

Lily was on her feet and upstairs in a hurry, jamming things in their bags. They were out the door and on the bike in five minutes, roaring through the gates and heading south.

She didn't even know where they were going, but this time she trusted Mac completely. The important thing was to get the virus away from whoever had shot Tom, whoever was after it.

Mac would keep it, and them, safe.

THIRTeen

THEY RODE HARD AND FOR A GREAT DISTANCE, ZIPPING THROUGH towns so fast Lily's head began to spin. Mac only stopped long enough for them to gas up the bike, use the bathroom, and grab a bite to eat and a drink, then they climbed back on and rode again. He made a quick phone call right after they left Tom's place when he'd stopped for gas, but other than that he didn't volunteer where they were going, and she didn't ask. She figured Mac knew what he was doing, and that was good enough. Besides, he seemed preoccupied—worried, even. About Tom, no doubt, and she couldn't blame him. Tom was a really nice guy. Lily was worried about him, too, wondering how badly he was hurt.

Adding to Mac's burden with a bunch of questions wasn't going to help, so she stayed silent. When he had something to tell her, he would, but she assumed that wouldn't be until they made their final stop.

She knew he was taking them someplace he thought was safe. They rode straight through Oklahoma and crossed the state line into Texas. Mac stayed as much as possible on the less traveled roads, even though they'd been followed before. He said he still didn't want to take the interstates, that they'd be safer on the back roads.

By the time they hit Dallas, it was nightfall. Lily was sore and exhausted, and utterly shocked to find herself back in the city where she grew up. Would they stop here, or keep going?

She got her answer a short time later. Mac took them to a secluded area where the houses were more spread out. He pulled into a ranch with a wired fence and a gate much like what Tom had. The house was set way back from the property line, but it was well lit, and even though it was dark it loomed before them like an imposing mansion.

Damn. Who lived here?

Mac pulled to the gate and waited while the security cameras scanned them. The gate opened slowly and he eased up the asphalt drive toward the house.

It was huge! Who did it belong to—another friend of Mac's? Another contact, maybe?

Mac wound around behind the house, where there was a long row of garages. One was already open and he pulled the bike inside. Lily climbed off, stunned to find several Harleys parked there, along with quite an awesome display of muscle cars.

"Where are we?" she asked.

"Wild Riders' headquarters."

"Oh." Her stomach knotted up in an instant. "What's your general going to think when he sees me?"

"No clue. We'll find out in a minute. But don't worry about it; I'll explain everything to him." He unpacked their things and slung the bag over his shoulder, then took her hand, which offered her a great deal of comfort. He led the way out of the garage and toward the back of the house.

Lily's throat had gone dry, but her palms were wet. She had no idea what to expect, but she figured General Grange Lee was not going to be happy to see her, considering Wild Riders was supposed to be a secret organization. And just how much of a secret did the government intend to keep this? How much of a liability was she? Was Mac's job in jeopardy? She hoped not.

The back door was an elevator, actually. Mac pushed a series of buttons on the keypad, and the doors opened. They stepped inside, and Mac entered more codes. The door closed and he pushed a button. Finally, the elevator started moving up.

"Damn. That's some security."

"We can't let just anyone in here."

"They saw you at the gate. They know you're coming."

"Never hurts to take extra precautions."

Okay, then. Now she was really confused about what she'd find when the doors opened. Some high-tech military operation? Guns drawn and pointed at her? She licked her desert-dry lips and prepared for the worst.

The elevator lurched to a stop and the doors drew open. Hard rock music filled the room. Loud music, blasting throughout the house. And leaning against the wall was a muscle-bound warrior.

Oh, my. Beefcake didn't even begin to describe him. Six foot four at least, with sandy brown hair, a T-shirt stretched tight over an impossibly muscled chest that led down to a lean waist, trim hips, and steely legs encased in camos. He was tan, with surfer boy blue eyes and a full, sensual mouth that seemed incongruous with the rest of his physique.

Lily was mad for Mac, but Jesus, this guy was gorgeous.

"You're in deep shit, Mac," the guy said with a smirk, in a voice that melted her panties on the spot. Deep and oh so dark.

"Suck my dick, Spencer."

Lily's gaze shot to Mac's, but he was grinning. When she looked back at Spencer, he was, too. Okay, so that must be *hello* in guyspeak. Mac stepped off the elevator, still holding onto Lily's hand.

"This is Lily."

Spencer raised a brow as he looked her over from head to toe. "Grange know about her?"

Nice to meet you, too, Spencer.

"No."

Spencer let out a hard laugh. "Oh, man, you *are* in deep shit."

She felt invisible. And irritated. "I am present, you know." She stuck out her hand. "Shall we try this again? Hi, Spencer, I'm Lily. Nice to meet you."

Spencer nodded as he looked from Mac back to Lily, then shook her hand. "Your lady has some balls. I like that. Nice to meet you, too, Lily."

"Spence is rude, crude, and completely without manners. We've tried our best to work with him, but he's hopeless."

Lily turned at the deep voice beside her. An older man in military uniform held out his hand. "I'm Grange Lee, Lily. Welcome to Wild Riders."

She shook his hand, feeling a lot less intimated by General Lee than she had been by Spencer. "Thank you."

"Spencer, go do something that doesn't require your presence in this immediate vicinity," Grange said.

"Yeah, yeah." Spencer turned and walked away, giving Lily a glimpse of one fine, tight ass. She blinked and turned back to Mac.

"Don't worry. He's the worst of the bunch," Mac said.

"There's more of them?"

He grinned. "A few."

"Any word on Tom?" Mac asked.

Grange looked at Lily.

"I already told her everything, and she was there when the call came in. You can talk in front of her."

"That's not the deal here and you know it."

Mac shrugged. "It couldn't be helped."

"It was my fault, I'm afraid," Lily said, feeling like she needed to intercede on Mac's behalf. "I did something really stupid and ran off with the virus. The only way Mac could stop me was to tell me everything. God knows he'd done everything he could to keep it from me, but I'm pushy as hell and refused to give up until I knew the truth."

"It didn't go down like that at all," Mac said.

"It most certainly did." Lily couldn't believe Mac was going to lie to Grange in order to protect her.

Grange frowned and crossed his arms. "Guess we'll sort this all out later."

"About Tom?" Mac asked.

"Nothing yet. Could be he's lying low and staying out of cell contact because he's been compromised."

"Let's hope that's all it is."

They started walking, and Lily followed them. The floor they were on was laid out like a normal house. Kitchen, living room, though every room was enormous in size. How many people lived in this place? Modern conveniences, big-screen television, and state-of-the-art stereo system—every gadget known to man in the space-age kitchen, too. Lily was in awe. The floors were wood throughout the house. Everything was open and expansive, with a loft and railings overhead leading to a second floor. There was also a second elevator that led upstairs. She heard noise and voices up there—and music, but so far she'd only met Spencer.

"Let's talk in my office where it's a little more quiet," Grange said, leading them down the hall and into another room.

This wasn't an office. It was a situation room, filled with maps and charts. Multiple televisions and computers lined the walls on either side of a desk, with long rows of chairs set up classroom style. Mac slid into a chair at the front of the room. Grange turned a chair around to face him and Lily sat in one next to Mac.

"Okay, now tell me what really happened," Grange said.

Mac filled Grange in on everything he knew so far, from how they met at the museum to all that had happened on their journey, up to and including Lily drugging him and Mac chasing after her last night. Damn, talk about coming clean. Lily blushed hot as she felt Grange's gaze on her while Mac recounted that part of the story. But she supposed it was vital that Grange know their entire history. At least Mac left the intimate details of their relationship out.

Mac pulled the vial out of his bag, handing it over to Grange. He took it out of the room and returned a few minutes later, then paused again when a call came in, indicating it was about Tom. Lily grasped Mac's hand while Grange chatted on the phone. Grange cast his gaze at their hands and shot a sideways look at Mac. Lily felt self-conscious about the intimacy of their hand holding, but Mac didn't seem inclined to let go of her.

She liked that.

"Okay," Grange said when he hung up the phone. "Tom's fine."

Lily exhaled. "That's great. What about the gunshot?"

"Superficial wound to his hand. He hightailed it to a safe zone where we have people who patched him right up."

"So he's secure," Mac said.

Grange nodded.

"What's a safe zone?" she asked.

"We have spots set up around the country. Places our contacts can go where they're secure, where they can get help if necessary. He's safe there."

"Okay. That's good."

"Any idea who hit him?" Mac asked.

Grange shook his head. "No. He was on the way back from a meeting when a black SUV pulled up beside his car and started firing at him. Tried to run his car off the road."

"I thought he took his boat?" Lily asked.

"He took the boat into town," Mac said. "A rental was waiting for him there. He had government meetings."

"Oh." So much she didn't know about this government stuff.

"They probably thought he had the virus," Mac continued "Which means they fingered us at Tom's location and figured him for a contact point."

"Maybe," Grange said, then looked at Lily. "Or they were contacted by someone who alerted them."

"No, man, you've got it wrong," Mac said.

Lily shook her head. "I didn't contact anyone. I've been with Mac since the museum."

Grange didn't look convinced. "She drugged you, she took the virus, and she had access to your cell phone while you were out cold."

"I also came back with him." Irritation pricked her nerve endings. She didn't like being accused. She was here, wasn't she? "I was with him last night and this morning."

"You could be gathering information about Wild Riders."

She rolled her eyes. "Oh for the love of God. Check Mac's cell phone. The only calls in or out are his. Easy enough to verify."

Mac tossed his phone at Grange.

"Did you check it?" Grange asked.

Mac shook his head. "I didn't need to. I trust Lily."

Warmth spread through her. He hadn't even checked. God, she loved his trust in her.

"Sorry, but I don't," Grange said. He stood and left the room with Mac's phone in hand.

"Don't take it personally," Mac said. "He doesn't know you and has to be certain you can be trusted."

"I understand." She looked down at her hands.

Mac reached for one, swirling his thumb over the center of her palm. The sensation shot between her legs. Even with the tension, their lack of privacy, he could still turn her on. She was amazed by her connection to him. "Thank you for believing in me. And I didn't use your phone."

His lips quirked. "I know you didn't."

His firm belief in her made her feel guilty that she hadn't trusted him all this time. She was almost ashamed for not believing in him when he'd asked her to at the beginning of all this. Then again, there had been mistrust on both sides, hadn't there? Ten years had separated them, had changed them both in so many ways. She still couldn't reconcile the Mac she'd known all those years ago with the man who sat next to her now. A government agent. She'd never have thought it.

"Phone's clean," Grange said as he came back in. "All the calls in and out were verified." He handed the phone back to Mac.

"I told you they would be," Mac said.

"I had to be sure," Grange said to Lily.

She nodded, not certain what she should say in reply. He didn't know her at all, so of course he didn't trust her. And Mac had violated his oath of secrecy about the Wild Riders and told Lily all about them. Well, mostly all about them. She really didn't know everything.

"Take her around. Introduce her to the guys. Then rest up," Grange said. "I need a few hours to get some information. We'll reconvene tonight and hopefully have something more to go on after I've had a chance to make some calls."

Mac arched a brow, then nodded. He stood. "Let's go," he said to Lily.

"Down this way are more offices," he said as they exited Grange's office. Mac pointed to the right where there were two closed doors. "Mainly tech stuff and storage."

She felt eyes on her—lots of eyes. When she looked above, she realized why. Several amazing-looking men were peering down over the railing at her.

"Dayum," she heard one of them say.

"Ignore them. You'll meet the other guys in a minute," Mac said, leading her toward the kitchen. "How about something to drink?"

Was he avoiding taking her upstairs to meet the others? That was . . . interesting. "I'm not thirsty."

"Well, I am."

He went into the kitchen and opened the refrigerator, grabbed a soda, and popped it open, offering it to her first. She shrugged and took a drink, then handed it back to him. He leaned against the counter and took a long swallow.

Lily guessed Mac was in no hurry to make introductions. "So tell me about this house."

"Grange was given this mansion and the assignment to start up Wild Riders after he came up with the idea to steal back vital government property that couldn't be retrieved under . . . more conventional and legitimate means."

"Ah. So this whole thing was General Lee's idea."

Mac grinned. "Yup."

She pulled out a chair from the kitchen table and took a seat. "How did he come up with it?"

"Frustration, mainly. He was involved with JAG, and if you think the conventional judicial system is screwed up, the military justice system is even worse."

Lily frowned. "What do you mean?"

"Everything's by the book, babe. Especially governmental procedures. When we're being screwed by foreign countries or even crime on our own soil, and we know damn well who did it and who has the goods, if the system isn't working in our favor there's nothing anyone can do about it."

She nodded. "I've seen that happen all too often."

"And with theft, Grange had a genius idea. We might not be able to see the bad guys brought to justice, but we could sure as hell take back what was stolen from us—and there wouldn't be a damn thing they could do about it."

She grinned. "Because they stole it in the first place, so it's not like they could report a theft."

"Exactly."

"You're right. It is genius."

"And the perfect career for a thief."

She laughed. "You get to do what you love most and you don't get in trouble for it."

"Not as long as we don't get caught." He polished off his soda and took her hand. "Let's go meet the other pros."

She was looking forward to it. If they were anything like Mac, this should be interesting.

He led her back to the elevators. "You've seen the main living area on this floor." He pushed the buttons. The rode to the next level and exited. "It's going to get a little crazy. Prepare yourself, and really, you've gotta ignore anything they say."

"You make it sound like we're entering a zoo."

Mac snorted.

In a matter of seconds she understood why. She was swarmed as soon as they stepped out the door. Five men poured out of the open rooms upstairs and descended on her. It was like an invasion of big, beefy testosterone.

And she thought Mac was sexy. She recognized Spence, who she'd met earlier. He was the biggest of the bunch—then again, none of these guys were small.

"Since when does Grange allow us to bring women here?" one of them asked.

"Yeah. I didn't get the memo," another said, tilting his head to the side and giving Lily the once-over.

They drew closer, giving her a head to toe inspection.

"Would you guys back up?" Mac rolled his eyes. "Jesus. It's not like you've never seen a woman before."

"We've never seen *your* woman," one of them said. "What's up with that?"

"Yeah. Introduce us."

Lily crossed her arms, not feeling the least bit threatened. She knew what this was about. They were testing her, seeing if she was skittish or afraid, if she'd run or hide behind Mac. Mac was giving her enough space to take care of herself. She appreciated that he was watching out for her, but not immediately coming to her aid.

She was no sissy. She'd weathered a lot worse her first year on the police force. Though lots of women became cops, in many precincts it was still a good ole boy network. Especially in Dallas, where she'd started.

"You can look all you want, guys," she said, making eye contact as they walked around her. "But if you touch, you'll be sorry."

"She's got a bark," one said behind her.

"But does she bite?" This from a guy in front of her.

"I might," she said, quirking her lips.

"I've got something you can bite, baby."

Someone whispered in her ear. She didn't know which one, and honestly, it didn't matter.

"I'm sorry, but I save everything oral for Mac."

That set them off and they all started laughing.

"Yeah, she'll do, Mac."

He slung his arm around her. "Guys, this is Lily, and if you didn't know it by now, let me make it real clear. She's mine."

Oh, she liked the sound of that.

"Lily, these are the guys. Biggest bunch of smart-asses you'll ever meet, but also my best friends. My brothers."

She sobered as she heard the sincerity in his tone, and shook hands with each of them—AJ, who was just as tall but not quite as broad as Spencer. His hair was darker, with eyes that looked like the sky before a summer storm. Paxton, lean, spiked dirty blond hair, and chiseled features that belonged on the cover of a magazine. Rick, quiet, with bedroom eyes that were dark to match his tan, unruly, thick black hair, and the kind of body a woman could run her hands over for hours and simply get lost in. Finally, Diaz, with dark good looks, perfect white teeth, and lips made to do sinful things to a woman's body. His smile was devastating.

All of this male beauty surrounding her, and she could think of only the man whose arm hung over her shoulder, whose finger toyed with her hair, whose body pressed close to hers.

Still, that didn't mean she couldn't tease him.

"So, is there a community sleeping area?" she asked.

"Oh, no you don't," Mac said, grabbing her hand. "I'll show you where you and I will sleep."

He dragged her down the hall in a hurry. She waved to the guys over her shoulder while they all laughed and walked away, heading into their own rooms. Mac's room was at the end of the hall. He opened the door and let Lily walk in, then closed it behind him.

Nice-sized room, double bed. Nothing fancy, but it was well kept. As far as decor, there wasn't any. Bed, dresser, a desk, and a closet. That was about it.

"There are bathrooms in each room," he said, pointing to the partially open door at the corner of his room. Plenty of bedrooms, too. "The guys stay on this side of the corridor, girls on the other side."

"Girls?" she asked, arching a brow.

"Jessie, mainly, since she hangs out here sometimes. Trust me, nobody brings girlfriends or dates or any women here. Grange would blow a gasket."

"You brought me."

"You're special," he said, his gaze dark with intent.

"Ah." She turned away to hide her smile at his comment, gazing out the double windows. The fence line indicated Grange had a sizeable amount of property. Shrubs and a ton of tall, thick trees littered the land, which provided good cover for the house. She saw AJ heading outside and toward the garage. Shortly thereafter she heard the sound of a rumble and saw a bike heading down the long drive. Lily watched until it disappeared into the trees.

She turned away from the window and toward Mac. "Interesting bunch of guys."

"You could say that."

She leaned against the windowsill. "They're all incredibly good-looking. Is that a requirement to be in your organization? Because a girl could get used to hanging around all that sexy testosterone." She fanned herself. "My, my, my."

He advanced on her, peeling off his jacket and tossing it onto the chair. "Don't even think about it."

"Think about what?" she asked, batting her lashes.

"You and any of those guys. Or for that matter, *any* other guy." He stopped in front of her.

Oh, this was fun. She stretched out her legs between his. "Are you getting possessive on me?"

Mac leaned over and placed his palms on either side of her, framing her within the windowsill. "I'm not getting possessive, baby. I just think of you as mine. And I don't share."

"Oh."

"Do you have a problem with that?"

He was so close his nose almost touched hers. She caught the faint scent of cinnamon on his breath from the gum he'd chewed earlier. She licked her lips, loving this side of him. "I don't have a problem with that."

"I don't like you ogling the other guys."

She snorted. "I wasn't ogling, but I have to admit they were damn fine specimens of the male species."

He narrowed his gaze. "Am I going to have to teach you a lesson?"

She loved this playful side of him, the one that could get down and dirty and role-play with her where it really counted—in the bedroom. It was a side of Mac, and frankly, of herself, that she never knew existed. She loved bringing it out of both of them. "I hardly think I need to be taught a lesson, Mac. If I want to look, I'll look."

"I don't think so."

He surprised her then by grasping her wrists and jerking her to her feet, then hauling her with him over to the bed. When he threw her over his lap, she let out a cry of surprise.

"Mac! What are you doing?"

"You've been a very bad girl, Lily."

A little thrill shivered up her spine at the way he talked to her, the promise of an exciting adventure. "Mac, the other guys—"

"Can hear us. Do you like knowing that they'll be able to hear me touching you?"

His hand came down hard on her buttocks, the loud smack echoing throughout his room.

"Ow! That hurt, goddamit!"

"Did it? Gee, Lily, I'm so sorry."

There wasn't an ounce of remorse in his words. She fumed, struggling to get off his lap. Then he surprised her by reaching underneath her to draw down the zipper on her jeans. When she felt him pulling them down, she started to struggle in earnest.

"Don't you dare."

Despite her kicking and fighting, she was no match for him, and soon her jeans were down around her knees and the only thing protecting her butt from his hand was a thin pair of panties.

"I like this color," he said, smoothing his hand over the lavender silk before smacking her rear end again. Loud enough for someone to hear, too.

"Stop that!" It stung, but what she found surprising was how much it turned her on. She was getting wet. But was that due to Mac's touch, the mental thrill of being spanked, or because the other guys might be listening in?

"I think you like this," he said. "I think knowing the guys might hear excites you."

"That's ridiculous." She wouldn't give him the satisfaction of admitting what she'd been thinking, even though every word he spoke made her cream in her panties.

He inhaled sharply. "I can smell you, Lily. When you're excited, I can smell your pussy. God, that's a sweet, hot scent. And it makes my dick hard."

He rubbed her ass, trailing his fingers down to her pussy.

"You're wet through your panties." He slipped his finger underneath her panties and drove two fingers inside her. "Goddamn, are you ever wet."

She couldn't help but moan when he entered her with his fingers. It just made her wetter, feeling her pussy convulse around him. She wanted his cock in there, filling her, fucking her, making her come.

The soft tear of fabric brought about a wrenching gasp from her as he ripped her panties away, lifting the material from her body so he could cup her pussy with the palm of his hand.

He caressed her sex, back and forth, rubbing her clit until she writhed against him, searching for that sweet spot she craved so desperately. He removed his fingers and coated her anus with her cream, then slid one finger inside her ass while he used his other hand to stimulate her clit.

His cock was hard as a rock against her hip. She wanted it out of his jeans and inside her. She wanted everything right now, and she found it hard to focus while his fingers were buried in her pussy and ass, doing delicious things to her.

"Mac. Oh, Mac," she cried, no longer caring at all who heard, or how loud she was. "Make me come."

He twisted his fingers inside her, pulling out, then pushing deep, withdrawing them to coat her clit with her juices. Tantalizing the tight knot while fucking her ass with relentless strokes was her undoing. She let out a cry as her orgasm rushed over her, quick, intense pulses that made her jerk against Mac's lap, shuddering as the waves of climax splintered her.

Mac withdrew and she lifted off him. He left for only a few seconds to use the bathroom and wash his hands, then he was back, undressing as he approached. She had already pulled off her shirt and bra, needing his cock inside her.

"On your knees," he commanded.

She dropped, eager for a taste of him, not waiting for him to tell her what he wanted. She knew.

Her mouth. On his cock. The musky scent of him compelled her, his cock head swollen, with a drop of pearly liquid pooling at the tip. She grasped the base of his shaft and brought it to her mouth, tilting her head back to look at him as her tongue snaked out to lick the salty fluid from the wide crest.

"Christ," he whispered, grasping the nape of her neck and guiding his cock onto her waiting tongue.

She swirled her tongue over his heated flesh, licking around every vein, each ridge, flicking the wide head before enveloping it between her lips and closing her mouth to suck him inside. She took him inch by inch, watching his face, his tortured expression as she engulfed his shaft completely.

His harsh intake of breath was music to her ears, letting her know he loved what she was doing. She took him deep, all the way to the back of her throat, swallowing him.

"God, Lily," he said, tightening his hold on the back of her hair, then setting the rhythm by pulling her head back and pushing it forward.

It excited her to have him control her movements, to know that he wanted her to take him deep. She loved pleasing him, because it heightened her senses, made her nipples tingle and her pussy quiver. She reached down and began to rub between her legs.

"You want to come again, baby?"

She couldn't answer, of course, because her mouth was filled with his hard cock. But she groaned, her throat vibrating against the soft tissue of his cock head.

"Jesus, you're making me crazy."

He withdrew, then dropped down to his knees in front of her, taking her mouth in a hard kiss. He drove his tongue inside, his lips rolling over hers in heated passion, his fingers tearing through her hair.

She loved this wild side of him, the part of him that was desperate to possess her and completely out of control.

He broke the kiss and picked her up, then deposited her on the bed, following her in a hurry. Lily barely had time to catch a breath before he spread her legs and plunged inside her. She responded with a shriek of pleasure that she knew every single guy on the floor had to hear, which only made her pussy tighten around his cock.

Mac lifted her arms over her head and licked her nipples, stopping every few seconds to kiss her, to talk to her and tease her about the noises she made.

"You know they can hear you," he said, his voice tight with strain.

"I don't care what they hear. Just keep fucking me."

She lifted and spread her legs, allowing Mac to sink deeper inside her, to rock his pelvis against her clit and take her closer to another orgasm. She wanted that—to come again, to splinter around his cock and squeeze the come right out of him.

"Come on, Mac, do it," she said, urging him on.

He responded by slamming into her, grasping her buttocks and lifting her legs so there wasn't a space of air separating them. She was sweating, crying out, so close she could feel the quivers inside.

Then she let go, shuddering as the sweetest sensations poured through her. She moaned her satisfaction, crying out Mac's name as she orgasmed. Mac stilled against her, burying his face in her neck as he came, then panted against her, resting his head on her shoulder.

Lily swept her hands over his back, realizing how much she'd changed since being with Mac. She was so bold now, unafraid to show him her wants and needs. And he always gave her what she craved, as if he could sense her desires.

Not that she hadn't liked sex before—she had. She'd loved experimenting, but she'd never given her all to any man before. Maybe she'd been saving it for Mac—that wild and uninhibited part of her that she always knew existed, but had never let out.

It was sure as hell out in the open now. She couldn't imagine being this free and open with any other man. But what would happen when this was all over? Would she stay with him, or would they part ways and go back to their respective lives?

She realized she didn't want to leave him, but that decision wasn't entirely up to her. Mac had a life—a very secret life, and he'd just recently let her in on it.

A lot of things between them were up in the air.

And they still had a long way to go before any decisions about their future could be decided.

FOURTEEN

LILY LOVED THESE GUYS. IT WAS LIKE HAVING BROTHERS. annoying brothers, but still, it was the closest thing to siblings she'd ever had. They'd made her feel welcome and like part of their family.

After she and Mac resurfaced from his room, she got looks, raised brows, and some snickers—pretty much what she'd expected after all the noise they'd made. She wasn't at all embarrassed about it, either. From what she could tell, the guys were jealous, but they took it well, and were surprisingly respectful to her. She liked that about them.

They'd gone downstairs to fix something to eat, and everyone pitched in. These guys were not incompetent, nor did they expect not to cook now that there was a woman on the premises. In fact, they kept pushing her out of the way, but she continued to butt her way back in. They finally let her slice vegetables for the salad, claiming "meat" was man's duty. She rolled her eyes and pronounced them all Neanderthals.

And oh, could they cook. The long table was covered with steaks, fried potatoes, salad, and warm bread. Who knew that men who looked like these guys also possessed culinary skills?

"If women around here knew guys like you existed, they'd be camped out at the gates," she said, finishing off the last juicy bite of meat.

"Maybe we should start advertising," Diaz said with a wink.

"I don't think so. Last thing we need is a bunch of squealing, hormonal females in our midst." AJ must have realized what he said, because his gaze shot to Lily. "Present company excepted, of course."

She tried to hide her smile. "Of course. So tell me what the 'AJ' stands for." she said.

"None of your business," he replied with a wink.

"He's never told any of us," Spence said. "It's some deep, dark secret."

"Which means it must be bad." Paxton looked over at AJ, who glared at him. "Really bad."

"Not that we haven't tried guessing," Rick said. "And believe me, we've come up with every name in the book. We figured we probably hit the nail on the head, but he won't admit it."

AJ kept his head down and ate, ignoring all of them.

"Adam James?" she offered.

AJ's lips curled, but he shook his head.

"He wishes it was that," Mac said. "We're thinking it's something like Alphonse. Or Armand."

"Adolph Junior."

"Alfalfa Jones."

"Alimentary Juice."

"Armpit Jolly."

Lily snorted. They acted like little boys—and she was already crazy about all of them. In a sisterly way, of course. Their good-natured teasing clearly defined their affection for each other.

"Better than Spencer. Or Paxton," AJ finally said. "Makes you both sound like rich boys."

"Yeah, well we know better than that, don't we, Pax?" Spence asked. He stood and began clearing plates.

"Sure as hell no money falling out of my family tree," Pax replied with a wink. "If there was, I'd have stolen it a long time ago."

They all laughed and moved the dirty dishes into the kitchen.

"I love how they insult each other and don't get mad." She leaned over to whisper at Mac.

"Water under the bridge. We all fought it out years ago. Insulted each other, really dug into the pain of our pasts. Grange made us."

She nodded. "I suppose it was like therapy."

He laughed. "You could say that. None of us have secrets, Lily. Not from each other. Grange made us lay it all out on the table, everything ugly, so there'd never be any skeletons in the closet."

"It drew you closer to each other, knowing you all had miserable upbringings."

"Yeah. Though we've had different experiences, we're the same, if that makes sense."

She rubbed his cheek, loving the feel of beard stubble on her hand. "It does."

He leaned over and kissed her, and what started out as a sweet gesture turned into something more passionate as he lingered, his tongue sliding between her lips. He cupped the back of her neck to draw her closer. She laid her palm on his chest and felt the way his heart picked up its pace.

"You two can have sex on the dining room table later. We need to have a meeting," Grange said as he walked by on the way to the kitchen.

Lily and Mac grinned into each other's mouths, then stood and helped the others in the kitchen. Once the dishes were done and the food was put away, they piled into Grange's office and took a seat.

"Tom's doing fine," Grange said. "The gunshot to his hand was minor. He lost a little blood, but that's about it."

Lily was relieved to hear that.

"I got some information from him. He said he recognized the guy who shot him."

"Who is it?" Mac asked.

"Some henchman for corporate bigwigs he's seen around before."

"Do we have a name?" Pax asked.

"Yeah. Belanfield."

"Name doesn't ring a bell with me," AJ said.

The rest of them responded in the same way.

But Lily's stomach tightened as recognition struck. She had to speak up. "I know that name."

Mac turned to her. "You do?"

"Yeah. At least I think I do. If it's the same guy, he's done business with my father and some of the other companies my father is associated with."

Grange leaned against his desk. "Who's your father?"

"John West, the CEO of West Industries here in Dallas."

Grange nodded. "That's interesting."

"Rich girl, huh? Way to go, Mac," Spence teased.

Lily rolled her eyes, taking no insult.

"Tell us what you know about him," Grange said.

Excited, she racked her brain to remember. "Not much, really, other than his name. I've heard my dad on the phone talking to him before."

"How long ago was this?"

"Oh, years ago. I live in Chicago now, not with my father. Still, I would imagine my dad's contacts haven't changed. He's deep with his old boy network. If this guy is a bodyguard or someone in with Dad's group of cronies, I'd bet money they're still tight." She realized then that all eyes were on her, and she was pleased she had something of value to offer. She just hoped her dad wasn't in any way involved with the theft of the virus. It would kill her to have to turn in her own father.

Grange nodded. "So your father owns a pretty big company with national ties."

"Yes. And he's on the board of quite a few other large companies."

"Which means," Mac said, "that this Belanfield is probably involved in one of those companies in some way having to do with the virus. If we can determine which company, we can figure out who's behind the theft of the virus."

Now she was really excited, especially when an idea popped into her head. "I'm not really sure what my father's current connection is to this Belanfield, but I'll bet with a little sleuthing, I could probably find out."

"How?" Grange asked.

"My dad keeps an extensive contact database on his computer. I used to help him when I was a teenager by keeping it updated for him, so I know the ins and outs of his home system. If I can tap into that, maybe we can track Belanfield's location."

"How dangerous is that for you?"

Lily laughed. "Not dangerous at all. I've avoided my father like Ebola for the past few years. Me showing up on his doorstep would be like Christmas. He'd be delighted to see me."

"No."

Her gaze shot to Mac. "What?"

"I don't like this, Grange," Mac said. "This puts Lily smack in the middle. It puts her in danger. She's not one of us."

"Are you kidding me? After everything *you've* put me through, you have the nerve to say that? I can't believe you're still trying to shut me out." She couldn't help it, but damn, she was irritated at Mac, and this time she wasn't going to allow him to try to protect her.

"It's too risky."

She rolled her eyes. "It's my father's house. He's hardly a danger to me. I can help."

"I have to admit she has a point, Mac," Grange said. "Lily is in the best position to get us the information we need and in a hurry. We need to find out who's behind this."

She crossed her arms and tried not to look smug.

"Besides, she has training in law enforcement and as a private investigator. It's not like she's green and untrained. I think she'd make a great addition to the team for this particular assignment."

"Ha! See?" she said, unable to hide her grin. She felt like she'd received the ultimate compliment. Too bad it had come from Grange and not from Mac.

Mac shook his head. "I don't like this."

"You don't have to like it. I'm going, and you're coming with me," she said.

"Oh yeah, your father will love that."

"No," she said, grinning. "He'll absolutely hate it. Which is why you're coming along."

"He'll detest every second." Mac laughed. "I can definitely see the merits of your plan."

Now he was warming up to the idea. Her idea. "Exactly."

"Well I don't get it at all," Rick said, looking confused.

"That's because you don't know my father. He's all about social class. If I bring Mac home with me, he'll be so worried about what I'm doing with Mac, and what Mac's doing skulking about the house, and following Mac around because he's afraid Mac will steal the family silver, that he'll never notice me poking around on the computer."

"Oh," Rick said, his lips curling into a grin as he nodded. "You would make a good Wild Rider. That's some devious thinking, darlin'."

"Why thank you." She felt rather proud of her impromptu plan.

"Then it's settled," Grange said. "When can you be ready to go?"

"Let me call my father and make sure he's in town first."

Grange nodded. "There's a secure line that can't be traced," he said, motioning over his shoulder at the landline on his credenza.

She stood and went over to the phone, her heart pounding as she dialed her father's number. How long had it been since she'd spoken to him. Six months? Longer?

He answered on the second ring, surprised to hear from her, and shocked when she told him she'd be arriving in Dallas tomorrow. She left the details purposely vague, only that she'd be coming for a short visit. He said he was looking forward to seeing her, and she hung up shortly thereafter.

"We'll head out first thing in the morning," she said. She couldn't wait to see her father. Actually, what she couldn't wait for was digging into his database and seeing what she could find. Seeing her father was going to be unpleasant, like always.

Frankly, she was thrilled Mac was going with her. Not only would she have backup, she was bringing the man she loved to her father. A father so consumed with a person's status and place in society that he'd probably choke when she rode up on the back of a Harley and walked in the door holding Mac's hand.

She owed her father a lot. For his interference in her life, for never thinking Mac was the kind of boy she should have been hanging out with when she was a teenager, for never believing the choices she made were good enough.

She'd always felt less than adequate in her father's eyes, had never felt truly loved for who and what she was.

Dammit, she was good enough, she had made decent choices, and she loved Mac.

It was payback time.

*　　*　　*

IN ALL THE TIME MAC HAD KNOWN LILY, HE'D NEVER BEEN TO HER house before. She'd always come to his apartment, or to the garage where he'd worked, but she'd never wanted him over at her place. She said her dad would give him a hard time and she didn't want that for him.

Of course, he could handle himself, and he didn't care if he ever saw John West. He'd just worried about Lily back then and didn't want to do anything to embarrass her.

He still worried about Lily. She was taking this all too lightly, looking on it as an adventure, when it was anything but. He knew how she felt about her father, knew there was some seriously uncomfortable history between the two of them: things that had been left unsaid and unsettled for a long time. He knew all about painful parental relationships. His parents were dead, though, and there was nothing left to say to them even if they had still been alive. The irreparable damage had been done in his childhood and nothing could change that.

Lily, on the other hand . . . she and her father saw things differently, and they'd argued, but he didn't think their relationship was unsalvageable.

But she seemed excited to be heading toward her dad's, though Mac figured that was more about getting to his database than facing her father and having any kind of serious discussion with him.

Mac followed Lily's directions and drove to the gated community, stopping at the security shack. Lily chatted up the guard, who recognized her immediately, seemed happy to see her, and buzzed them through.

Nice houses, no doubt worth millions, and on sizeable lots, too. Perfectly manicured lawns, nothing out of place. A slice of suburban utopia. Mac could already feel himself suffocating in a place like this.

He pulled into the long driveway leading up to the West mansion. God, this place was ostentatious. It was like a dark brick version of the White House in D.C., with tall columns bordering the wide front porch. The only thing missing was the dome over the roof flying the American flag.

John West was standing on the front porch as they pulled around the circular drive. He was tall and looked to be in his sixties, with a thick head of silvery hair combed in waves away from his face. He wore jeans, a white shirt, and silver-tipped cowboy boots. His arms were crossed.

Man, he didn't look at all happy to see his daughter riding up on the back of a Harley, either. His brows were knit so tightly together they looked like one. Mac resisted the urge to smirk as he parked, and they climbed off the bike.

Lily's dad frowned even more when she grabbed Mac's hand.

"Daddy," she said as they walked up the white steps onto the pristine white porch.

His frown turned to a wary smile of greeting. "Lily. You didn't tell me you were bringing a . . . friend."

Ignoring his comment, she kissed her father on the cheek, then turned to Mac. "Surely you remember Mac Canfield, don't you, Daddy?"

West's brows raised in tandem, then the frown returned. "Oh. Canfield. Yes, I do remember you as a matter of fact."

Not fondly, either, from the look on his face. "And I remember you, too. Last time we met you were dragging your daughter out of my garage." That was about a week before Mac took Lily's virginity, though it wouldn't be a good idea to tell John West that story.

"Lily had other things to do besides waste her time in a dirty, greasy garage, hanging around fast cars and motorcycles."

Lily snorted. "And look at me now, riding on the back of a Harley."

She was just daring the old man to make a comment, wasn't she?

"Well, come inside," John said with a heaving sigh. "Will you be staying, too, Canfield, or did you just drop Lily off?"

"He goes where I go, Dad." Lily once again clasped Mac's hand and shot a glare at her father that just dared him to snatch up the welcome mat. Mac really had a hard time holding back his laugh. If Lily thought his feelings could be hurt by the likes of a snob like John West, then she had a lot to learn about him. People like West could never hurt him, because he didn't care what they thought.

Inside the house was even fancier, the kind of place one would never think about bringing small children. Did Lily grow up here? He couldn't imagine running wild and free in a place like this, with fragile vases sitting on narrow tabletops and expensive-looking knickknacks everywhere. Not a speck of dust and nothing out of place. Everything was cold, austere, and damned expensive looking.

Lily squeezed his hand. "Disgustingly pretentious, isn't it?" she whispered as they followed her father down a long hallway.

"It just doesn't feel like a place you'd call home."

She shrugged. "My room is warmer."

They were escorted into what Lily explained was the library. Made sense, since it was filled with books. Floor to ceiling bookshelves lined every wall, with the exception of a stone fireplace that took up an entire wall. A leather sofa and matching chairs were centered in front of the fireplace. John directed them to sit.

"Drink?" John asked, as a diminutive woman entered the room.

"New staff?" Lily asked. "And I can get my own, thank you."

Again, that frown. "We have servants to do that."

Lily waved the servant off. "I'm sure they have plenty to do." She turned to Mac. "What would you like?"

"Whiskey." He didn't really want a whiskey, just figured it would irritate Lily's father and make her happy. It did. She turned her back on her dad and her lips curled. John West did frown. Lily splashed two fingers of whiskey over some ice and poured a matching glass for herself, then sat on the sofa next to Mac. Practically on top of Mac, she scooted so close, which resulted in yet another scowl from John.

"So what brings you here?" he asked.

Lily shrugged. "Mac and I took a road trip on his bike."

"All the way from Chicago on that thing?" he asked, casting a glower in Mac's direction.

"Yes, all the way from Chicago. We made quite a few stops, too, and we're having a great time."

"Motorcycles are dangerous."

He was still staring daggers at Mac. Mac was still ignoring him.

So, apparently, was Lily. "Anyway, since we'd come this far south and were in the neighborhood, I thought we'd stop by and visit for a day."

John finally dragged his venomous gaze away from Mac and placed it back on Lily, his demeanor immediately changing. He smiled, his facial features relaxing, his voice softer. "I'm glad you did. I don't see nearly enough of you anymore."

"My job keeps me busy."

"You could do the same work here in Dallas."

"So you could continue to run my life and interfere like you did when I was on the force? I don't think so."

John lifted his chin and sniffed. "I never interfered in your life or your job."

"Oh, please, Daddy," Lily said, rolling her eyes. "You did everything but have me fired."

"You chose a very dangerous line of work. I insured your safety."

"You meddled."

Mac leaned back and got comfortable while the two of them

bickered back and forth. This was interesting, and he enjoyed see-ing Lily get riled, especially if it meant standing up to her old man, something she hadn't done nearly enough of when she was a teen-ager. If he hadn't been one hundred percent certain John West could have had him tossed into jail, he would have stepped in the day he'd shown up at the garage and dragged Lily out, claiming she was too good to be hanging out with a loser like Mac.

Not that he had disagreed with the old man at the time.

The next day Lily had been back at the garage, leaning over the hood of the car Mac was working on, vowing that her father was not going to dictate the terms of her life, wasn't going to force her to attend a college she didn't want to go to. Then she claimed in no uncertain terms that it would be a cold day in hell before she joined her father's company. She'd told Mac that she intended to live her own life as she pleased and not according to the whims of her dad.

Mac hadn't believed she'd be strong enough to break the iron grip John West held over her. He'd always told her to be her own woman, stand up for herself, and not let her dad lead her around on a chain, but he didn't think she'd actually do it.

He'd been wrong. He would have liked to have been there when she'd stood up to her father and refused to attend the col-lege of his choice, refused to major in business, instead opting for police science. He'd bet John West was near apoplexy that day.

"It really doesn't matter how long we argue about this, Dad," she finally said. "I'm not moving back here. I like my job in Chi-cago, and I intend to stay there."

Interesting. Mac wondered if she really meant that or if she'd just said it to dig at her father.

Her dad didn't get a chance to respond, because a servant stepped into the doorway. "I have the rooms made up for Miss West and her guest."

John nodded and looked back at Lily. "Your room is the same

as always," he said to Lily. "We had a guest room prepared for Mac."

Lily snorted. "Totally unnecessary, Daddy, since Mac will be sleeping in my room with me."

Zing.

John stood, his face darkening. "That's unacceptable."

Lily stood, too, crossing her arms. "I'm an adult now and can make my own decisions. If you have a problem with that, Mac and I can leave."

Mac was still enjoying the show and wasn't about to get involved. Besides, Lily was handling herself great and no way was he going to interfere in her moment of triumph over her father.

"Lily," her father said, his tone harsh. "I will not tolerate you sharing a bed with—"

"One more word and I'm out of here," she warned. "I will not allow you to insult Mac or me with your snooty, antiquated notions of propriety. I'm well over twenty-one and capable of making decisions about my sex life without your input, thank you. If you don't want me here, fine. Say so now and I'm gone. But let me make this perfectly clear: If I stay, Mac stays. In my room with me. That's the way it will be and I don't want to hear another word about it. If you can't live with that, then now is the time to speak up."

John's face was red. Mac just knew the man wanted to blow up at her, to read her the riot act about how he felt about Mac. He stared down his daughter for a few seconds, and Lily calmly stared back at him.

John finally sighed. "You know I want you here. I don't see you enough as it is. You're welcome to stay."

She waited, her booted foot tapping on the wood floor.

"You and Mac are welcome to stay here. In fact, dinner will be ready shortly."

She nodded. "Good." Lily turned to Mac. "Why don't you get our things and bring them inside?"

"Fine with me." Mac went out, grabbed their things, brought them in, and laid the bag at the foot of the stairs, then rejoined Lily and her father in the library.

"Would you two like to freshen up and change before dinner?" her father asked, eying them up and down.

Mac arched a brow and glanced over at Lily. "Damn. Left my suit in my other Harley."

She snickered, then shook her head at her father. "No, we're good, thanks."

"Very well." He led them down the hall and through double doors into the dining room.

Mac really did need a suit for this. A white tablecloth covered what had to be a ten-foot oval table with twelve chairs that gleamed with dark, polished wood. The cushions were white. Guess he'd better not drop any food on them. He waited for John and Lily to take their seats—John at one end, Lily to his left. He sat on the other side of Lily.

Was he out of his element here or what? Lily, of course, seemed right at home, taking the cloth napkin and flipping it out to her side, then letting it sail over her lap as if she'd done it thousands of times. Then again, she probably had, so it was second nature to her. Mac was lucky if he remembered to use napkins when he ate. Weren't they just for wiping the dripping stuff off your fingers and mouth?

He'd rather sit in the kitchen and eat with the help. This was uncomfortable.

At least until Lily turned her head, smiled at him, and said, "Relax, will you?"

Two servants came in and poured wine in one of the glasses, ice tea in the other, then proceeded to bring in their meal. Salad first. Mac was hungry, but he waited while Lily and her father passed around a silver bowl that he guessed contained the salad dressing.

He loaded his salad with dressing and started eating, grateful when the staff brought bread.

They hadn't eaten much on the drive down, so his stomach made loud rumbles. He caught the disgusted look John cast his way, but could care less. The guy might be an ass, but at least he served good food. Mac ate every bite of each course offered. He was going to have to thank the folks in the kitchen. Those people could cook.

"How is your work progressing, Lily?" John asked.

"Fine."

"Chicago is a very dangerous city to do private investigative work."

"Dallas can be the same way," she said, taking a sip of her wine.

"At least here you had friends on the police force."

"I have friends in Chicago, too. And I'd still have been on the police force here, if not for your interference."

"I hardly think we need to rehash this. You shouldn't have become a police officer in the first place. You should have joined me in the family business."

Lily lifted her shoulders, then dropped them as she exhaled. Mac could only imagine her tension, though outwardly she seemed calm enough. He wanted nothing more than to pull her out of there, take her up to her room, and massage the stress away.

"I did exactly what I wanted to do, as we discussed when I graduated high school."

John laid his fork across his plate and dabbed at his lips with the napkin. "I can't help but think those decisions were somehow . . . influenced by others." He cast his gaze to Mac.

"Oh, please," Lily said. "Mac had nothing to do with my decision. This is what I wanted to do. Do you think I was so brainless that I couldn't come up with an original idea on my own?"

"You never mentioned the police academy to me."

"Why would I have? You'd have just shot the idea down as ridiculous. You had it set in your mind what I was going to do from the time I was five years old. Nothing I wanted would have mattered."

"That's not true. I would have listened."

"Bull. You never listened to me when I tried to talk to you about what I wanted."

"I would have. Had you anything of value to say."

Mac really wanted to come to Lily's defense, to tell John West that his daughter was capable and intelligent. But he wanted Lily to fight her own battles, knew she wouldn't appreciate his interference, so he let it slide. But the way John continued to berate Lily really grated on Mac's nerves. He poured another glass of wine.

"I had plenty to say. Only no one was listening." She didn't look at Mac, but he felt like her words were meant for him, too. *Damn.*

He almost cringed. He hadn't listened to her either. Even he had pushed her away. In a way, he'd been like her father, thinking he knew what was best for her. He had a hell of a lot of nerve being angry at her dad, when he had done the same thing.

He gave Lily a lot of credit for thumbing her nose at both of them and going her own way.

"You were only eighteen," John continued. "You didn't know what you wanted. And you always made the most idiotic choices." Again, he slid a sideways glance at Mac. "Sadly, I'm not sure you've changed all that much."

Lily calmly cut a piece of chicken and shrugged, not even looking at him when she replied. "You never had faith in me, never believed in me. I guess you haven't changed all that much, either."

She stated it matter-of-factly, as if her father's words didn't hurt.

Did she grow up with this every single day, having to endure this man berating her, never feeling as if she measured up, as if what she wanted hadn't mattered? How frustrating that must have been for her. John West treated his daughter like an employee asking for a raise—with complete disregard for her needs, wants, and desires. He was the coldest man Mac had ever known.

Mac seethed inside, wanted to climb across the table and knock the son of a bitch across the room.

For so long he thought Lily had everything, that she'd gone slumming when she'd come after him. Mac always thought he and Lily had nothing in common. Hell, they had everything in common. No wonder she'd clung to him. And he'd failed her, hadn't given her what she'd needed most.

She'd needed him, and he hadn't been there for her.

He was no better than her old man. He felt ashamed, and he didn't like that feeling at all. It burned like a knife in his gut.

After dinner they moved back into the library for brandy. With this kind of ritual it was a miracle the family wasn't a bunch of alcoholics. Drinks before dinner, wine with dinner, brandy after dinner. Mac liked a drink now and then, but damn, these people were lushes. He and Lily both declined the brandy, deciding instead on coffee. Mac excused himself to find the kitchen so he could tell the staff how much he enjoyed dinner. Their wide-eyed looks of shock told him they weren't appreciated all that often, but they smiled and nodded their thanks.

As he made his way back to the library, he could hear that the arguing between Lily and her father was on again. He hung back in the hall, waiting to make his reappearance.

"I suppose Mac isn't invited?" Lily asked.

"Your friend would not be comfortable at the country club."

"You mean he's not welcome there."

No response from Lily's dad on that one. Mac smirked.

"Which is precisely why I'm not going. They're nothing but a bunch of nose-in-the-air snobs."

"It would be nice if you'd make an appearance. My friends at the club haven't seen you in years."

"*Your* friends at the country club don't give a damn about me and you know it. You just want to parade me around like some grand prize at the county fair. I don't even remember half those people."

"It wouldn't hurt you to be social. Many of those people give large amounts to the endowment fund."

"I came to see you, not them."

John just didn't get it, did he? Mac pushed off the wall and strolled back into the library with a casual smile, seating himself next to Lily and reaching for his coffee. He leaned over and pressed a light kiss to her lips, which brightened up her face. She smiled at him, her cheeks turning pink.

Lily needed to smile more often.

John was scowling. Again. Screw the old man. Mac could care less if John didn't like him showing affection to Lily. He'd had more than enough of the way the man treated his daughter.

"Besides," Lily said, turning back to her father, a wicked grin on her face. "I'd rather stay here tonight. Mac and I are going to bed so we can fuck."

FIFTEEN

MAC NEARLY CHOKED ON HIS COFFEE. JOHN'S FACE WENT STARK red, his cheeks puffed out, and Mac prepared to do CPR.

Holy shit, her father was mad. Lily leaned back with a serene smile on her face.

At that moment, he didn't think he could ever love her more.

"I'm ready now if you are," Mac said, standing and holding out his hand. "It's been a long damn day."

She slid her hand in his. "Night, Daddy."

"Thank you for dinner, Mr. West," Mac said, wrapping an arm around Lily's waist.

John didn't say a word as Mac turned away and headed out of the room with Lily. When they got to the foot of the stairs, he swooped her up into his arms. She let out a shriek of delight, laughing as he bounded up.

"First door on the right," she said when they reached the landing.

She helped by turning the knob on the door. He nudged it

the rest of the way open and found the light switch, immediately blasted by a plethora of Pepto-Bismol pink.

"Good God," he said, setting Lily on her feet.

"I know. Disgusting, isn't it?"

He didn't have words. A double bed with frilly pink bedspread. Pink walls in a contrasting shade. Pink lampshade, pink curtains. Pink shelves. Every-freakin-thing in the room was pink.

"You don't really expect me to sleep in here, do you? I'll wake up emasculated, my balls shriveled."

Lily giggled and wrapped her arms around him, pressing a soft kiss on his mouth. "I think you can handle it, macho man."

"I don't know. I feel weak. Must. Sit."

She snorted and pushed at his chest, then wandered over to the window seat, which was adorned with, of course, thick pink pillows. She flounced down on it and looked at him.

"I used to think about you while I spent time in here."

"Oh yeah?" He arched a brow and moved toward her.

She kicked her feet up in the air, locking her ankles together. "Yup."

"You mean you fantasized about me." He grabbed her boots and pulled them off, then her socks. Her window was half-open, bringing in a breeze that ruffled the lacy curtains in his direction.

"That's exactly what I mean. I'd sit here at my window seat every night and write in my diary about this boy who made me hot."

He toed off his boots, then flipped open the button on his jeans. "Naughty girl."

"Scandalous," she said with a saucy smile, unzipping her jeans and lifting her hips. "I'll bet the maids found my diary and read it."

He pulled the bottom hem of her jeans, sliding them down her legs. "And what did the maids read in your diary?" He threw the jeans to the floor, mesmerized by Lily's slender legs.

"They read about how it felt to stand next to you every day, to feel your hard body brushing against mine." She pulled her shirt off, leaving her in only a black bra and matching panties. "About how much I ached to have you touch me. But you wouldn't, so I had to touch myself, fantasizing it was your hands on me."

She demonstrated by palming the swells of her breasts, teasing him by slipping her fingertips inside the fabric of her bra to skim across her nipples. Her breath caught and Mac could only imagine what she was feeling. She was touching her nipples, making them hard, feeling that sensation shoot between her legs.

"Did you touch yourself here in your room at night, and think about me when you were doing it?" He dragged the zipper down on his jeans, making sure to take his time since Lily was watching. He pushed them over his hips and let them drop to the floor. His boxers went next and he grasped his already hard cock in his hand.

Lily licked her lips, her gaze riveted on his shaft. She moved one hand to her panties, letting her fingers drift under the satin fabric. "Yes, Mac. I often touched myself and thought about you."

He fisted his cock in a hard grip and began to stroke.

Lily spread her legs, dipping her hand fully inside her panties. "I'd sit like this at my window seat. The windows would be partially open and the summer breeze streamed in, helping to cool my heated skin. I'd lean back against the wall and touch my pussy, wishing you were here with your hand in my panties."

His cock leapt forward, his balls tightening at the visual she presented, both present and past.

"My pussy's so wet, Mac."

"Take your panties off. Let me watch."

She pulled her panties down, kicking them away, then spread her legs, skimming her fingers over her pussy lips. They glistened with moisture in the soft light cast by the table lamp, making her pussy look like it was adorned by crystals.

Lily's eyes were half-closed as she ran two fingers over those sweet lips. She swept her fingers over her cunt, tantalizing him with her movements, then tucked them inside. Her lips parted and she sucked in a breath, thrusting her fingers in and out between the swollen folds.

"Oh, yeah. I love watching you touch yourself." He tightened his grip on his cock, plunging it in and out of his hand. He moved closer, needing to see her, to inhale the musky scent of her pussy and watch her pleasure herself.

With her fingers embedded in her pussy, she pressed the heel of her palm against her clit, lifting her hips. Panting, she looked at him with blatant desire in her eyes, a glassy look that screamed "fuck me now."

Exactly his thought. But first, he was going to taste her. He dropped to his knees between her widespread legs, planting his fingers against her thighs to hold them in place. He felt her muscles quiver there, smiling as he went down on her. The first taste of her was hot, spicy, her sweet cream flowing against his tongue as he licked her from pussy to clit. Lily let out a low moan and slid down in the window seat, clutching the sheer curtains in a death grip.

Mac slid his tongue inside her pussy, using his thumb to caress her clit.

"Oh. Oh, God, Mac."

She came in a rush, her eyes widening as she jerked against his face and jammed her pussy against his mouth. He licked her until her trembling subsided, then stood, yanking her from the window seat and taking her spot, pulling her astride him. She settled over him, sliding over his swollen cock with a whimper of pleasure.

She began to ride him. "This is what I wanted, what I fantasized about all those nights when I sat alone here in my room," she said, her voice husky and raw. "I thought about all the different ways you would kiss me, undress me, make love to me. You have no idea how much I wanted it."

Yeah, he did, because he'd wanted the same thing.

She leaned over him and tangled her fingers in his hair, pulling his face to hers and covering his mouth with hers. She licked her own cream from his mouth, her tongue washing over his lips before diving between them.

He held onto her hips, setting their rhythm by lifting her, then pulling her down over his cock. She was slick, rocking back and forth against him, sliding over his balls until he gritted his teeth to keep from erupting inside her.

"I used to fantasize about you, too," he said, letting go of her hips only long enough to reach for her breasts, cupping them in his hands and using his thumbs to graze her nipples.

She moaned. "Did you?"

"Yes. I wanted you. You were everything that was good and pure in my life back then. So sweet, so untainted. I'd jack off thinking about your sexy legs in those short skirts you wore, wondering what kind of panties you had on, and fantasizing about tossing you on the hood of my car and eating your pussy until you screamed."

"Oh, God," she whispered. "I would have loved that. I'd still love that."

He surged upward, burying his cock deep. "Remind me to do that later." Because right now he couldn't think anymore. His balls tightened and he needed to come inside her. He slipped his hand between her legs and strummed her clit. Lily tilted her head back; her muscles tensed, she jerked forward and began to shudder. Her pussy squeezed his cock in tight spasms as she came with loud cries, her nails digging into his shoulders.

That was as long as he could hold out. He let go, releasing inside her with a shuddering groan, clasping onto her hips and grinding her pussy against him until he was empty.

Lily laid her forehead against his, her warm breath panting against his cheek.

"That was better than anything I ever wrote in my diary," she said.

He laughed. "Glad to hear that. It was kind of kinky to fuck you in here, knowing you had all those fantasies about me."

She grinned and kissed him. "I had a *lot* of fantasies."

He wrapped his hands around her buttocks and lifted her, carrying her into the adjoining bathroom, which, thank God, wasn't pink. They showered together, Mac soaping every inch of her body. He couldn't get enough of running his hands over her skin, making sure to spend time massaging her shoulders until he'd released the knots of tension her father had put there. When they were finished, they dried off and fell into bed. Lily lay against his side, her head on his shoulder.

"Your dad's an asshole," he whispered against her hair.

She laughed. "Yes, he is."

"He hurts you with his words. I'd like to kick his ass."

"Don't bother. It used to make me feel insecure. I never felt as if I could measure up to his expectations of me, but I eventually got over it when I realized that no matter what I did, it wouldn't please him. He no longer has the power to hurt me. I'm immune."

He'd still like to make the old man pay for hurting her. He lay there for a while, holding her and listening to the night sounds, trying to figure out how he was going to say what needed saying.

"I'm sorry," he finally said.

"For what?"

They'd turned off the light, so the only illumination was the moon filtering in through the windows.

"For being the same kind of dickhead as your dad all those years ago."

She sat up and switched on the bedside lamp. Soft pink light filtered the room, casting a glow over Lily's frowning face.

"What? You're nothing at all like my father."

"Yeah, actually, I am. You needed me to believe in you, to have faith in the decisions you made and what you wanted. I wasn't there for you, just like he wasn't there for you. I pushed you away, believing I knew what was best for you. I was as full of shit as he was. Only you knew what was right for you."

She was quiet for several minutes, her palm resting on his chest.

"I love you, Mac."

His heart slammed against his chest. Jesus Christ, he hadn't expected that.

She smiled down at him. "I've always loved you. When I was eighteen I fell in love with who you were, at first because you were so different from any guy I'd ever known. I was crazy about your bad boy image, your independent nature, the fact that you threw caution to the wind and did whatever you wanted. I craved that kind of life because I was imprisoned here; my life had been entirely laid out before me and I wanted to be free.

"But as I got to know you, I realized you were more than just this image I had of you. There was an inherent kindness within you, an honor and integrity that you couldn't hide, no matter how hard you tried. That's the Mac Canfield I fell in love with, the one I wanted to give my body and heart to."

He closed his eyes. And he'd taken her heart and stomped on it, tossing it carelessly back at her as if she'd meant nothing.

When he opened his eyes again, he looked up at Lily.

"Lily, I need you to know—what happened that last night we saw each other . . ."

"I know. You did what you thought was best for me. You didn't want to take me down with you. You weren't trying to run my life for me, Mac. You're nothing like my father."

"I loved you." As soon as he said the words, he realized they were true. He wasn't just making excuses for the way he'd treated Lily. He'd dumped her because he loved her, because he was scared to death she would follow him down the black road of his life, that she would end up miserable if she'd stayed with him. "I didn't want you to be with me because I was afraid of where I was going, and I didn't want to tell you how I felt, didn't want you to be able to see it in my eyes. If I didn't let you go after I made love to you, if I didn't walk away after that first night, I would have never let you go."

Tears streamed down her face. "Thank you. I needed to hear that."

"I'm not finished." He brushed a tear away with his thumb. "I loved you back then and I didn't tell you. I'm telling you now that I still do."

Those words were true, too. He'd spent a lifetime running from them, but he'd never been able to run far enough. Lily had always been in his heart, had never left. She never would. "I love you, Lily."

"You've never said that to anyone before, have you?" she asked, sniffling.

"I've never loved anyone before." He was on unfamiliar ground now, and it felt strange. Good, but really strange.

She was still crying when she leaned over and kissed him, the salt from her tears searing him. God, she was sweet. He'd always thought she was too good for him, but maybe he'd earned the right to love her—maybe he did deserve someone like Lily now.

He didn't know what the future held for them. His life had always been about right now, not tomorrow. And right now he wanted to love her again—really love her.

He tunneled his fingers in her hair and deepened the kiss, letting his tongue slide over hers, licking her, moving his lips in slow motion. It was tender, something he wasn't used to, but it made his dick hard to love her this way. She moaned against his mouth.

He swept her underneath him, using his knee to part her legs and ease inside her. There was no hurry this time, just a slow lovemaking as he moved in and out of her, stopping when he was deep inside to grind against her clit, wanting to feel her come apart around him one more time.

With the light on he could watch her eyes, see them widen when he hit a spot that felt good to her. Her body and her face told him everything as she lifted toward him, tightened around his cock, and whimpered her need.

He cupped her cheek with one hand, wrapped the other around her butt to bring her closer, kissing her as she spasmed around him with her orgasm. He drank in her shuddering cries and came with her, surprised at the tenderness and emotion of the moment. Afterward, he drew her to his side and wrapped his arms around her, content to hold her.

If he could have his way, he'd shut out the world. Leave this mess they were in behind them and run, so they could just be Mac and Lily, a couple. They needed time to discover each other without all this bullshit going on around them.

But that wasn't going to happen. The world intruded in a big way.

"Time's running out," she whispered against him.

Didn't he know it. "Yeah. What do you want to do?"

She lifted her head to peer at the clock on the nightstand. "It's still plenty early. Daddy won't be in bed yet, and I need to slip into his office and get on the computer."

"Do you want to wait until he's asleep?"

"No, because then he'll be upstairs, and he's a light sleeper. This will be easier to do when he's awake."

He nodded. "Okay, you're in charge. Tell me your plan."

"Why don't you go downstairs and distract him?"

"How do you suggest I do that?"

She sat up. "You won't have to do anything, knowing my father. Tell him I'm asleep and you came down to get something to drink. Once he has you to himself and away from me, he'll no doubt try to convince you to leave me. He'll probably try to pay you off or something equally repulsive, but at least it'll give me enough time to hack into his database while you have him engaged."

Mac grinned. "You have a wicked and devious mind, Lily West."

She winked. "That's why you love me."

They hopped out of bed to clean up and get dressed.

Lily's adrenaline was pumping. She was excited about this, didn't think twice about tapping into her father's computer. To her, this was a job. She wasn't in any way hurting her dad by looking into his files. Instinct told her he wasn't involved in this—her father might be a lot of things, but he wasn't a criminal. He was just a means to get information on Belanfield, a stopping point along the way.

She hovered in her room to make sure her father wasn't upstairs, while Mac headed downstairs. Her plan was to listen for their voices. Once she was assured her father was down there and engaged with Mac, she'd slip into his office.

Her door open just a crack, she waited what seemed like forever, though in reality she was certain it had only been a few minutes. Mac made sure to be loud enough to alert her father that someone was downstairs in the kitchen. Lily knew her dad never went to bed early, so he had to be roaming the house. She tiptoed out of her room and leaned over the railing, leaning back as she saw her father leave the library and head down the hall toward the kitchen. *Perfect!*

She crept down the stairs, lingering at the landing. Soon, she heard Mac and her father talking together. *Okay, good enough.* Mac would keep him busy for a while. She hurried upstairs and opened the door to her father's office. Thankfully, his computer was on.

Now the big moment—had he changed his password? Though she'd helped him out when she was in high school, he changed his password after she went to college. But when she wanted on his system during her breaks, she'd fiddled with a few combinations and figured it out, though he'd never known about it. She typed in the code, nearly whooping for joy when she was granted access. Heart pounding, she inserted the jump drive and opened his contact database. It, too, was password protected, so it proved more difficult to access. But her father wasn't all that sophisticated with his passwords, so she tried several combinations, rolling her eyes when she entered her own date of birth and the program opened.

Really, Dad, how simple could that be? She made a mental note to someday teach him how to guard his data a little more carefully, but at the moment she was glad he hadn't. She copied the database files onto the jump drive, closed all the files, pocketed the drive, and hightailed it out of his office.

That was almost too easy.

As soon as she closed the door to her father's office, she heard Mac and her father's voices raised in anger. Curious, she crept downstairs and headed down the hall toward the kitchen, lingering at the doorway.

"I could make you a rich man, Canfield."

No surprise there. She knew her father was going to try and buy Mac off. She hated that her dad was so predictable. To him, everything was about money.

"I've got everything I need already. I don't want your money."

"You don't need Lily."

"That's where you're wrong. I do need her."

Lily's heart squeezed.

"You have nothing to offer her. I could give her so much more."

Mac snorted. "You are so blind. If you hadn't tried to tie such a tight leash around Lily, make her fit into your preconceived notions of what you thought she should be, then maybe you wouldn't have lost your daughter."

Oh, Mac was really letting her father have it, wasn't he? She crossed her arms and smirked into the darkness. He never held back, with her or with anyone else. She loved that he didn't let her father intimidate him.

"You know nothing about my relationship with my daughter," John sniffed.

"I know all I need to know. You pushed her right out the door—hell, right out of the state. She ran as far away from you as she could and you're too proud to admit the mistakes you made."

"She made the mistakes, starting with taking up with you."

"No, you and I were the ones who screwed up. I let her think I didn't want her, that she should do what you wanted her to do. I was wrong. So are you. If you open your eyes and accept her for who and what she is, give her the freedom to live the life she wants rather than some mapped-out plan that you designed for her, then maybe she'd open her heart to you. Instead, you still insist you know what's best for her. Keep that up and you're going to lose her forever."

"You have no idea what you're talking about." Her father was about to say something more, but he turned and spotted her.

Lily swiped at the tears, hating herself for letting them fall. Her father would never, ever understand. Nor would he ever change. She'd always known that, but somehow she'd hoped . . .

"I wish just once you would listen to someone. But you will never see reason. You'll never change. We're leaving, Mac," she said, then turned and walked out of the room.

Mac caught up with her and put his arm around her.

"It's done," she whispered. "Let's get out of here. I don't want to spend a night under his roof."

He squeezed her shoulder. "You got it, babe. A little too much pink for me, anyway."

She laughed, thankful to have Mac at her side.

He didn't coddle her as they packed up, and she appreciated that. She'd long ago gotten over her father's inability to see her point of view, but admittedly, it still stung that he wouldn't give, even a little. Mac's words held such power, such an important message, and her father wouldn't yield.

He would never change.

She forced thoughts of him aside as they left the house. Mercifully, her dad wasn't hovering nearby when they walked out the door and climbed on the bike. Not that she expected him to. John West had too much pride to beg his daughter to stay. He'd rather be right than loved.

She almost felt sorry for him.

Mac revved the engine after he started it up, and Lily grinned, knowing it would irk her father. They roared out of there and into the night, back to Wild Riders headquarters.

Back to her current "home," much better than the one they'd left. She felt like she could breathe again as soon as she left her father's.

At Wild Riders, the guys were all waiting for them, and when she produced the jump drive and pronounced her mission a success, she was greeted with whoops and hollers and clapped on the back, as if she was one of them. Admittedly, that felt damn good.

Grange smiled as she handed over the jump drive.

"Well done, Lily," he said. "Now let's see what we've got here."

Mac took her hand and pulled her aside as the rest of them headed into Grange's office.

"I know you're upset about your dad, even though you like to act as if you don't care."

She shrugged. "I'm fine with it. Used to it."

He smiled, the tenderness in his eyes unnerving. "I know how that feels. But you have no family other than your father, and I know what it's like to feel alone. Even when I had family, I was alone. My parents were drunks; they didn't want the responsibility of having a kid around and wished I'd just as soon disappear off the face of the earth. They didn't want me, so I made sure to stay as far away from them as I could."

Her heart ached for him, for the way he grew up. She cupped his cheek and pressed a soft kiss to his lips. "I'm sorry for what you had to go through."

He grasped her wrist and pressed a kiss to the palm of her hand. "It's okay. It toughened me up for what was to come. But what I need you to know is that you're not alone anymore. You have me. I can be your family. I'll be here to share the burden with you."

She couldn't believe what he was saying, the things he'd told her today. He loved her, he was offering to—what? To take care of her? Not exactly a marriage proposal, but for Mac, it was a huge step. For a man who prided himself on no ties, it meant everything that he made this kind of offer to her. The depth of caring that caused him to make this admission was overwhelming.

Her knees were shaking. "I love you, Mac."

"I love you, too."

The words spilled easily from him. She knew in her heart he meant them, and that made all the difference in the world to her. She wrapped her arms around him and held him tight, not wanting to break the spell of the moment.

"Christ, Lily, do you know how scary this is?"

She pulled back and frowned. "What?"

"These feelings."

She nodded. "Yes."

"I don't want to let you go. Ever. But what kind of life is this for a woman who grew up in luxury and wealth?"

She inhaled, let it out slow and easy. She knew it cost him to bare his soul to her. That loving her scared the hell out of him. She didn't take it lightly, nor did she think he wanted to rush headfirst into any kind of lifelong commitment.

"I live a very simple life in Chicago, not in any kind of luxury. You should see my apartment. It's a mess. Not a servant around for miles. And not a spec of pink in the whole place."

He grinned. "Thank God."

"You two aren't going to be having sex or anything out here, are you? Because Grange is waiting."

Lily smiled at Mac, who said, "No, AJ. We'll go outside and have sex later."

"Great," AJ said. "I'll be sure to get the video camera set up for that one. Now move your asses and get in here."

By the time they settled in Grange's office, he had the database up on the big screen and was scrolling down the list of names and corporations.

"Tell me about this database, Lily," Grange said.

"My father keeps a contact database of everyone he's affiliated with in some way or another. Company names, and who works for whom. Basically, how everyone is connected," she said, moving to the front of the room. Grange stood and let Lily take a seat at the computer, so she could manipulate the data. "I didn't have a chance to look at anything while I was at my father's house, because I only had a few minutes to make a copy."

She studied the information now. "Each person is linked with a corporation or with individuals within corporations." She searched until she found the name she sought. "Okay, here's Belanfield. It's kind of like a flowchart, each person's name linked to everyone he's connected to." She demonstrated by clicking on Belanfield's name. The screen expanded to showcase every person, every company, that Belanfield had contact with.

The list was extensive.

"Damn," Rick said. "That guy gets around."

She nodded. "I'll say. The list of corporations and bigwigs connected to Belanfield is impressive."

"Major corporations, from the looks of them," Mac said.

"So I see," Grange said. "If Belanfield was in the car and shooting at Tom, that means he's dirty. And if he's dirty for any of these companies, we need to look closely at all of them to see which could be involved with the virus."

Lily scanned the list, zeroing in right away on one that caught her attention. "What about Delor Pharmaceuticals?"

"What about them?" Mac asked.

"I remember reading an article last year about Delor having financial difficulties due to a recall of one of their prominent drugs. It hit them pretty hard."

"Interesting," Grange said. "I wonder what a pharmaceutical company would be willing to do to get hold of a potentially harmful virus?"

"A company cornering the market on the cure for a virus no one has ever seen could make billions," Mac added.

"Oh, my God," Lily said. "You're right."

"Good plan from a business standpoint," Mac said. "They want the virus, they want to develop the drug for it, then they want to let loose the virus on the population and be the first to come up with the drug to cure it."

"Damn," Spence said. "That's vicious."

"Sadly, it's often how big business works. They don't care about hurting the little guy," Lily said, shaking her head. Now she really wanted to nail them.

"Which means, if we can tie Delor to the attempts to steal the virus, we've got this case nailed," Grange said.

Excited, Lily clicked on Delor Pharmaceuticals. "Let's see what we can find out about them."

Of course, they already knew Belanfield was tied into Delor, which in itself wasn't damning evidence, since Belanfield was affiliated with several major companies. His front was a security company, though that was bullshit, of course. He was hired muscle, and obviously a hit man, since he was involved in Tom's attempted murder.

But there had to be more, because Belanfield took orders—he didn't give them. They had to find out who was directly responsible for putting this together.

"Got it," she said. "Monty Richardson."

"Who's that?" Mac asked.

"He's on the board at the museum in Chicago. He was my contact, employed my firm to test the new security team they'd hired. If you look at the chart here, he's also on the board of directors for Delor Pharmaceuticals."

"So there's your connection," Pax said.

She nodded. "He knew night security was lax at the museum. He thought he was doing the right thing by making sure it was tight. The last thing he wanted was to have that artifact, aka the virus, stolen."

"Which is exactly what happened when Mac lifted it," Grange said.

"They had to know that could happen, that someone would eventually figure out where the virus might be," Mac said.

"And Richardson couldn't afford to have anyone not affiliated with the museum covering security. It would arouse suspicion."

"Which meant he had to keep Belanfield outside," Mac said. "Which I'd bet is exactly where he was. He was the one who shot at us that night," he said to Lily.

"Of course," Lily said. "Belanfield saw you break in and take the virus. It was his job as outside man to insure no one took it."

"And when we disappeared with it, both Richardson and Delor were all over Belanfield's ass, leading Belanfield to climb all over ours in a big way," Mac said.

"Well, aren't you two popular," Spence teased.

Mac laughed. "Not in a way we wanted to be."

"Okay, so now we have the players figured out," Lily said. "What next? I assume we can't just call in the cops with this information?"

"Not exactly," Grange said. "We don't have proof, just supposition. But Delor's corporate headquarters are here in Dallas. Which means we need to set a trap, and we need to do this ourselves, under the radar, as always."

"My favorite part," Diaz said with a grin.

"Okay, this is easy," AJ said. "Bargain with the virus."

"How?" Mac asked.

"Contact Richardson directly. Tell him you have the virus and you're willing to deal for money."

"Do you think he'd buy that?" Lily asked.

AJ shrugged. "I don't see why not. Dirty guys like that think anyone can be bought for the right price. I see it all the time."

"He's right," Grange said.

"But who's going to contact him?" Rick asked.

"I will," Lily said.

"I don't think so."

She looked at Mac. "Why not?"

"Too dangerous."

She rolled her eyes. "Are we going to do this again?"

"Lily. This isn't small chips. This is major."

"I realize that. But I'm the logical choice. I already know him. Richardson hired me. Belanfield knows I hopped on the back of your bike after you took the virus."

"She's right," Grange said. "She is the logical choice as contact person."

Mac stood and brushed his fingers through his hair. "I don't like this."

"I know you don't, but it makes sense. I contact Richardson, tell him I've nabbed the virus away from you and I'm willing to sell it to him. You know he'll fall over himself to get it back. Then all we have to do is wait and see what he does with it."

"Right," Spence said. "And we'll be there, ready to protect Lily as well as track Richardson."

"Exactly," Grange said.

"I know. It does make sense. And of course we'll expect him to take the bait, buy the virus, and run it right over to Delor Pharmaceuticals," Mac said.

Lily nodded, excitement making the blood rush through her veins. She could hardly sit still. "And then we somehow figure out how to call in the authorities once we have Richardson tied firmly into Delor, with the stolen virus on the premises."

"I'll take care of that part," Grange said.

"But we don't want to give him the actual virus," Lily said. "Right?"

"No, we'll mix up a fake batch," Pax said. "I'll take care of that."

"Weird science in action," Spence said, rolling his eyes. "Try not to blow up the lab this time."

"That wasn't my fault," Pax said.

"There's a story I want to hear someday," Lily said.

"All right." Grange stepped to the front of the classroom. "We need to get our assignments in order and set up a time line. First thing we need to do is have Lily make a call and see if Richardson will take the bait."

Lily nodded and looked up Richardson's cell phone number, the one he'd given her when he'd hired her firm to test security. She moved over to the secure line and made the call, with Grange listening in. Richardson answered on the second ring.

"Hello?"

"Mr. Richardson, this is Lily West."

He paused for only a second, no doubt shocked as hell to hear from her.

"Miss West, we've been so worried about you after the theft at the museum. Are you all right?"

"I'm fine."

"We assumed you'd been kidnapped. Where are you?"

"Mr. Richardson, let's cut through the bullshit right away, shall we? I know all about the virus hidden in the artifact, and how deeply you're involved in all this."

He went silent again for a few seconds. "I don't know what you're talking about."

"Yes you do. There's a potentially fatal virus that was hidden in the traveling artifacts. That's what you hired me to protect, that's what you were afraid would be stolen because of the lack of adequate security at the museum. And you were right. It was stolen. The good news for you is that I've finally stolen it back."

"How do I know you're not working for the police?"

She snorted. "I was a cop once, Mr. Richardson, and I could have been one for my lifetime and never made any money. Now, are you interested, or do I go find another buyer? I need some cash."

Another few seconds of silence. This time his voice wasn't as friendly. "What do you want?"

"One million dollars in exchange for the virus."

"That's insane."

"You want this virus back, don't you?"

"Where are you?"

"Dallas."

"I can be there tomorrow night."

"With the money?" she reiterated, trying to sound impatient, as if she was anxious for cash.

"Yes, Miss West. With the money. You just make sure you're there with the virus."

They made arrangements for a time and meeting place, then Lily hung up, her palms sweating and her heart pounding against her chest.

"You did great." Grange stood and squeezed her shoulder. "Relax now. We have a lot to do before tomorrow night."

She stood, rolled her shoulders back to ease the tension, and turned to Mac. The others had already filed out, working on their assigned tasks.

"Shall we go join them?" she asked.

"I guess."

"What's wrong? You're worried about me, aren't you?"

"I'm trying not to be. I know you're capable."

"Thanks. For both the compliment and the concern."

"I just don't like this setup. It puts you front and center in the danger zone. This isn't your deal. You didn't sign up for this life."

She shrugged. "This is what I've always wanted to do, Mac. This kind of life, this adventure. The hint of danger, the chance to right a wrong—all those things my father kept me from doing when I was on the force."

"And it's a part of you I love. When I saw you that night at the museum—how much you'd changed—I was stunned, but I loved how kick-ass and competent you were. It was like you'd grown into your own skin, Lily, like you were doing what you were born to do. So while I'll always worry about you, I would never stand in the way of you doing something you love, something you're damn good at."

She smiled at him, understood exactly where he was coming from. "Knowing what I know now, the danger you're in, I feel the same way. I'm so proud of you for what you've done with your life, the way you've turned it around, but I'll always be concerned when you go on an assignment. I can't help it, because I'm in love with you."

"Doesn't make sense, does it?"

"Actually, it does. If we didn't love each other, we wouldn't care about the danger. When I go out there tomorrow night, I'll feel safe because I know your eyes will be on my back."

He took her hand and they moved into the lab, watching Pax create a duplicate of the virus, laughing when he called it green alien goo. By the time he was finished, Lily couldn't tell the difference between the original and the copy, down to the Plexiglas container housing the vial. It was a perfect replica, even to the fluorescent green color.

"How very comic book this color is," Pax said dryly.

They spent time working on the meeting spot. Lily was going to meet Richardson at a public restaurant at a busy intersection, which would give the Wild Riders plenty of places to hide in plain sight. They'd be on bikes and in cars, ready to move in just in case anything happened. Lily's purse and her car were going to be wired so she could record what went down.

It was late, and they'd gone over the plan several times. Grange told them they'd review the details again tomorrow, but that she looked like she needed some sleep.

She *was* tired. It had been an eventful night, and it was already three in the morning. Mac led her upstairs and closed the door to his room. She yawned and stretched, ready to climb into bed and pass out, but he grabbed her around the waist and pulled her against him, covering her mouth with a kiss that stole her breath.

Tiredness evaporated in an instant as he slammed her against the wall, pressing his hard body against hers. Pinned, her senses went on overload as she felt every steely inch of him, from the wall of his chest to his quickly hardening cock sliding against her hip.

Passion exploded as she felt the wild, urgent need within him, as if he wanted this because it could be the last time they would be together. She knew better, but she understood him better than he gave her credit for. She loved this side of him, this primitive, animalistic instinct. His mouth still against hers, he jerked at the button of her jeans, slamming the zipper down and pushing her jeans and panties to the floor. She stepped out of them in a hurry while he unzipped his jeans, drawing them open only enough to pull out his cock.

She reached for it, wrapping her fingers around his pulsing heat. He gripped her buttocks, lifting her onto his cock then pushing into her until he was buried deep. She whimpered against his mouth, pushing her tongue against his.

The ride was wild and harsh. She tore her fingers through his hair, pulled at him as he thrust deeply inside her with relentless strokes. He demanded, and she responded, knowing she wasn't going to last long, feeling the insane rush to completion tunneling through her.

Mac tensed, shuddering against her.

"Dammit," he said, "Come."

Knowing he was so close so fast was her undoing. She shrieked as she came in a lightning burst of sensation that ended their play all too quickly.

Oh, but she was wrong. It wasn't over, because he wasn't going to let her off that easily. He kept at her, still holding her up with his hands as he powered inside her. She was so wet she poured over him, mindless with ecstasy as he brought her to the brink again. This time, he went with her, yelling out as he came, pushing her back against the wall and groaning against her sweat-soaked neck.

She felt limp as a dishrag when he finally set her back on her feet. Good thing he kept his arm wrapped around her. In fact, he didn't seem to want to let go, just stepped backward, stumbling over whatever was on the floor, and fell onto the bed, carrying her with him.

He kissed the top of her head, pulled her next to him, and yanked the covers over them both.

She smiled and sighed in utter contentment. If this was how the rest of her life played out, she'd be one happy woman.

sixteen

BY THE TIME EVENING HIT THE NEXT DAY, LILY HAD GONE OVER the plan so many times she could recite it by memory. The route was lined out; she had practiced every possible conversation and scenario that could go down with Richardson. She knew which way she could turn and run if she got into trouble, not that she'd even have to, because one signal from her and someone would be at her side in a second.

Since they'd be in a public place, the chance of Richardson pulling a gun on her was very slim. She was going to be fine. In fact, she wasn't worried at all. Excited, yes, but not scared.

Mac had been pacing like a caged animal all day, making her repeat the plan, role-play potential scenarios so she'd know what to do in case Richardson did something unexpected. She'd never been so well prepared. She was so ready, in fact, that she was about to scream if they didn't get moving.

She'd eaten, showered, and dressed, and Mac had shadowed her every step of the way. She loved him, she really did, but if he didn't give her some space and soon, she was going to have to shoot him. Though she understood his protectiveness, he was starting to annoy her.

And the other guys had noticed it, though Mac was so coiled with tension even they kept their distance, didn't offer up any teasing comments like they normally would. Lily just shook her head and told him to relax.

"I am relaxed."

"You are not. You're so wound up you're liable to shoot some poor senior citizen who walks out of the restaurant and crosses in front of me."

He tilted his head to the side. "Give me a little credit, Lily."

She laughed. "Just trying to get you to lighten up a bit."

"You worry about your part. I'll take care of my own."

They had an hour before they had to leave, because Grange wanted everyone in position well before Lily was due to meet Richardson, just in case he showed up early or put some of his people in strategic positions. Lily picked up a book to read. The rest of the guys were otherwise occupied.

Mac paced.

"Does he always do this before a job?" she asked AJ.

"Hell no. Usually he takes a nap."

"So it's me."

"Yeah, babe, sorry. It's you."

She sighed and resumed reading, trying to ignore the man attempting to wear a hole in the wood floor in front of her.

Except his boots squeaked, which made ignoring him impossible.

Squick, squick, squick.

She heaved a disgusted sigh and dropped the book in her lap.

"Mac, I'm armed," she said, glaring at him in the hopes he would understand her utter frustration. She had reached the end of her rope. "If you don't stop that goddamn pacing I'm going to conduct target practice on your feet."

It wasn't just her, either, because the others in the living area were staring at Mac, too, and not in a nice way.

"Fine," he shot back, dropping into the nearest chair.

"Thank you." She just wanted quiet. A few minutes of silence to relax and get her thoughts in order. She knew the next several hours were going to be intense and she didn't want to get nervous now. Calm was essential because if she fell apart in a jittery mess when this went down, they were going to lose everything, including the chance to bring down Richardson and Delor Pharmaceuticals.

Fortunately, Mac calmed down. She dove into her book and felt the tension melt away. At least until Grange walked out.

"Everyone ready?"

So much for relaxing.

She stood and nodded as Grange approached her and Mac.

"Don't worry about anything. We'll all be there to take care of you."

"I'm not worried." *Much.*

She slid into a vehicle they'd equipped with a tracking device, just in case. The guys following in cars had her monitored on GPS. Every contingency had been planned for, "just in case."

She drove slow, the others hightailing it out of there, some on bikes, others in cars. A couple of them drove muscle cars, one a pretty fancy Lexus, and another a beat-up Impala. They'd all blend in one way or the other, though the bikes weren't going to be parked where Richardson could spot them. Since she and Mac had left the museum on one, they didn't want to give him or Belanfield, if he happened to be there, any reason to think this was a setup.

They wanted Richardson to think Lily was doing this on her own.

By the time Lily got to the restaurant, she knew the others were already in place. She'd taken the city streets instead of the highway, had made multiple turns and backtracked a couple of times.

The restaurant was one of those big chain places, really popular. The menu offered a variety of dishes, and the place was always packed.

She pulled into the parking lot, lucky enough to find a spot right in front as a car pulled away just as she drove up. A quick glance at her watch told her she had about ten minutes to spare before her designated meet time with Richardson. The fake virus was tucked neatly into a purselike bag so she wouldn't call attention to herself when she stood out in front. The restaurant was very well lit, so she foresaw no problems.

Those ten minutes were the longest of her life. She stayed in the car, looking around her, in her side mirrors and rearview mirror, every passing minute tying her stomach up in knots. She practiced deep, even breathing, reassuring herself that this plan was going to go off without a single hitch.

FINALLY, IT WAS TIME. SHE SLUNG THE PURSE OVER HER SHOULDER and stepped out of the car, searching the parking lot and intersection. Even she couldn't spot the other Wild Riders. The guys really were good at hiding in plain sight.

There was a bench out front. Since it was eight o'clock at night and well into prime dinner hour, the place was busy. People were going inside, a few loitering around outside, no doubt waiting for tables. Exactly the way they'd wanted it so she wouldn't be alone when she met Richardson. Lily sat on the bench and affected a casual pose, trying to look as if she was waiting for someone to join her.

A black sedan pulled into the parking lot, its windows tinted so dark she couldn't see through any except the front windshield. The driver wore a black hat shielding his face, so she couldn't make him out. Lily tensed as the car pulled past the front of the restaurant, then slowed to a stop. The back door opened and a man stepped out, the cut of his clothes spelling out money. He stood and commanded attention, from his steel gray eyes to his slicked back, shocking white hair and the take-no-shit look on his patrician features. He motioned to her and she stood, walking over to his car.

That had to be Richardson, though she'd never met the man. He'd dealt with her boss in person and with her by telephone only.

"Miss West?"

"Mr. Richardson."

"We cannot possibly do this here," he said. "It's too busy."

She let her lips curl in a smile. "That's the whole idea, isn't it?"

"It's totally unacceptable. Even the police prowl this area to keep it safe."

She shrugged. "Not my problem."

He arched a brow. "Is that what you want? The police to catch us?"

She snorted and leaned against his shiny sedan, earning her a frown. "Hardly. Then I wouldn't get my money."

"If I hand you a suitcase full of money and you in turn hand over the virus out here in front of this restaurant, it's going to look like a drug deal going down. Plus, there are surveillance cameras."

"What?"

He inclined his head toward the front of the restaurant and the parking area.

"Do be discreet when you're gawking at them," he added.

She turned as unobtrusively as she could, but sure enough, he was right. Cameras were mounted on the corners of the restaurant, shooting toward the parking area, and on the parking lot poles, their viewpoint toward the front of the restaurant.

"Smile," Richardson said. "You're on *Candid Camera*."

Shit. "I didn't know about the cameras." That part was honest. She hadn't paid the slightest attention to those. Did Grange know about them when they'd selected the restaurant? She wished she was in contact with him. With the wire hidden in her purse, she knew they were hearing her, but she couldn't communicate with the other Wild Riders.

Dammit. Now what?

"Slide into the car with me. We'll take a little ride."

Her heart pounded so hard the blood rushed in her ears and she could barely hear herself think. But she maintained her cool, crossing her arms. "Said the spider to the fly. How dumb do you think I am?"

"Miss West, as I previously stated, there are surveillance cameras here. If you turn up missing or dead, my face is now on those cameras as the last person to meet with you. That would immediately make me the prime suspect. So to use your own words . . . how dumb do you think I am?"

Okay, he had a point. She didn't like this, but the key was to turn over the virus to him and see where he took it. Her slipping into his car meant that the guys were going to follow. Was Richardson really stupid enough to do her harm?

She had mere seconds to make this decision and she didn't want to lose him. Not when they were this close to breaking this case wide open.

"I want my money." She tried to look greedy and desperate.

"Then let's go. This will only take a moment and you can be on your way. I just don't want to do this so publicly."

"I have a better idea." The thought struck her. "I'll follow you in my car. It's the blue Mustang right over there." *Much safer.*

She tilted her head back and he followed with his eyes, then looked back at her. "Ever the cautious one, aren't you?"

"It's what's kept me alive this long, Mr. Richardson. Not that I think you have any unsavory plans or anything, but I'm not really comfortable sliding into your car there and taking off to parts unknown. Can you blame me for that?"

Now it was his turn to consider. She waited.

"Very well," he said. "We'll only go a few short blocks. Someplace a little less . . . populated, and with no cameras to implicate either of us."

She nodded. "Fine with me. I'll follow you."

She pushed off his car and walked back to hers, hoping like hell the guys would figure out how to follow her without being seen. She trusted them to know their job.

Richardson's car pulled away and she followed, out of the parking lot and into the main intersection. She kept watch behind her, but didn't recognize any of the Wild Riders' cars or bikes.

They were somewhere out there, though. She knew it.

"I hope you guys heard all that," she said into the wireless mic hidden in her car.

True to his word, they didn't drive far. There was a strip mall nearby, and they pulled into that lot. She drove up next to him. The shopping center wasn't very well attended, a lot of the stores closed, but at least he hadn't led her into an alley. There were plenty of places for the guys to keep watch and pull into the lot should she need help.

Still, the venue had changed. She might just be on her own. As she saw it she had two choices here—walk away and lose the chance to follow Richardson after he got the virus in hand, or take a chance that he was on the up-and-up and simply didn't want witnesses to them making the exchange. She was operating on instinct here, and she got the feeling that Richardson just wanted the virus.

She got out of her car and Richardson opened the back door, beckoning to her. A breeze had picked up, whipping her hair. She looked around, once again not seeing the guys. Still, she knew they were somewhere close.

They had to be.

She moved over to the car door.

"I need my man to pat you down, make sure you're not wearing a wire."

She expected that. That's why the car and her bags were equipped with the wires for communication, not her. "Fine."

The driver did a quick pat down and nodded at Richardson.

"Where is it?" Richardson asked.

She leaned against the side of the car.

"In this bag."

"Step inside the car, please."

The driver held the door for her. She kept her distance. "Tell him to get in the front passenger seat and I will. I want my door left open."

Richardson shot her a look of utter exasperation, as if she was inconveniencing him. Too bad. But he did nod to his driver. "Do it."

The driver moved around and slid in, and Richardson scooted over to make room for her in the back. Only then did Lily slide into the seat vacated by Richardson, but she left the door open.

"Do you have the money?" She wanted to make sure he thought the money was her primary motivation.

"Right here." He patted a hard-sided briefcase next to him.

"Let me see it."

Richardson drew the case onto his lap, flipped the latches open, and pulled the lid up. Lily did a quick calculation of the bills she saw on the top, though the money wasn't relevant.

She made sure to look appropriately wide-eyed and hungry.

"Considering your father's vast wealth, I'm surprised the money is so important to you," Richardson said.

Lily arched a brow. "How did you know?"

He closed the briefcase with a smug smile. "I make it my business to know who I'm dealing with, Miss West. I know everything about you, from where you went to high school and college, to your service record with the Dallas PD and your current position with the private investigation firm in Chicago."

This guy was good.

"So answer my question. Your father is a very rich man. I'm sure you could have everything you want. Why are you doing this?"

She shrugged and leaned back against the seat, stretching out her legs. "My father isn't happy with my choice of career. He wanted me to go into business with him. We've been . . . at odds ever since I entered the police academy."

Richardson nodded. "He cut you off financially."

"Yes. Several years ago."

"You didn't like that."

She snorted. "I hated it. I might have wanted to take my career in my own direction at first, but I started to miss the finer things, the lifestyle I'd grown accustomed to."

His lips lifted in a faint hint of a smile. "I can appreciate a woman who enjoys luxuries."

"That money will go a long way to insuring I can once again live the kind of life I was used to. And no one will ever know how I got it since I am related to a very rich man. It wouldn't be at all unusual for me to live an opulent lifestyle, knowing who my father is."

"You have this all planned out, don't you?"

"I didn't at first, but after I got involved in all this, after I found out what was *really* stolen from the museum, I developed a plan. I just had to find the right moment to get the vial and run off with it, then I put the pieces together and figured out it was you who wanted it back."

"You're very good at your job."

She smiled, thinking of the ultimate satisfaction she was going to get when Richardson was behind bars. "Thank you."

"Let me have the vial, please."

She handed over the bag. Richardson pulled the Plexiglas container out, inspected the vial within it, and nodded. He handed the briefcase over to her.

"So, what are you planning to do with that stuff?" she asked.

He frowned. "Do you have any idea what this is?"

"No. The guy I was with didn't tell me. He said he didn't know, only that it was worth a lot of money, so I pretended to throw in with him for a piece of the action. It was only a matter of time before he started to trust me, then I gave him the slip and contacted you."

Richardson seemed to consider that for a moment. "I can only imagine how you did that."

"I have my ways," she said, batting her lashes so he had no doubt of her meaning.

"I'm certain you do."

The way he looked at her—God, this guy was a creep. She couldn't wait to get away from him. "So are you going to tell me what that stuff is?"

Richardson slid his finger under her chin and tipped it up. "It's best you remain ignorant of some things, Miss West."

She shrugged, wanting to slap his hand away, but maintaining her calm. "Makes no difference to me, as long as I have this." She patted the case and held out her hand to shake his. "Nice doing business with you, Mr. Richardson. Hopefully we'll cross paths again. If you ever need my services . . ."

"Does it bother you that you've given up your good ways and turned to a life of . . . crime?"

She snorted. "A girl's gotta do what's necessary to survive."

Richardson smiled and nodded. "You're a very resourceful young woman, Miss West. I'll be sure to contact you should I ever have need of someone with your unique . . . talents."

"You do that. I like money." She stepped out of the car and moved back to her own, making sure she didn't look back as Richardson drove away. She didn't want to give the impression she was watching him, though she knew the others were. It wasn't more than a minute before she heard the revving engine of a vehicle pulling up next to hers.

It was Mac, in a sweet-looking Trans Am, circa midseventies or so.

She tossed the briefcase in the back and slipped into the passenger seat, relieved to see him. "Sorry. I didn't know what else to do. He insisted on the change in location because of the security cameras."

"Yeah, we heard you on the mic. Tricky, but it worked out fine. The restaurant recently installed the security cameras out front. We didn't know about them either, or that Richardson would freak out about them. Major fuckup. Sorry."

She shrugged. "Like you said, it worked out. We still have to link him to Delor or Belanfield."

"We'll figure that out at his next stop."

"What about my car?" she asked.

"Somone's gonna pick it up and take it back to headquarters. Don't worry."

Mac gunned the engine and Lily's head shot back against the headrest. She grabbed for her seat belt as he pulled out onto the street. "The others already picked up his tail and are following. We'll lag behind and join in, taking over a few blocks down the road. That way if his driver is watching the rearview mirror for cars, he'll keep seeing different ones and won't think he's being followed."

The Wild Riders all kept in touch via a communication system that the government supplied them. It was pretty slick, just a clip-on earpiece with internal voice mic in one self-contained unit. It was hands free, so even the guys on bikes could stay in touch. In this way, when one veered off, the others knew exactly where the others were. Whoever was following Richardson could let the others know.

Right now it was Rick in charge of tailing Richardson.

"He's going north on Fifth Street," Rick said, the sound of his bike revving clear as a bell on their communication system.

Mac had handed her an earpiece to wear so she could stay abreast of the action. Every mile or so the cars would switch out. Soon it was their turn, and Mac made a smooth transition, sliding onto the street as Pax pulled off. Mac pulled within three cars of Richardson, leaving him in the left-hand lane while they stayed in the right.

"Isn't that a little risky? What if he turns left?"

Mac grinned. "This car handles great. I can zip into the left lane and make a turn if I need to. Besides, AJ is running parallel one street over. He'll pick him up on the next block if we miss a turn."

"You all have it covered, don't you?"

Mac laughed. "We hope so."

They followed Richardson only a short distance, as the car pulled into a condominium complex. Mac went on ahead and Spence took over.

"Where's he going?" Lily asked.

"No clue."

"He's picking up someone," Spence said. "Tall, beefy guy. Bald. Dressed all in black."

Lily wrinkled her nose. "That sounds like Belanfield."

"He's getting into the front passenger seat and they're taking off now," Spence said. "I'll follow for the next leg."

Within ten miles it was Mac and Lily's turn again. They were on the interstate now, and it was easier to keep an eye on Richardson's vehicle as well as stay far enough back and hidden within the flow of traffic.

He exited the interstate and they followed, discreetly of course. Traffic was heavy so they were about four cars behind. Richardson's car pulled onto a side street almost immediately. Diaz picked them up on his bike, weaving in and out of traffic while Mac drove off.

"They're stopping at a convenience store," Diaz said.

"Delor Pharmaceuticals is within that complex of buildings," Lily said, pointing off to their right.

"Okay, this is all going according to plan," Grange said. "We're going to assume they're heading to Delor. Everyone roll. Diaz, stay on them."

Mac pushed it, hard, careening around the corner and gunning the engine. The side street he took was deserted, so he cranked up the speed. Mac parked on the east side of the building, where it was dark, well hidden, and out of view of the security cameras. The rest of them were already there.

Mac and Lily were going inside. Mac with a camera to record what they could, Lily because she might recognize some of the higher-ups at Delor.

Mac had hated that part, but Lily insisted. Besides, it wasn't as if she was untrained. She could handle it, and she was excited to be a part of taking down Richardson and Belanfield. Rick would go with them since he was their breaking and entering expert. The rest of them would stay outside and monitor.

Mac and Lily put on white coats with IDs denoting them as Delor research personnel. Grange didn't think they'd need them, but just in case they ran into security, they'd need covers and a plausible reason for wandering the hallways. Everyone would be armed.

"Okay," Rick said. "Their codes are simple, nothing as complex as government codes. A simple keypad structure at the side doors. Code was like child's play to break. Front door is trickier, with armed security and card pass required, but we won't be going in that way."

"AJ is masquerading as the local delivery guy," Grange reminded them, going over each step again. "He'll be making a rush delivery when Belanfield and Richardson come in through the front door. While AJ's getting his late delivery package signed for by night security, he'll be able to tell us what direction our guys go. By then, we'll already be through the side door, ready to pick up two men on infrared."

"Infrared is already set up so we can track body count," Spence said. "I'll monitor from out here and let you know who's in there and where they are. At this late hour, the place is a ghost town. Mainly security."

"Which is exactly what Richardson wants," Lily said. "Fewer curious eyes when he drops off the virus."

"And exactly what we want. Easier to follow them. Get going," Grange said.

"We've set up interference for their monitoring systems so when we open the door it won't show on security's detail," Rick said. He punched in the seven-digit security code and pulled the heavy door. Lily held her breath as it clicked, expecting to hear alarms sound. But when Rick turned the handle, the door opened, and she exhaled in relief. They stepped inside the semidark hallway and started moving toward the front of the building. Austere white walls and nondescript gray carpet. Their feet made no noise at all on the floor. They advanced down the hall as if they had a purpose.

"Your earsets are tuned into voices," Spence said. "You'll have to get close to them to pick theirs up."

"Try to look like you belong there," Grange reminded them.

By the time they got to the end of the corridor, there was no one at the front desk. They pulled into a nearby hallway and waited.

"Belanfield and Richardson headed straight for the elevators," Diaz said into their earsets. "I was there long enough to watch the elevator stop at the second floor."

"Let's go," Mac said, leading the way toward the stairway door.

Though there were open stairs in the center lobby, they were located directly behind the reception desk, and Mac didn't want to risk the guards' scrutiny.

He pushed open the door at the top of the second floor. "Clear."

"Infrared is picking up two people in a room just to the left of the stairwell," Spence said. "Otherwise the floor is empty."

"That's got to be them." Mac opened the door and they stepped out of the stairwell and into the corridor, moving to the right instead of the left. He peered around the corner. "The conference room is all glass. Belanfield and Richardson are the only ones in there." He lifted his tiny video camera and started filming

Lily peered over his shoulder, getting a perfect view of the Delor Pharmaceuticals sign in the back of the conference room, with Belanfield and Richardson standing directly to the left of the sign. It was absolutely perfect.

"I'm getting their voices," she said.

"Camera is sensitive enough to pick it up, too," Mac whispered over his shoulder.

Lily turned around, making sure Rick was right behind her and in position, watching their backs. She and Rick had their guns drawn, prepared in case of . . . anything. Mac was in charge of videotaping the exchange in the conference room.

Belanfield looked at his watch. "Where is he? I don't have all night."

"He'll be arriving shortly," Richardson said.

So, they were meeting someone. Who?

"Someone's coming in," Diaz signaled. "One man just pulled up in front and parked in the executive spot."

Lily hoped this was who and what they were waiting for. She wanted this over with.

"You've got company," Spence said. "He's coming up in the elevator."

They ducked back into the stairwell until Spencer gave them the okay.

"You're clear. He's in the conference room now with the other two," Spence said after a few minutes.

They moved out again and Mac took up position with the camera.

"Do you have the vial?" the man asked.

"Yes."

"I know him," Lily said. "That's Mitchell Delor, chairman of the board of Delor Pharmaceuticals. He took over about ten years ago after his father died. His father was very conservative, a really nice man. Ran the company well and legitimately. Mitchell is arrogant and likes to take risks."

"Risky enough to get his corporation in deep shit?" Mac whispered.

Lily nodded. "Likely."

Richardson handed Lily's bag over to Belanfield, who took the virus out of the bag and brought it over to Mitchell.

"Finally," Mitchell said. "You did well. I trust there will be no more trouble."

"It's all under control now," Richardson said. "We retrieved the virus and the woman who had it was paid off."

Mitchell frowned. "I don't like loose ends."

"She didn't even know what she had," Richardson argued.

Mitchell looked at Belanfield. "She knows enough. Take care of her."

Belanfield nodded. "I'll find her. It'll be dealt with."

Lily's throat went dry. Good thing Belanfield hadn't been in the car with Richardson, or she'd have been fighting for her life—or possibly losing it.

"That's unnecessary." Richardson seemed uncomfortable.

"Do you realize what's at stake here?" Mitchell asked. "Bil-

lions of dollars, and you stand to profit handsomely when I turn
this company around. So spare me your thoughts because I'm not
interested in hearing them. You let me take care of the minor details, since you botched this up from the start. Having this virus
and letting it loose on a small section of the population, then suddenly cornering the market on a miracle cure will bring Delor out
of potential bankruptcy. We'll all be rich."

Lily was seething. The bastard. How could he be so heartless?
To use innocent people that way, to risk their lives, all in the name
of capitalism and saving his own ass?

"You've got enough," Grange said. "Get out of here."

They started to back up so they could move down the stairwell,
but their movements must have caught Belanfield's eye, because
he frowned, pulled a gun out of his pocket, and pushed through
the conference room door in a flash, shouting down at the security
guards for assistance.

"We've been made," Mac said, taking a step forward.

Mac didn't even have his gun out. She did. "Get that camera
out of here," she said to Mac. "It's the only evidence we have."
She swerved in front of Mac, wanting to protect him and the video
he'd made. "I'll take care of this."

It all happened so quick. Belanfield rushing them from the
front, security guards coming at them from the open stairwell behind them. She wanted to help Rick, but she had to take on Belanfield. She aimed her gun, but Belanfield already had his out and
targeting—for Mac. She took aim and fired at Belanfield, hitting
him at the same time he fired off a shot.

Oh God, don't hit Mac. Please, no. She did her best to shove Mac
out of the way. It must have worked, because she was slammed
against the wall and a rush of searing hot pain hit her left shoulder. Her left hand didn't work; she was suddenly numb, and cold.
She sank to the floor and everything went fuzzy. She heard shout-

ing and saw a tangle of feet around her, but she was sick to her stomach.

Don't throw up. There was a battle going on and she so didn't want to throw up when she really should be shooting someone.

SON OF A BITCH, THIS WAS GOING DOWN SO FAST MAC'S HEAD was spinning. Lily had taken a hit and was crumbling down the wall. He wanted to stop and run to her, but he couldn't. Belanfield, though limping, was still shooting. Mac ducked, took aim, and hit him point-blank in the chest. Belanfield went facedown on the carpet.

Mac pivoted back to the stairwell to help Rick, who fortunately already had his gun drawn on the two security guards. Mac ran into the conference room where Delor and Richardson were holed up.

"Don't move!" he hollered, training his weapon on them.

Rick moved into the room with the security guards

"Grange, we need damage control in here now!" Mac yelled.

But Grange was obviously already aware of what was going on, because the rest of the guys stormed in within seconds.

"See to Lily," Grange said to Mac.

That was all he needed. He nodded and ran to Lily. Her eyes were closed.

"Lily, can you hear me?"

He checked her pulse, which was a little fast, but at least her heart was beating. Her shoulder was bleeding bad. He ripped the white lab coat and pressed pieces of cloth inside her shirt, right against the wound.

"Need help?" Spence asked.

"I need to get her out of here."

Spence nodded. "Let's go. I'll drive."

"You can't take her to a hospital. I'll have medical personal at headquarters standing by." Grange was already taking out his cell phone.

Mac nodded and carefully lifted Lily into his arms. He didn't care where they went as long as someone could help her when they got there.

seventeen

"DON'T MOVE."

Lily swung her legs over the side of the bed, letting them dangle there. That was as far as Mac was going to let her get. Her mutinous stare was met by his equally determined one.

"Mac, I'm fine. Honestly. If I don't get out of this bed and go downstairs, I'm going to scream. And if I scream, I'll rip these stitches. You don't want that, do you?"

Mac thought Lily was the worst patient ever. She woke up when he got to the car, threw up down the side of his Trans Am, laughed about it, apologized for barfing all over the new paint job, then proceeded to complain all the way back to the house about having to leave Delor before all the good stuff happened.

True to his word, Grange had a doctor and nurse waiting for them at the house when they arrived. The bullet was lodged just at the edge of Lily's upper shoulder muscle; it had come out easily, and only required a few stitches. Doc said she passed out because she hit her head on the wall when the force of the bullet slammed her against it, and she probably had a slight concussion, then gave Mac instructions to watch her for the next twenty-four hours.

He gave Lily a shot of antibiotics and some pain medication should she need it and told her to rest for a few days. Other than that, he indicated she should be fine. She'd slept for a few hours, but woke up as soon as the guys started filing in.

"You stay here. I'll get details and tell you everything later."

"Bullshit. I'm going downstairs."

"You are the most stubborn woman I have ever met."

She smiled at him. "And you love me because of it."

He rolled his eyes. "No, I love you in spite of it."

"I'm going downstairs, Mac. With or without your help. But honestly, I'm still a little shaky so I could use your assistance."

Obviously he wasn't going to win this one. With a reluctant sigh he scooped her up in his arms. He'd cleaned her up after the doctor left. She was wearing shorts and a tank top, which meant he got to feel the smooth skin of her thighs against his arms as he carried her downstairs.

So not a good time to think sexual thoughts. It would be a while before Lily was ready for sex, but he was so damned relieved she was okay he wanted to jump her right now.

He was such a pervert.

"Hey, how's the patient?" AJ asked as the elevator door opened and they stepped out into the living room.

They were all gathered around, everyone just about to take a seat.

"I'm fine. Just a few stitches."

"You're tough," Spence said as Mac sat her down in the recliner. "Not a sissy, you know your stuff, and you take a bullet like a guy."

"Oh right. Just like a guy," she said, laughing. "Except for the passing out and throwing up part."

Spence shrugged. "Yeah, well, that couldn't be helped. I think you'd make a great addition to the Wild Riders."

Mac shot him a warning glare. "Don't even think about it."

As he perched on the side of the chair, Lily took his hand and gave it a gentle squeeze. "Don't be too sure about that," she said. "And thanks, Spence."

Paxton brought her a cup of coffee.

"Oooh, thank you. This is just what I needed."

She sipped and smiled at all the guys, who all looked adoringly at her. *Uh-huh.* They were all getting way too comfortable around Lily, making her feel like she was part of the gang.

She wasn't. He couldn't allow it.

They needed to have a talk. Seeing her crumple to the floor after getting shot reaffirmed she had no business in this line of work. Yes, she was a former cop and a private investigator, but she hadn't signed on to do this. He'd almost lost her. Anything could have happened, and she'd thrown herself in front of him without thinking about her own safety. She was entirely too daring. She didn't understand the risks.

And he couldn't do his job if he had to worry about Lily.

"So tell me everything," she said, pulling her legs up on the chair and tucking them behind her, cradling the cup between her hands. "I'm pissed I wasn't there to finish things up."

"Well, you were kind of busy bleeding and passing out," Rick said with a half grin.

"And taking a bullet for your guy," AJ said. "How sweet."

"Shut up," she said with a smile. "I was protecting the video camera."

"You were not," Spence said. "You just didn't want pretty boy here to get hurt."

"Hey." Mac shoved Spence, wondering sometimes if he was still in high school. "I can take care of myself. I didn't need Lily's help."

"You're welcome," Lily said with a frown.

"That's not what I meant."

"Whatever." She turned her gaze away from Mac and toward the others. "Fill me in."

"After Mac took you out, we brought the security guards into the conference room," Rick said.

"Though the security guys weren't implicated in this, we couldn't allow them to contact the police," Grange added. "So we had to tie them up in the conference room, along with Delor and Richardson. We left the video tape on the table and contacted the authorities, cleaned up any evidence, then left."

Lily nodded. "Because the Wild Riders work under the radar, you couldn't afford to be there when the authorities arrived, or to become directly involved as witnesses."

"Exactly. But we did leave Delor's video confession as evidence, and the real virus, and notified both the local police and the FBI. The virus will be recovered, and Delor and Richardson are all in very deep shit."

"Belanfield?" she asked.

"Dead," Diaz said.

"Good. He was bad news, doing dirty deeds for a lot of companies for a long time. I never trusted the man."

"Besides the fact that he shot you. We'd have had to kill him for that alone," Pax said.

"Awww, how sweet." She felt herself blush at Paxton's wayward compliment.

"I've heard from our government contact that the FBI swooped in and took control of the virus. It should be back where it belongs shortly," Grange said.

"Thank God." That was Lily's biggest worry the entire time.

"And with the video in hand, we won't have to worry about Delor or Richardson. They're history."

"So why was the virus transported within the artifact?" Lily asked. "I never could figure that out."

"Delor had the virus manufactured overseas," Grange explained. "It wasn't like Richardson could ship it through regular channels, so they hid it in the Egyptian museum exhibit. And the exhibit was heavily guarded, so their people couldn't simply retrieve the artifact whenever they wanted."

"Were they intending to steal it at some point?"

"My guess is they were planning either a switch or an outright theft of the artifact once the exhibit made its way to Dallas," Grange said.

"Ah. That makes sense," she said. "Right under the noses of the police and the government, and no one would be the wiser."

"Exactly. The virus was cradled in the artifact, safely transported into the United States and from state to state. And because the museum exhibit was owned by another coutry, our government didn't have legal right to seize it."

Lily nodded. "Frightening to think what might have happened had the virus made its way into Delor Pharmaceuticals' hands."

"But it didn't," Mac reminded her.

"Because you're such a great thief." she teased.

"That's what I do, babe."

"Case closed?" she asked.

"Yup," Mac said.

She sighed and leaned back in the chair. "So now what?"

"Now you're free to go back to Chicago. Call your boss and let him know what's been going on."

"What you're saying is, you don't want me around here anymore."

"Oh, you can heal and stuff. But I think it would be best if you left."

Lily discarded the immediate urge to dump her cup of coffee in Mac's lap. Yes, he was acting like a caveman and a total ass, but she knew why.

He was afraid of losing her.

So while she was angry as hell about his alpha male insensitive behavior, she also knew he was trying to protect her by pushing her out of his life, because he loved her.

She wasn't going to let him.

"You think it would be better if I left."

"Wow, I think my favorite television show is on," AJ said, shooting up off the couch as if it had been set on fire.

"Mine, too." Rick was right behind him.

"Stay right there," Lily said. "There's no need to run off, any of you."

"There's an argument brewing. A man/woman argument. We don't want any part of it," Spence said.

Lily arched a brow. "And here all this time I thought you guys were tough."

"Angry females are worse than any enemy we could face," AJ said.

"Funny. And for your information, I'm not going anywhere, unless you all took some secret vote and decided I was a nuisance and unwanted." She laid her cup down on the end table and crossed her arms.

They all went silent, obviously not sure whether they wanted to take sides against Mac or incur her wrath.

"I think you're brave, talented, and gutsy, and you have a lot to offer our organization. You can be trusted, you're well trained, and you got off a nice shot to Belanfield before he took you down." Grange stood in front of her. "I do believe you could use a little training, like when *not* to step in front one of your team members in order to take a bullet, and when to keep emotion out of the game, but other than that, I think you'd make a fine team member of the Wild Riders. But if you work for us, you won't be assigned cases with Mac. You two could be a danger to each other."

Obviously Grange had no problem speaking his mind. She beamed under his praise, and understood his concerns. "Thank you. And you're right. I let my worry for Mac cloud my judgment. It won't happen again."

"It's not going to happen at all. She's not staying."

Lily refused to listen to Mac's railing, especially since his argument had no validity.

"I need a bath. Mac, would you mind helping me upstairs?"

He couldn't very well argue about that, so he picked her up and she said good night to the guys—God, what time was it, anyway—it had to be the middle of the night.

He took her to their room and set her on the bed.

"I'll run the tub water for you. Stay here. You'll need me to help you."

She nodded, not wanting to argue with him. She felt grimy, blood still caked her wound, and she wanted to wash her hair. Mac helped her into the tub. The bath felt wonderful, and she kept her injured arm above the level of the water. She closed her eyes and relaxed.

"I can wash your hair for you, if you'd like."

She smiled, knowing Mac hadn't left the bathroom, wouldn't leave her there alone. He'd been watching over her since the moment he'd run into her at the museum in Chicago. In his own misguided way, his idea to get rid of her was still watching over her.

Only it wasn't going to work—she wasn't leaving.

"I'd like that."

He left her only long enough to find a plastic pitcher, then filled it with warm water, wetting her hair and lathering shampoo onto his hands. Lily let out a low moan of utter ecstasy as he massaged her head.

"Your fingers are magic."

"I like touching you."

She sighed. He really was very good at washing her hair, tenderly rubbing her scalp and neck, lingering over the task instead of performing it as if it were something to be done in a hurry. He laid her head back and cupped her neck in the palm of his hand as he poured clean water over her hair to rinse it. He even did the whole process over again with conditioner.

He grabbed the sponge and soaped her body, dipping it into the water and rubbing it over her legs, her hips, her arms, circumventing her injury. He took special care of where she'd been shot, using a washcloth to gently scrub away the dried blood.

"Does it hurt?"

He was bent over the tub, his face only inches from hers.

"No."

"You were shot in almost the same place I was that night at the museum."

She offered the hint of a smile. "We'll have matching scars."

He pressed his lips to hers, a gentle sweep. Her breath caught and held, the moment so sweet and magical. The steam from the bathwater rose between them, and her heart pounded.

He pulled away, his gaze dark. "Seeing you shot scared the hell out of me, Lily."

Now he wasn't acting stupid, and she realized the depth of emotion reflected in his eyes. "I'm sorry. I wasn't trying to get shot."

"I had to do my job, ignoring you lying out there in the hallway, possibly bleeding to death, maybe even dead already. Do you know how that made me feel?"

"Yes." Because if their situations had been reversed, she'd have gone crazy. She reached up and cupped his cheek. "I wanted to protect you, thought I had a good shot at Belanfield."

"Like Grange said, you can't do that stuff. I was about to pull my gun when you pushed me to the side like you were some kind of superhero, and you ended up getting yourself shot. You can't let your emotions run the game, Lily."

"Yes. But I love you."

"I love you, too. But we have to put that love aside when we're working together. I can't work with you, knowing you'll put your own life on the line for mine."

She smiled. "That's what people who love each other do. Don't ever ask me to change that, because I won't. Would you?"

He closed his eyes for a second, then opened them and shook his head. "No. I guess I wouldn't."

"So where does that leave us?"

"I don't know. I don't want you to take those kinds of risks."

She sighed. "Okay. I'll work on it."

"You're going to have to. You can't do this and let emotion rule your judgment. Grange would never let you stay if you do."

"Grange said we couldn't work together," she said, her lips turned down in disappointment.

"I can change his mind. But he was right. We have to be able to do our jobs—both of us—without emotion."

"Can either of us do that?" she asked.

Mac shrugged. "I don't know, babe. I worry about you."

She studied him a minute, then nodded. "I don't ever want to be afraid to do what I love to do, Mac. My father tried to prevent me from following my dream. I really like this lifestyle. It's exciting, it fuels my love of adventure and law enforcement. It's everything I've ever wanted, and not within reach of my father's influence."

"And if I told you that you couldn't do this, that I refused to work with you because it was too dangerous for you, I'd be no better than your dad."

"I didn't say that."

"You didn't have to. I just did."

She knew this was difficult for him, that he did love her and want to protect her. But she also knew that she had to be allowed to stand on her own two feet, that she had to be allowed the freedom to grow and do what she really wanted to do—what she loved to do.

"I love you, Lily. I'll never stop worrying about you every time you're doing something dangerous. If I didn't worry, it would mean I didn't care. But I'd be ten times an asshole if I got in the way of you living your dream. If this is what you really want, then I won't stand in your way."

Her eyes filled with tears. He really did understand.

"Help me up."

He slipped his hand under her arms, then grabbed a towel and wrapped it around her, gently drying her off after he pulled her out of the tub.

"What now?" he asked.

"Love me. Make love to me. I need to feel you inside me."

He glanced down at her shoulder. "Your arm—"

"Is fine. I'm tough, Mac. I won't break. Try me."

He shook his head and picked her up, dragging his lips over hers.

Lily felt the rush of power—that same zing she'd felt with Mac since the very first time, and probably always would. Her body flushed with heat, her nipples tightening as Mac crushed her against him. Even though she felt the tension of his need, he was careful of her shoulder, easing her onto the bed.

He followed her there, sweeping his hand over her hip. His touch was so tender, as if he stroked her with reverence.

"I told you I won't break," she said.

"I know you won't, but I thought I'd lost you tonight. You're just going to have to deal with the fact that I want to learn every inch of your body again."

Her tough guy, the one she thought didn't care about her at all. She was oh so wrong. The depth of Mac's soul astounded her—the way he touched her was lava, his fingertips like molten fire along her skin.

He lay next to her, his body pressed up against hers. His cock was hard, so rigid and beautiful she wanted to touch it. She reached down, but Mac took her hand and laid it on the bed.

"Relax. Let me touch you."

He brushed his hand along her hip, down her thigh, letting his fingers sweep along her inner thigh. She sighed, spread her legs, needing to feel his fingers parting the folds of her pussy and dipping inside where she was wet and needy for him. She needed Mac to release the tension inside her.

But he didn't touch her there, instead bypassing her sweet spot to sweep over her hip again, palming her belly, swirling his fingers around her navel. The muscles of her abdomen rippled as she laughed.

"That tickles. I thought you were supposed to be relaxing me."

He cast her a devilish smile. "Workin' on it."

She raised her knees, planting her feet on the mattress. "I have a great idea. Rub my clit. Make me come. Very relaxing."

"You're so direct."

"I know what I like."

"I'll get there. Be patient. I'm still touching."

She blew out a breath. A loud breath, just so he'd know how fast she was losing patience.

Apparently he didn't care, because he grinned down at her with an evil leer and swept his hand upward, toward her breasts.

No. Not up! Down. But then he cupped her breast, letting his hand slide underneath to squeeze it between his fingers. Then he bent his head and took her nipple in his mouth, and oh, it was so sweet. The sensation shot fast and straight south, pooling low and hot in her core, making her clit quiver. She arched her back and immediately winced at the pain in her shoulder.

"Baby," he said, pressing down on her middle. "Lie down and relax."

"I can't. I need—"

"Shhh, I know what you need."

He moved down between her legs, lying on his belly and kissing her inner thigh.

"Don't lift your shoulder. Don't move," he said, murmuring against her leg. "If you hurt yourself again, I'll stop."

"Yes, sir." She pressed back against the mattress, determined to not move her upper half. She wanted him to lick her pussy, and she'd do anything for an orgasm.

But when his tongue snaked out and licked along her vulva, sweeping upward across her clit, she knew it was going to be torture to stay still, because she wanted to come up off the mattress. Sensation rocketed through her, every nerve ending coming to life. His tongue was like hot velvet along her sensitive flesh, making her arch her hips to get more.

Then he pressed his lips against her, covering her clit, using his mouth and his tongue to drive her to the brink. When he added his fingers, sliding two into her pussy, she knew all was lost. She tried to be gentle, she really did, but by now she didn't care whether she hurt her shoulder or not. She was beyond feeling pain anyway. Pure pleasure had taken over. Mac was the devil and he was taking her on the ride of her life, straight through the sweetest fires of hell, twisting his fingers inside her, swirling his tongue over her and sucking on her clit.

She fisted the sheets, lifted her ass, and sailed over the edge into orgasm, letting out a hoarse cry as hot fluid spilled from within her. She shuddered and rocked against his face, while he continued to torture her all the way through the aftershocks until she gasped for breath.

Then he crawled up, fitting his cock against her pussy, and thrust inside her at the same time he took her mouth. Salt and the sweet taste of Mac mingled on her tongue as he drove his cock in deep, but with gentle strokes. She wrapped her legs around him and welcomed his heat and thickness, this joining that meant as much to her heart as it did to her body. With her good arm, she touched him—his face, his shoulders, entwining her fingers with his as he lifted her arm above her head and tightened his hold on her hand, moving against her with increasing rhythm.

She opened her eyes, lost in the depths of the whiskey brown ones looking back at her. Love was reflected there, something she never thought she'd see. It intensified every sensation, every stroke of his cock inside her. She belonged to him, and he to her, and they would always care for each other. There would never be another man who was so much a part of her like Mac. No other man understood her like Mac did.

He tucked his hand underneath her, lifting her buttocks, tightening their connection.

"Come again for me, Lily. Squeeze my cock."

Again and again he dragged his cock almost all the way out, only to slide inside her again. Each time he pushed inside her she felt the hot tingles as he rubbed her G-spot. There wasn't a part of her body he didn't know, hadn't explored, didn't own.

She was his, and proved it to him by exploding around him, weeping for him, inside and out. He kissed her, murmuring her name as he came.

It had never been more perfect.

Afterward, he rolled off and let her lie on her back while he stroked her hair.

"Thank you," he said.

"For what?"

"For trusting me. For understanding me. Sometimes I think you know me better than I know myself."

She smiled, half turning to face him. "I don't know about that. I'm learning about you. We're learning about each other. It's a long process."

"We'll both make mistakes."

"No doubt."

"I'll probably make you mad or hurt you a hundred times."

She loved this side of him. "Probably. And I'll frustrate you, and infuriate you with my stubborn nature."

"So this is love."

"Yes, Mac. This is love."

He leaned over and kissed her, and her toes curled.

"Welcome to the Wild Riders, Lily."